THE CRITICS PRAISE
THE VALLEY OF BONES

"Balances expertly between the comic and the serious. . . .
Characters are . . . substantially developed—especially
Gwatkin and Bithel, two memorable creations."
—*New York Times Book Review*

* * *

"Throughout the present performance, Anthony Powell is
seen most often as a first-rate entertainer. But he appears
too as an artist. . . . And at his best he is a swift, laughing,
charitable, beautifully intelligent observer: a writer who
knows who he is, what he believes, and why he is writing."
—*Harper's Magazine*

* * *

"Mr. Powell has been justly celebrated as a master of comic
understatement, and this quality is elegantly present in
The Valley of Bones. But his comedy has also become more
broad and grotesque then heretofore, since army life makes
men more ridiculous than they usually are. As the novels
move on, Mr. Powell looms less as a funnyman and more
as a writer of poignant tragicomedy."
—*Atlantic Monthly*

A Dance to the Music of Time
by Anthony Powell

A Question of Upbringing
A Buyer's Market
The Acceptance World
At Lady Molly's
Casanova's Chinese Restaurant
The Kindly Ones
The Valley of Bones
The Soldier's Art*
The Military Philosophers*
Books Do Furnish a Room*
Temporary Kings*
Hearing Secret Harmonies*

Published by
POPULAR LIBRARY

*forthcoming

A DANCE TO THE MUSIC OF TIME № 7

THE VALLEY OF BONES

ANTHONY POWELL

POPULAR LIBRARY

An Imprint of Warner Books, Inc.

A Warner Communications Company

POPULAR LIBRARY EDITION

Copyright © 1964 by Anthony Powell
All rights reserved.

Popular Library® is a registered trademark of Warner Books, Inc.

This Popular Library Edition is published by arrangement with
Little, Brown and Company, 34 Beacon Street, Boston, Mass. 02106

Cover design by Rolf Erickson
Cover art by Max Ginsburg

Popular Library books are published by
Warner Books, Inc.
666 Fifth Avenue
New York, N.Y. 10103

 A Warner Communications Company

Printed in the United States of America

First Popular Library/Warner Books, Inc., Printing: October, 1985

10 9 8 7 6 5 4 3 2 1

For Arthur
and Rosemary

One

SNOW from yesterday's fall still lay in patches and the morning air was glacial. No one was about the streets at this hour. On either side of me in the half-light Kedward and the Company Sergeant-Major stepped out briskly as if on parade. Some time in the past — long, long ago in another existence, an earlier, less demanding incarnation — I had stayed a night in this town, idly come here to cast an eye over a countryside where my own family had lived a century or more before. One of them (rather a hard case by the look of it, from whom Uncle Giles's failings perhaps stemmed) had come west from the Marches to marry the heiress of a small property overlooking a bay on this lost, lonely shore. The cliffs below the site of the house, where all but foundations had been obliterated by the seasons, enclosed untidy banks of piled-up rock against which spent Atlantic waters ceaselessly dissolved, ceaselessly renewed steaming greenish spray: *la mer, la mer, toujours recommençée,* as Moreland was fond of quoting, an everyday landscape of heaving billows too consciously dramatic for my own taste. Afterwards, in the same country, they moved to a grassy peninsula of the estuary, where the narrowing sea penetrated deep inland. There moss and ivy spread over ruined, roofless walls on which broad sheets of rain were descending. In the church nearby, a white marble tablet had been raised *in memoriam.* Those were the visible remains. I did not remember much of the town itself. The streets, built at constantly

1

changing levels, were not without a bleak charm, an illusion of tramping through Greco's Toledo in winter, or one of those castellated upland townships of Tuscany, represented without great regard for perspective in the background of *quattrocento* portraits. For some reason one was always aware, without knowing why the fact should be so inescapable, that the sea was not far away. The poem's emphasis on ocean's aqueous reiterations provoked in the mind a thousand fleeting images, scraps of verse, fragments of painting, forgotten tunes, disordered souvenirs of every kind: anything, in fact, but the practical matters required of one. When I tried to pull myself together, fresh daydreams overwhelmed me.

Although they had remained in these parts only a couple of generations, there was an aptness, something fairly inexorable, in reporting under the badges of second-lieutenant to a spot from which quite a handful of forerunners of the same blood had set out to become unnoticed officers of Marines or the East India Company; as often as not to lay twenty-year-old bones in the cemeteries of Bombay and Mysore. I was not exactly surprised to find myself committed to the same condition of service, in a sense always knowing that part of a required pattern, the fulfilment of which was in some ways a relief. Nevertheless, whatever military associations were to be claimed with these regions, Bonaparte's expressed conviction was irrefutable—French phrases seemed to offer support at that moment—*A partir de trente ans on commence à être moins propre à faire la guerre*. That was exactly how I felt myself; no more, no less. Perhaps others of the stock, too, had embarked with reservations on a career by the sword. Certainly there had been no name of the least distinction for four or five hundred years. In mediaeval times they had been of more account in war; once, a long way back—in the disconcerting, free-for-all manner of Celtic lineage—even reigning, improbable as that might now appear, in this southern kingdom of a much disputed land. One wondered what on earth such predecessors had been like personally; certainly not above blinding and castrating when in the mood. A pale, mysterious sun opaquely glittered on the circlet of gold round their helmets, as armed men, ever fainter in outline and less substantial, receded into the vaporous, shining mists towards intermediate, timeless beings, at once measurably historical, yet at the same time mythically heroic: Llywarch the Old, a discontented guest at the Arthurian Table: Cunedda—though only in the female line—whose horsemen had mounted guard on the Wall. For some reason the Brython, Cunedda, imposed himself on the imagination. Had his expulsion of the Goidels with great slaughter been at the express order of Stilicho, that Vandal captain who all but won the Empire for himself? I reviewed the possibility as we ascended, without breaking step, a short, very steep, very slippery incline of pavement. At the summit of this little hill stood a building of grey stone surrounded by rows of spiked railings, a chapel or meeting house, reposing in icy gloom. Under the heavy portico a carved scroll was inscribed:

S A R D I S
1874

Kedward came smartly to a halt at the entrance of this tabernacle. The Sergeant-Major and I drew up beside him. A gale began to blow noisily up the street. Muffled yet disturbing, the war horns of Cunedda moaned in the frozen wind, as far away he rode upon the cloud.

"This is the Company's billet," said Kedward, "Rowland is meeting us here."

"Was he in the Mess last night?"

"Not when you were there. He was on his rounds as Captain of the Week."

I followed Kedward through the forbidding portals of Sardis—one of the Seven Churches of Asia, I recollected—immediately entering a kind of cave, darker than the streets, though a shade warmer. The Sergeant-Major formally called the room to attention, although no visible presence stirred in an ominous twilight heavy with the smell of men recently departed, a scent on which the odour of escaping gas had been superimposed. Kedward bade the same unrevealed beings "carry on." He had explained earlier that "as bloody usual" the Company was "on fatigues" that week. At first it was not easy to discern what lay about us in a Daumier world of threatening, fiercely slanted shadows, in the midst of which two feeble jets of bluish gas, from which the pungent smell came, gave irregular, ever-changing contours to an amorphous mass of foggy cubes and pyramids. Gradually the adjacent shapes contracted into asymmetrical rows of double-decker bunks upon which piles of grey-brown blankets were folded in a regulated manner. Then suddenly at the far end of the cave, like the anthem of the soloist bursting gloriously from a hidden choir, a man's voice, deep throated and penetrating, sounded, rose, swelled, in a lament of heartbreaking melancholy:

> "That's where I fell in love,
> While stars above
> Came out to play;
> For it was *mañana*,
> And we were so gay,
> South of the border,
> Down Mexico way . . ."

Another barrack-room orderly, for that was whom I rightly judged the unseen singer to be, now loomed up from the darkness at my elbow, joining in powerfully with the last two lines. At the same time, he swung his broom with considerable violence backwards and forwards through the air, like a conductor's baton, finally banging it with all his force against the wooden legs of one of the bunks.

"All right, all right, there," shouted the Sergeant-Major, who had at first not disallowed the mere singing. "Not so much noise am I telling you."

As one's eye grew used to the gloom, gothic letters of enormous size appeared on the walls of the edifice, picked out in red and black and gold above the flickering gas-jets, a text whose message read straight across the open pages of a huge volume miraculously confronting us high above the paved floor, like the mural warning at Belshazzar's feast:

"Thou hast a few names even in Sardis
which have not defiled their garments:
and they shall walk with me in white:
for they are worthy."
Rev. III. 4.

"Some of these blankets aren't laid out right yet, Sergeant-Major," said Kedward. "It won't do, you know."

He spoke gravely, as if emphasising the Apocalyptic verdict of the walls. Although he had assured me he was nearly twenty-two, Kedward's air was that of a small boy who had dressed up for a lark in officer's uniform, completing the rag by rubbing his upper lip with burnt cork. He looked young enough to be the Sergeant-Major's son, his grandson almost. At the same time, he had a kind of childish dignity, an urchin swagger, in its way quite impressive, which lent him a right to be obeyed.

"Some of the new intake was taught different to fold them blankets," said the Sergeant-Major cautiously.

"Look at that—and those."

"I thought the lads was getting the idea better now, as it was."

"Never saw anything like it."

"A Persian market, you might think," agreed the Sergeant-Major.

Cleanshaven, with the severely puritanical countenance of an Ironside in a Victorian illustration to a Cavalier-and-Roundhead romance, CSM Cadwallader was not as old as he looked, nor for that matter—as I discovered in due course—nearly so puritanical. His resounding surname conjoined him with those half-historical, half-mythical times through which my mind had been straying a minute or two before, the stern nobility of his features suggesting a warrior from an heroic epoch, returned with dragon banners to sustain an army in time of war. Like the rest of the "other ranks" of the Battalion, he was a miner. His smooth skull, entirely hairless, was streaked with an intricate pattern of blue veins, where coal dust of accumulated years beneath the ground had found its way under the skin, spreading into a design that resembled an astrological nativity—his own perhaps—cast in tattoo over the ochre-coloured surface of the cranium. He wore a Coronation medal ribbon and the yellow-and-green one for Territorial long service. The three of us strolled round the bunks.

"Carry on with the cleaning," said Kedward sharply.

He addressed the barrack-room orderlies, who, taking CSM Cadwallader's rebuke as an injunction to cease from all work until our party was gone, now stood fidgeting and whispering by the wall. They were familiar later as Jones, D., small and fair, with almost white hair, a rarity in the Battalion, and Williams, W. H., tall and dark, his face covered with spots. Jones, D., had led the singing. Now they began to sweep again energetically, at the same time accepting this bidding as also granting permission to sing once more, for, as we moved to the further end of the room, Jones, D., returned to the chant, though more restrainedly than before, perhaps on account of the song's change of mood:

> "There in a gown of white,
> By candlelight,
> She stooped to pray . . ."

The mournful, long-drawn-out notes died for a moment. Glancing round, I thought the singer, too, was praying; then saw his crouched position had been adopted the better to sweep under one of the bunks. This cramped attitude no doubt impeded the rendering, or perhaps he had paused for a second or two, desire provoked by the charming thought of a young girl lightly clothed in shimmering white—like the worthy ones of Sardis—a picture of peace and innocence and promise of a good time, very different from the stale, cheerless atmosphere of the barrack-room. Rising, he burst out again with renewed, agonised persistence:

> ". . . The Mission bell told me
> That I mustn't stay

South of the border,
Down Mexico way . . ."

The message of the bell, the singer's tragic tone announcing it, underlined life's inflexible call to order, reaffirming the illusory nature of love and pleasure. Even as the words trailed away, heavy steps sounded from the other end of the chapel, as if forces of authority were already on the move to effect the unhappy lover's expulsion from the Mission premises and delights of Mexico. Two persons had just come through the door. Kedward and the Sergeant-Major were still leaning critically over one of the bunks, discussing the many enormities of its incorrectly folded bed clothes. I turned from them and saw an officer approaching, accompanied by a sergeant. The officer was a captain, smallish, with a black moustache like Kedward's, though much better grown; the sergeant, a tall, broad shouldered, beefy young man, with fair hair and very blue eyes—another Brythonic type, no doubt—that reminded me of Peter Templer's. The singing had died down again, but the little captain stared angrily at the bunks, as if they greatly offended him.

"Don't you call the room to attention when your Company Commander comes in, Sergeant-Major?" he asked harshly.

Kedward and CSM Cadwallader hastily straightened themselves and saluted. I did the same. The captain returned a stiff salute, keeping his hand up at the peak of the cap longer than any of the rest of us.

"Indeed, I'm sorry, sir," said the Sergeant-Major, beginning to shout again, though apparently not much put out by this asperity of manner. "See you at first, I did not, sir."

Kedward stepped forward, as if to put an end to further fault finding, if that were possible.

"This is Mr. Jenkins," he said. "He joined yesterday and has been posted to your company, Captain Gwatkin."

Gwatkin fixed me with his angry little black eyes. In appearance, he was in several respects an older version of Kedward. I judged him to be about my own age, perhaps a year or two younger. Almost every officer in the unit looked alike to me at that very early stage; Maelgwyn-Jones, the Adjutant, and Parry, his assistant sitting beside him at the table, indistinguishable as Tweedledum and Tweedledee, when I first reported to the Orderly Room the evening before. Later, it was incredible persons so dissimilar could ever for one moment have appeared to resemble one another in any but the most superficial aspects. Gwatkin, although he may have had something of Kedward's look, was at the same time very different. Even this first sight of him revealed a novelty of character, at once apparent, though hard to define. There was, in the first place, some style about him. However much he might physically resemble the rest, something in his air and movements also showed a divergence from the humdrum routine of men; if, indeed, there is a humdrum routine.

"It's no more normal to be a bank-manager or a bus-conductor, than to be Baudelaire or Genghis Khan," Moreland had once remarked. "It just happens there are more of the former types."

Satisfied at last that he had taken in sufficient of my appearance through the dim light of the barrack-room, Gwatkin held out his hand.

"Your name was in Part II Orders, Mr. Jenkins," he said without smiling. "The Adjutant spoke to me about you, too. I welcome you to the Company. We are going to make it the best company in the Battalion. That has not been brought about yet. I know I can rely on your support in trying to achieve it."

He spoke this very formal speech in a rough tone, with the barest suggestion of sing-song, his voice authoritative, at the same time not altogether assured.

"Mr. Kedward," he went on, "have the new intake laid out their blankets properly this morning?"

"Not all of them," said Kedward.

"Why not, Sergeant-Major?"

"It takes some learning, sir. Some of them is not used to our ways yet. They are good boys."

"Never mind whether they are good boys, Sergeant-Major, those blankets must be correct."

"Indeed, they should, sir."

"See to it, Sergeant-Major."

"That I will, sir."

"When was the last rifle inspection?"

"At the pay parade, sir."

"Were the Company's rifles correct?"

"Except for Williams, T., sir, that is gone on the MT course and taken his rifle with him, and Jones, A., that is sick with the ring-worm, and Williams, H., that is on leave, and those two rifles the Sergeant-Armourer did want to look at that I told you of, sir, and the one with the faulty bolt in the Company Store for the time being, you said, and I will see about. Oh, yes, and Williams, G. E., that has been lent to Brigade for a week and has his rifle with him. That is the lot I do believe, sir."

Gwatkin seemed satisfied with this reckoning.

"Have you rendered your report?" he asked.

"Not yet, sir."

"See I have the nominal roll this evening, Sergeant-Major, by sixteen-hundred hours."

"That I will, sir."

"Mr. Kedward."

"Sir?"

"Your cap badge is not level with the top seam of the cap band."

"I'll see to it as soon as I get back to the Mess."

Gwatkin turned to me.

"Officers of our Battalion wear bronze pips, Mr. Jenkins."

"The Quartermaster told me in the Mess last night he could get me correct pips by this evening."

"See the QM does so, Mr. Jenkins. Officers incorrectly dressed are a bad example. Now it happens that Sergeant Pendry here, who is Battalion Orderly Sergeant this week, will be your own Platoon Sergeant."

Sergeant Pendry grinned with great friendliness, his blue eyes flashing in high-lights caught by the gas-jets, making them more than ever like Peter Templer's in the old days. He held out his hand. I took it, not sure whether this familiarity would conform with Gwatkin's ideas about discipline. However, Gwatkin seemed to regard a handshake as normal in the circumstances. His tone had been austere until that moment; intentionally, though perhaps rather unconvincingly austere. Now he spoke in a more friendly manner.

"What is your Christian name, Mr. Jenkins?"

"Nicholas."

"Mine is Rowland. The Commanding Officer says we should not be formal with each other off parade. We are brother officers—like a family, you see. So, when off duty, Rowland is what you should call me. I shall say Nicholas. Mr. Kedward told you his name is Idwal."

"He has. I'm calling him that. In practice, it's Nick for me."

Gwatkin gazed at me fixedly, as if not altogether sure what I meant by "in practice," or whether it was a term properly to be used by a subaltern to his Company Commander, but he did not comment.

"Come along, Sergeant Pendry," he said, "I want to look at those urine buckets."

We saluted. Gwatkin set off on his further duties as Captain of the Week—like the Book of the Month, I frivolously thought to myself.

"That went off all right," said Kedward, as if presentation to Gwatkin might have proved disastrous. "I don't think he took against you. What must I show you now? I know, the ablutions."

That was my first sight of Rowland Gwatkin. It could hardly have been more characteristic, in so much as he appeared on that occasion almost to perfection in the part for which he had cast himself: in command, something of a martinet, a trifle unapproachable to his subordinates, at the same time not without his human side, above all a man dedicated to duty. It was a clear-cut, hard-edged picture, into which Gwatkin himself, for some reason, never quite managed to fit. Even his name seemed to split him into two halves, poetic and prosaic, "Rowland" at once suggesting high deeds:

... When Rowland brave, and Olivier,
And every paladin and peer,
    On Roncesvalles died!

"Gwatkin," on the other hand, insinuated nothing more impressive than "little Walter," which was not altogether inappropriate.

"Rowland can be a bloody nuisance sometimes," said Kedward, when we knew each other better. "He thinks such a mighty lot of himself, do you know. Lyn Craddock's dad is manager of Rowland's branch, and he told Lyn, Rowland's not all that bloody marvellous at banking. Not the sort that will join the Inspectorate, or anything like that, not by a long chalk. Rowland doesn't care much about that, I expect. He just fancies himself as a great soldier. You should keep the right side of Rowland. He can be a tricky customer."

That was precisely the impression of Gwatkin I had myself formed; that he took himself very seriously, was eminently capable of becoming disagreeable if he conceived a dislike for someone. At the same time, I felt an odd kind of interest in him, even attraction towards him. There was about him something melancholy, perhaps even tragic, that was hard to define. His excessively "regimental" manner was certainly over and above anything as yet encountered among other officers of the Battalion. We were still, of course, existing in the comparatively halcyon days at the beginning of the war, when there was plenty to eat and drink, tempers better than they subsequently became. If you were over thirty, you thought yourself adroit to have managed to get into uniform at all, everyone behaving almost as if they were attending a peacetime practice camp (this was a Territorial unit), to be home again after a few weeks' change of routine. Gwatkin's manner was different from that. He gave the impression of being something more than a civilian keen on his new military role, anxious to make a success of an unaccustomed job. There was an air of resolve about him, the consciousness of playing a part to which a high destiny had summoned him. I suspected

he saw himself in much the same terms as those heroes of
Stendhal—not a Stendhalian lover, like Barnby, far from
that—an aspiring, restless spirit, who, released at last by
war from the cramping bonds of life in a provincial town,
was about to cut a dashing military figure against a backcloth
of Meissonier-like imagery of plume and breast plate: dragoons
walking their horses through the wheat, grenadiers at ease
in a tavern with girls bearing flagons of wine. Esteem for the
army—never in this country regarded, in the continental
manner, as a popular expression of the national will—implies
a kind of innocence. This was something quite different from
Kedward's hope to succeed. Kedward, so I found, did not deal
in dreams, military or otherwise. By that time he and I were
on our way back to the Mess. Kedward gratifyingly treated
me as if we had known each other all our lives, not entirely
disregarding our difference in age, it is true, but at least
accepting that as a reason for benevolence.

"I expect you're with one of the Big Five, Nick," he said.

"Big five what?"

"Why, banks, of course."

"I'm not in a bank."

"Oh, aren't you. You'll be the exception in our Battalion."

"Is that what most of the officers do?"

"All but about three or four. Where do you work?"

"London."

Banks expunged from Kedward's mind as a presumptive
vocation, he showed little further curiosity as to how otherwise I might keep going.

"What's London like?"

"Not bad."

"Don't you ever get sick of living in such a big place?"

"You do sometimes."

"I've been in London twice," Kedward said. "I've got an
aunt who lives there—Croydon—and I stayed with her. I
went up to the West End several times. The shops are bloody
marvellous. I wouldn't like to work there though."

"You get used to it."

"I don't believe I would."

"Different people like different places."

"That's true. I like it where I was born. That's quite a long way from where we are now, but it's not all that different. I believe you'd like it where my home is. Most of our officers come from round there. By the by, we were going to get another officer reinforcement yesterday, as well as yourself, but he never turned up."

"Emergency commission?"

"No, Territorial Army Reserve."

"What's he called?"

"Bithel—brother of the VC. Wouldn't it be great to win a VC."

"He must be years younger than his elder brother then. Bithel got his VC commanding one of the regular battalions in 1915 or 1916. I've heard my father speak of him. That Bithel must be in his sixties at least."

"Why shouldn't he be much younger than his brother? This one played rugger for Wales once, I was told. That must be great too. But I think you're right. This Bithel is not all that young. The CO was complaining about the age of the officers they are sending him. He said it was dreadful, you are much too old. Bithel will probably be even older than you."

"Not possible."

"You never know. Somebody said they thought he was thirty-seven. He couldn't be as old as that, could he. If so, they'll have to find him an administrative job after the Division moves."

"Are we moving?"

"Quite soon, they say."

"Where?"

"No one knows. It's a secret, of course. Some say Scotland, some Northern Ireland. Rowland thinks it will be Egypt or India. Rowland always has these big ideas. It might be, of course. I hope we do go abroad. My dad was in this battalion in the last war and got sent to the Holy Land. He brought me back a prayer-book bound in wood from the Cedars of Lebanon. I wasn't born then, of course, but he got the prayer-book for his son, if he had one. Of course that was if he didn't get killed. He hadn't even asked my mum to marry him then."

"Do you use it every Sunday?"

"Not in the army. Not bloody likely. Somebody would pinch it. I want to hand it on to my own son, you see, when I have one. Are you engaged?"

"I was once. I'm married as a consequence."

"Are you really. Well, I suppose you would be at your age. Yanto Breeze—that's Rowland's other Platoon Commander— is married now. The wedding was a month ago. Yanto's nearly twenty-five, of course. What's your wife's name?"

"Isobel."

"Is she in London?"

"She's living in the country with her sister. She's waiting to have a baby."

"Oh, you are lucky," said Kedward, "I wonder whether it will be a daughter. I'd love a little daughter. I'm engaged. Would you like me to show you a photograph of my fiancée?"

"Very much."

Kedward unbuttoned the breast-pocket of his tunic. He took out a wallet from one of the compartments of which he extracted a snapshot. This he handed over. Much worn by constant affectionate reference, the features of the subject, recognisably the likeness of a girl, were otherwise all but effaced. I expressed appreciation.

"Bloody marvellous, isn't she," said Kedward.

He kissed the faded outlines before returning the portrait to the notecase.

"We're going to get married if I become a captain," he said.

"When will that be, do you think?"

Kedward laughed.

"Not for ages, I suppose," he said. "But I don't see why I shouldn't be promoted one of these days, if the war goes on for a while and I work hard. Perhaps you will too, Nick. You never know. There's this bloody eighteen months to get through as second-lieutenant before you get your second pip. I think the war is going on, don't you? The French will hold them in the Maginot Line until this country builds up her air strength. Then, when the Germans try to advance, chaps like you and me will come in, do you see. Of course we might be sent to the help of Finland before that, fight the Russkis instead of the Germans. In any case, the decisive arm is infantry. Everybody agrees about that—except Yanto Breeze who says it's the tank."

"We shall see."

"Yanto says he's sure he will remain with two pips all the war. He doesn't care. Yanto has no ambition."

I had met Evan Breeze—usually known by the diminutive "Yanto"—in the Mess the previous night, a tall, shambling, unmoustached figure, not at all military, who, as an accountant, stood like myself a little apart from the norm of working in a bank. Gwatkin, so I found in due course, did not much like Breeze. In fact it would be true to say he hated him, a sentiment Breeze quietly returned. Mutual antipathy was in general attributed to Gwatkin's disapproval of Breeze's un-smart appearance, and unwillingness to adapt himself to army methods and phraseology. That attitude certainly brought him some persecution at the hands of Gwatkin and others in authority. Besides, Breeze always managed to give the impression that he was laughing at Gwatkin, while at the same time allowing no word or act of his to give reasonable cause for offence. However, there was apparently another matter. When we knew each other better, Kedward revealed that Gwatkin, before his marriage, had been in love with Breeze's sister; had been fairly roughly treated by her.

"Rowland falls like a ton of bricks when he does, believe me," Kedward said, "when he takes a fancy to a girl. He was so stuck on Gwenllian Breeze, you would have thought he had the measles."

"What happened?"

"She wouldn't look at him. Married a college professor. One of those Swansea people."

"And Rowland married someone else?"

"Oh, yes, of course. He married Blodwen Davies that had lived next door all their lives."

"How did that work out?"

Kedward looked at me uncomprehendingly.

"Why, what do you mean?" he said. "All right. Why should it not? They've been married a long time now, though they haven't any kids. All that about Gwen Breeze was years ago. Yanto must have forgotten by now that Rowland could ever have been his brother-in-law. What a couple they would have been in one family. They would have been at each other like a dog-fight. Rowland always knows best. He likes bossing it. Yanto likes his own way too, but different. Yanto should clean himself up. He looks like an old hen in uniform."

All the same, although Breeze might not possess Kedward's liveliness, ambition, capacity for doing everything with concentrated energy, I found later that he was not, in his own way, a bad officer, however unkempt his turnout. The men liked him; he was worth consulting about the men.

"Keep an eye on Sergeant Pendry, Nick," he said, when he heard Pendry was my Platoon Sergeant. "He is making a great show-off now, but I am not sure he is going on that way. He has only just been promoted and at present is very keen. But he was in my platoon for a time as a corporal and I am not certain about him, that he can last. He may be one of those NCOs who put everything into it for two or three weeks, then go to pieces. You'll find a lot like that. They have to be stripped. There is nothing else to do."

It was Breeze, on the evening of the day I had been shown round the lines by Kedward, who took me to the bar of the hotel where the officers of the unit were billeted. After dinner, subalterns were inclined to leave the ante-room of the Mess to the majors and captains, retiring to where talk was less restricted and rounds of drinks could be "stood." This saloon bar was smoky and very crowded. In addition to a large civilian clientele and a sprinkling of our own Regiment, were several officers from the Divisional signals unit located in the town, also two or three from the RAF. Pumphrey, one of our subalterns, was leaning against the bar talking to a couple of army chaplains, and a lieutenant I had not seen before, wearing the Regiment's badges. This officer had a large, round, pasty face and a ragged moustache, the tangled hairs of which glistened with beer. His thick lips were closed on the stub of a cigar. In spite of the moustache and the fact that he was rather bald, he shared some of Kedward's look of a small boy dressed up in uniform for fun, though giving that impression for quite different reasons. In strong contrast with Kedward's demeanour, this man had an extraordinary air of guilt which somehow suggested juvenility; a schoolboy wearing a false moustache (something more than burnt cork this time), who only a few minutes before had done something perfectly disgusting, and was pretty sure that act was about to be detected by the headmaster with whom he had often been in trouble before. Before I could diagnose more, Kedward himself came into the bar. He joined us.

"I will buy you a bitter, Idwal," said Breeze.

Kedward accepted the offer.

"Finland is still knocking the Red Army about on the news," he said. "We may go there yet."

Pumphrey, another of our non-banking officers (he sold second-hand cars), beckoned us to join the group with the chaplains. Red-haired, noisy, rather aggressive, Pumphrey was always talking of exchanging from the army into the RAF.

"This is our new reinforcement, Yanto," he shouted. "Lieutenant Bithel. He's just reported his arrival at the Orderly Room and has been shown his quarters. Now he's wetting his whistle with me and the padres."

We pushed through the crowd towards them.

"Here is Iltyd Popkiss, the C. of E.," said Breeze, "and Ambrose Dooley that saves the souls of the RCs, and is a man to tell you some stories to make you sit up."

Popkiss was small and pale. It was at once evident that he had a hard time of it keeping up with his Roman Catholic colleague in heartiness and avoidance of seeming strait-laced. Dooley, a large dark man with an oily complexion and appearance of not having shaved too well that morning, accepted with complaisance this reputation as a retailer of hair-raising anecdote. The two chaplains seemed on the best of terms. Bithel himself smiled timidly, revealing under his straggling moustache a double row of astonishingly badly fitting false teeth. He hesitantly proffered a flabby hand. His furtiveness was quite disturbing.

"I've just been telling them what an awful journey I had coming here from where I live," he said. "The Adjutant was very decent about the muddle that had been made. It was the fault of the War Office as usual. Anyway, I'm here now, glad to be back with the Regiment and having a drink, after all I've been through."

I thought at first he might be a commercial traveller by profession, as he spoke as if accustomed to making social contacts by way of a kind of patter, though he seemed scarcely sure enough of himself for that profession. The way he talked might be caused by mere embarrassment. The cloth of his tunic was stained on the lapels with what seemed egg, the trousers ancient and baggy. He looked as if he had consumed quite a few drinks already. There could be no doubt, I saw with relief, that he was older than myself. If he had ever played rugby for Wales, he had certainly allowed himself to run disastrously to seed. There could be no doubt about that either. He seemed almost painfully aware of his own dilapidation, also of the impaired state of his uniform, at which he now looked down apologetically, holding out the flap of one of the pockets from its tarnished button for our inspection.

"When I'm allotted a batman, I'll have to get this tunic pressed," he said. "Haven't worn it since I was in Territorial camp fifteen or more years ago. Managed to spill a glass of gin-and-italian over the trousers on the way here, I don't know how."

"You won't get any bloody marvellous valeting from your batman here, I'm telling you," said Pumphrey. "He'll be more used to hewing coal than pressing suits, and you'll be lucky if he even gets a decent polish on those buttons of yours, which are needing a rub up."

"I suppose we mustn't expect too much now there's a war on," said Bithel, unhappy that he might have committed a social blunder by speaking of pressing tunics. "But what about another round. It's my turn, padre."

He addressed himself to the Anglican chaplain, but Father Dooley broke in vigorously.

"If I go on drinking so much of this beer, it will have a strong effect on my bowels," he said, "but all the same I will oblige you, my friend."

Bithel smiled doubtfully, evidently not much at ease with such plain speaking in the mouth of the clergy.

"I don't think one more will do us any harm," he said. "I drink a fair amount of ale myself in civilian life without bad results."

"You want to keep your bowels open anyway," said Dooley, pursuing the subject. "That's what I believe in. Have a good sluicing every day. Nothing like it."

He held up his glass to the light, as if assessing the aperient potentialities of the contents.

"Army food gives me squitters anyway," he went on, roaring with delight at the thought. "I've hardly had a moment's peace since we mobilized."

"It makes me as constipated as an owl," said Pumphrey. "I should just about say so."

Dooley finished his beer at a gulp, again giving his jolly monk's laugh at the thought of man's digestive vicissitudes.

"Even if I'm all bound up, I always carry plenty of toilet paper round with me," he said. "Never be without it. That's my rule. You can't know when you're not going to be taken short in the army."

"That's a good notion," said Pumphrey, "we must follow His Reverence's advice, mustn't we. Take proper precautions in case we have to spend a penny. Perhaps you do already, Iltyd. The Church seems to teach these things."

"Oh, why, yes, I do indeed," said Popkiss.

"What do you take Iltyd for?" said Dooley. "He's an old campaigner, aren't you, Iltyd?"

"Why, yes, indeed," said Popkiss, evidently pleased to be given this opening, "and what do you think? In my last unit, when I took off my tunic to play billiards one night, they did such a trick on me. You'd never guess. They wrapped a french letter, do you know, between those sheets of toilet paper in my pocket."

There was a good deal of laughter at this, in which the RC chaplain amicably joined, although it was clear from his expression that he recognised Popkiss to have played a card he himself might find hard to trump.

"And did it fall out in the middle of Church Parade?" asked Pumphrey, after he had finished guffawing.

"No, indeed, thank to goodness. I just found it next day on my dressing table by my dog-collar. I threw it down the lavatory and pulled the chain. Very thankful I was when it went away, which was not for a long time. I pulled the chain half a dozen times, I do believe."

"Now listen to what happened to me when I was with the 2nd/14th—" began Father Dooley.

I never heard the climax of this anecdote, no doubt calculated totally to eclipse in rough simplicity of language and narrative force anything further Popkiss might attempt to offer, in short to blow the Anglican totally out of the water. I was sorry to miss this consummation, because Dooley obviously felt his own reputation as a raconteur at stake, a position he was determined to retrieve. However, before the story was properly begun, Bithel drew me to one side.

"I'm not sure I like all this sort of talk," he muttered in an undertone. "Not used to it yet, I suppose. You must feel the same. You're not the rough type. You were at the University, weren't you?"

I admitted to that.

"Which one?"

I told him. Bithel had certainly had plenty to drink that day. He smelt strongly of alcohol even in the thick atmosphere of the saloon bar. Now, he sighed deeply.

"I was going to the 'varsity myself," he said. "Then my father decided he couldn't afford it. Business was a bit rocky at that moment. He was an auctioneer, you know, and had run into a spot of trouble as it happened. Nothing serious, though people in the neighbourhood said a lot of untrue and nasty things at the time. Nothing people won't say. He passed away soon after that. I suppose I could have sent myself up to college, so to speak. The money would just about have run to it in those days. Somehow, it seemed too late by then. I've always regretted it. Makes a difference to a man, you know. You've only got to look round this bar."

He swayed a little, adjusting his balance by clinging to the counter.

"Had a tiring day," he said. "Think I'll smoke just one more cigar and go to bed. Soothing to the nerves, a cigar. Will you have one? They're cheap, but not bad."

"No, thanks very much."

"Come on. I've got a whole box with me."

"Don't really like them, thanks all the same."

"A 'varsity man and don't smoke cigars," said Bithel, speaking with disappointment. "I shouldn't have expected that. What about sleeping pills? I've got some splendid ones, if you'd like to try them. Must use them if you've had just the wrong amount to drink. Fatal to wake up in the night when that's happened."

By this time I had begun to feel pretty tired myself, in no need of sleeping pills. The bar was closing. There was a general move towards bed. Bithel, after gulping down a final drink by himself, went off unsteadily to search for a greatcoat he had mislaid. The rest of us, including the chaplains, made our way upstairs. I was sleeping in the same bedroom as Kedward, Breeze and Pumphrey.

"Old Bithel's been allotted that attic on the top floor to himself," said Pumphrey. "He'll feel pretty lonely up there. We ought to make a surprise for him when he comes to bed. Let's give him a good laugh."

"Oh, he'll just want to go quietly to bed," said Breeze, "not wish for any tomfoolery tonight."

Kedward took the opposite view.

"Why, yes," he said, "Bithel seems a good chap. He would like some sort of a rag. Make him feel at home. Show him that we like him."

I was glad no such welcome had been thought necessary

for myself the previous night, when there had been no sign of horseplay, merely a glass or two of beer before bed. There was perhaps something about Bithel that brought into being such schemes. What shape the joke should best take was further discussed. The end of it was we all climbed the stairs to the top floor of the hotel, where Bithel was housed in one of the attics. The chaplains came too, Dooley particularly entering into the idea of a rag. At first I had envied Bithel the luxury of a room to himself, but, when we arrived there, it became clear that such privacy, whatever its advantages, was paid for by a severe absence of other comfort. The room was fairly big, with a low ceiling under the eaves. Deep shelves had been built along one side, so that in normal times the attic was probably used as a large linen cupboard. The walls were unpapered. There was a strong smell of mice.

"What shall we do?" asked Kedward.

"Put his bed upside down," suggested Pumphrey.

"No," said Breeze, "that's plain silly."

"Make it apple-pie."

"That's stale."

The padres wanted to see the fun, but without too deeply involving themselves. The idea that we should all lie on the shelves, then, when Bithel was already in bed, appear as a horde of ghosts, was abandoned as impracticable. Someone put forward the project of making an effigy. This was accepted as a suitable solution to the problem. Pumphrey and Kedward therefore set about creating a figure to rest in Bithel's camp-bed, the theory being that such a dummy would make Bithel suppose that he had come into the wrong room. The shape of a man that was now put together was chiefly contrived by rolling up the canvas cover of Bithel's valise, which, under the blankets, gave the fair semblance of a body. Two of Bithel's boots were placed so that they stuck out at the foot of the bed, a head on the pillow represented by his sponge-bag, surmounted by Bithel's "fore-and-aft" khaki cap. No doubt there were other properties too, which I have forgotten. The thing was quite well done in the time available, a mild enough joke, perfectly good natured, as the whole affair would not take more than a couple of minutes to dismantle when Bithel himself wanted to go to bed. The effigy was just completed when the sound came of Bithel plodding heavily up the stairs.

"Here he is," said Kedward.

We all went out on to the landing.

"Oh, Mr. Bithel," shouted Pumphrey. "There is something you should look at here. Something very worrying."

Bithel came slowly on up the stairs. He was still puffing at his cigar as he held the rail of the banisters to help him on his way. He seemed not to hear Pumphrey's voice. We stood aside for him to enter the room.

"Such a fat officer has got into your bed, Bithel," shouted Pumphrey, hardly able to control himself with laughter.

Bithel lurched through the door of the attic. He stood for several seconds looking hard at the bed, as if he could not believe his eyes; not believe his luck either, for a broad smile spread over his face, as if he were delighted beyond words. He took the cigar from his mouth and placed it with great care in the crevice of a large glass ashtray marked with a coloured advertisement for some brand of beer, the sole ornament in the room. This ashtray stood on a small table, which, with a broken chair and Bithel's camp-bed, were its only furniture. Then, clasping his hands together above his head, Bithel began to dance.

"Oh, my," said Breeze. "Oh, my."

Bithel, now gesticulating whimsically with his hands, tripped slowly round the bed, regularly changing from one foot to the other, as if following the known steps of a ritual dance.

"A song of love . . ." he intoned gently. "A song of love . . ."

From time to time he darted his head forward and down, like one longing to embrace the figure on the bed, always stopping short at the moment, overcome by coyness at being seen to offer this mark of affection—perhaps passion—in the presence of onlookers. At first everyone, including myself, was in fits of laughter. It was, indeed, an extraordinary spectacle, unlike anything before seen, utterly unexpected, fascinating in its strangeness. Pumphrey was quite scarlet in the face, as if about to have an apoplectic fit, Breeze and Kedward equally amused. The chaplains, too, seemed to be greatly enjoying themselves. However, as Bithel's dance continued, its contortions became increasingly grotesque. He circled round the bed quicker and quicker, writhing his body, undulating his arms in oriental fashion. I became gradually aware that, so far as I was myself concerned, I had had sufficient. A certain embarrassment was making itself felt. The joke had gone on long enough, perhaps too long. Bithel's comic turn should be brought to a close. It was time for him, and everyone else, to get some sleep. That was how I felt. All the same, I had nothing but admiration for the manner in which Bithel had shown himself equal to being ragged; indeed, the way in which he had come out completely on top of those who had tried to make him look silly. In similar circumstances I should myself have fallen far short of any such mastery of the situation. Nevertheless, an end should now be made. We had seen enough. You could have too much of a good thing. It must, in any case, stop soon. These were idle hopes. Bithel showed no sign whatever of wanting to terminate his dance. Now he placed the palms of his hands together as if in the semblance of prayer, now violently rocked his body from side to side in religious ecstasy, now whirled past kicking out his feet before him in a country measure. All the time he danced, he chanted endearments to the dummy on the bed. I think Popkiss was the first, after myself, to begin to tire of the scene. He took Dooley by the arm.

"Come along, Ambrose," he said, "Sunday tomorrow. Busy day. It's our bedtime."

At that moment, Bithel, no doubt by this time dizzy with beer and dervish-like dancing, collapsed on top of the dummy. The camp-bed creaked ominously on its trestles, but did not buckle under him. Throwing his arms round the outline of the valise, he squeezed it with abandon, at the same time covering the sponge-bag with kisses.

"Love o' mine . . ." he mumbled, "Love o' mine . . ."

I was wondering what would happen next, when I realized

that he and I were alone in the room. Quite suddenly the others must have decided to leave, drifting off to bed, bored, embarrassed, or merely tired. The last seemed the most probable. Their instincts told them the rag was at an end; that time had come for sleep. Bithel still lay face-downwards on the bed, fondling and crooning.

"Will you be all right, Bithel? We are all going to bed now."

"What's that?"

"We're all going to bed."

"You lucky people, all going to bed . . ."

"I'll say good night, Bithel."

"Night-night," he said, "Night-night. Wish I'd decided to be a 'varsity man."

He rolled over on his side, reaching across the dummy for the remains of his cigar. It had gone out. He managed to extract a lighter from his trouser pocket and began to strike wildly at its mechanism. Hoping he would not set fire to the hotel during the night, I shut the door and went down the stairs. The others in the room were at various stages of turning in for the night.

"He's a funny one is old Bithel," said Breeze, who was already in bed.

"A regular caution," said Kedward. "Never saw anything like that dance."

"Went on a bit long, didn't it," said Pumphrey, removing a toothbrush from his mouth to speak. "Thought he'd be at it all night till he fell down."

However, although there was general agreement that Bithel had unnecessarily prolonged the dance, he did not, so far as his own personality was concerned, seem to have made a bad impression. On the contrary, he had established a certain undoubted prestige. I did not have much time to think over the incident, because I was very tired. In spite of unfamiliar surroundings, I went to sleep immediately and slept soundly. The following morning, although there was much talk while we dressed, nothing further was said of Bithel. He was forgotten in conversation about Church Parade and the day's routine. Breeze and Pumphrey had already finished their dressing and gone downstairs, when Pumphrey's soldier-servant (later to be identified as Williams, I.G.) came up to Kedward in the passage as we were on the way to breakfast. He was grinning.

"Excuse me, sir."

"What is it, Williams?"

"I was ordered to look after the new officer till he had a batman for hisself."

"Mr. Bithel?"

"The officer don't seem well."

"What's wrong with him?"

"Better see, sir."

Williams, I.G., enjoyed giving this information.

"We'll have a look," said Kedward.

We went upstairs again to the attic. Kedward opened the door. I followed him, entering a stratosphere of stale, sickly beer-and-cigar fumes. I half expected to find Bithel, still wearing his clothes, sleeping on the floor; the cap-surmounted sponge-bag still resting on the pillow. However, in the manner of persons long used to turning in for the night the worse for drink, he had managed to undress and get to bed, even to make himself reasonably comfortable there. His clothes were carefully folded on the floor beside him, one of the habits of the confirmed alcoholic, who knows himself incapable of arranging garments on a chair. The dummy had been ejected from the bed, which Bithel himself now occupied. He lay under the grey-brown blankets in a suit of yellow pyjamas, filthy and faded, knees raised to his chin. His body in this position looked like a corpse exhumed intact from some primitive burial ground for display in the showcase of a museum. Except that he was snoring savagely, cheeks puffing in and out, the colour of his face, too, suggested death. Watch, cigar-case, sleeping pills, stood on the broken chair beside the bed. In addition to these objects was another exhibit, something of peculiar horror. At first I could not imagine what this might be. It seemed either an ornament or a mechanical contrivance of complicated design. I looked closer. Was it apparatus or artifact? Then the truth was suddenly made plain. Before going to sleep, Bithel had placed his false teeth in the ashtray. He had removed the set from his mouth bodily, the jaws still clenched on the stub of the cigar. The effect created by this synthesis was extraordinary, macabre, surrealist. Again one thought of an excavated tomb, the fascination aroused in archaeologists of a thousand years hence at finding these fossilized vestiges beside Bithel's hunched skeleton; the speculations aroused as to the cultural significance of such related objects. Kedward shook Bithel. This had no effect whatever. He did not even open his eyes, though for a moment he ceased to snore. The sleeping pills must have been every bit as effective as Bithel himself had proclaimed them. Apart from gasping, snorting, animal sounds, which issued again as soon as his head touched the pillow, he gave no sign of life. Kedward turned to Williams, I.G., who had followed us up the stairs and was now standing in the doorway, still grinning.

"Tell the Orderly Corporal Mr. Bithel is reporting sick this morning, Williams," he said.

"Right you are, sir."

Williams went off down the stairs two at a time.

"I'll come and have a look at old Bithel later," said Kedward. "Tell him he's been reported sick. Nothing much will be expected of him this morning, Sunday and newly joined."

This was prudent handling of the situation. Kedward clearly knew how to act in an emergency. I suspected that Gwatkin, confronted with the same situation, might have made a fuss about Bithel's state. This show of good sense on Kedward's part impressed me. I indicated to him the false teeth gripping the cigar, but their horror left him cold. We moved on to breakfast. It had to be admitted Bithel had not made an ideal start to his renewed army career.

"I expect old Bithel had a glass too much last night," said Kedward, as we breakfasted. "I once drank more than I ought. You feel terrible. Ever done that, Nick?"

"Yes."

"Awful, isn't it?"

"Awful, Idwal."

"We'll go along early together, and you can take over your platoon for Church Parade."

He told me where to meet him. However, very unexpectedly, Bithel himself appeared downstairs before it was time for church. He smiled uncomfortably when he saw me.

"Never feel much like breakfast on Sundays for some reason," he said.

I warned him that he had been reported sick.

"I found that out from the boy, Williams, who is acting as my batman," said Bithel. "Got it cancelled. While I was talking to him, I discovered there was another boy called Daniels from my home town who might take on being my regular servant. Williams got hold of him for me. I liked the look of him."

We set off up the street together. Bithel was wearing the khaki side-cap that had been set on the sponge-bag the night before. A size too small for him, it was placed correctly according to Standing Orders—in this respect generally disregarded in wartime—squarely on the centre of his head. The cap was also cut higher than normal (like Saint-Loup's, I thought), which gave Bithel the look of a sprite in pantomime; perhaps rather—taking into consideration his age, bulk, moustache—some comic puppet halfway between the Walrus and the Carpenter. His face was pitted and blotched like the surface of a Gruyère cheese, otherwise he seemed none the worse from the night before, except for some shortness of breath. He must have seen me glance at his cap, because he smiled ingratiatingly.

"Regulations allow these caps," he said. "They're more comfortable than those peaked SD affairs. Cheaper, too. Got this one for seventeen bob, two shillings off because slightly shop-soiled. You don't notice the small stain on top, do you?"

"Not at all."

He looked behind us and lowered his voice.

"None of the rest of them were at the 'varsity," he said. "I've been making inquiries. What do you do in Civvy Street— that's the correct army phrase, I believe."

I indicated that I wrote for the papers, not mentioning

books because, if not specifically in your line, authorship is an embarrassing subject for all concerned. Besides, it never sounds like a serious occupation. Up to that moment, no one had pressed inquiries further than that, satisfied that journalism was a known form of keeping body and soul together, even if an esoteric one.

"I thought you might do something of the sort," said Bithel, speaking with respect. "I was trained for professional life too—intended for an auctioneer, like my pa. Never cared for the work somehow. Didn't even finish my training, as a matter of fact. Always been more or less interested in the theatre. Had walk-on parts once or twice but I'm no actor. I'm quite aware of that. I like doing odd jobs in any case. Can't bear being tied down. Worked for a time in our local cinema, for instance. Didn't have to do much except turn up in the evening wearing a dinner jacket."

"Does that sort of thing bring in enough?"

"Not much cash in it, of course. You'll never make a fortune that way, but I rub along all right with the few pennies I have already. Helps not being married. I expect you're married?"

"I am, as a matter of fact."

He made marriage sound as if it required some excuse.

"I thought you would be," he said. "As I mentioned, I'm not. Never found the right girl somehow."

Bithel looked infinitely uncomfortable when he admitted that. There was a pause in our conversation. I could not think of anything to suggest. Girls certainly did not appear much in his line, though you never could tell. I asked how he came to be in the Territorial Army Reserve, which seemed to require explanation.

"Joined the Terriers years ago," he said. "Seemed the thing to do. Never thought I'd wear uniform again when I gave them up. Rather glad to get back now and have some regular money rolling in. I've been out of a job, as a matter of fact, and what I've got doesn't support me. We draw Field Allowance here, so I heard last night. I expect you know that already. Makes a nice addition to the pay. Funds were running rather low, to tell the truth. Always such a lot to spend money on. Reading, for instance. I expect you're an omnivorous reader, if you're a journalist. What digests do you take?"

At first I thought he referred to some sort of medical treatment, harking back to the conversation of the chaplains the night before, then realized the question had something to do with reading. I had to admit I did not take any digests. Bithel seemed disappointed at this answer.

"I don't really buy a lot of digests myself," he admitted. "Perhaps not as many as I should. They have interesting articles in them sometimes. About sex, for instance. Sex psychology, I mean. Do you know about that?"

"I've heard of it."

"I don't mean the cheap stuff just to catch the eye, girls and legs, all that. There are abnormal sides you'd never guess. It's wiser to know about such things, don't you think?"

"Certainly."

Bithel moved nearer as we walked, lowering his voice again. There was a faint suggestion of scented soap at this close, too close, range.

"Did they say anything about me before I arrived?" he asked in a troubled tone.

"Who?"

"Anybody in the Battalion?"

"How do you mean?"

"Any details about my family?"

"Somebody said you were a brother of the VC."

"They did?"

"Yes."

"What did you say when they told you that?"

"I thought you must be too young to be his brother—more likely his nephew."

"Quite right. I'm not Bithel VC's brother."

"You are his nephew?"

"I never said so, did I? But don't let's talk any more about that. There was something else I wanted to ask you. Did they say anything about games?"

"What sort of games?"

"Did they say I played any special game?"

"There was some talk of your having played rugger for Wales."

Bithel groaned.

"There was talk of that?" he asked, as if to make sure he had heard right.

"Yes."

"I knew there'd been a misunderstanding," he said.

"What about?"

"Why, about my playing football—about rugger. You know what it is when you've had a few drinks. Very easy to give a wrong impression. I must have done that when I phoned that officer dealing with TA Reservists. Talked too much about local matters, sport, other people of the name of Bithel and so on."

"So the VC is no relation, and you didn't play rugger for Wales?"

"I wouldn't go so far as to say he was no relation. Never know who you may be related to in this part of the world. He's not a brother or uncle anyway. I must have managed to mislead that fellow completely if he got that idea into his head. He didn't sound very bright on the phone. I thought so at the time. One of these old dug-outs, I suppose. Colonel Blimp type. But it isn't Bithel VC who worries me so much. It's this rugger misunderstanding."

"How did it arise?"

"God knows. Something misheard on the phone too, I should think. I believe there was a merchant called Bithel in the Welsh Fifteen one year. Perhaps there was a Bithel who played cricket for Glamorgan and I've muddled it. One or the other, I'm sure. It was a few years back anyway. I must have mentioned it for some reason."

"It doesn't really matter, does it?"

"It would if we had to play rugger."

"That isn't very likely."

"The fact is I've never played rugger in my life," said Bithel. "Never had the chance. Not particularly keen to either. Do you think we shall have to play?"

"Not much time with all the training, I should imagine."

"I hope not," he said, rather desperately. "There's a rumour we're going to move almost at once in any case."

"Any idea where?"

"People seem to think Northern Ireland. I say, this parade ground is a long way off, isn't it. Hope we shan't be inspected too closely, I'm not all that well shaved. I cut myself this morning. Hand shaky, for some reason."

"That dance was a splendid affair."

"What dance?"

"The dance you did round the dummy in your bed last night."

"Ah," said Bithel laughing, "I've heard that one before—having somebody on by pretending he made a fool of himself the night before. I know when I'm having my leg pulled. As a matter of fact I was rather relieved when everyone went off quietly to bed last night. I thought there might be some ragging, and I was feeling tired after the journey. They used to rag a lot when I was in Territorial camp years ago. I never liked it. Not cut out for that sort of thing. But to get back to razors—what shaving soap do you use? I'm trying a new kind. Saw it advertised in *Health and Strength*. Thought I'd experiment. I like a change of soaps from time to time. It freshens you up."

By that time we had reached the parade ground. Kedward was already there. He took me off to the platoon I was to command. Bithel disappeared in another direction. Kedward explained certain matters, then we marched up and down side by side until officers were ordered to fall in. The service was held in one of the parish churches of the town. Later, from the pulpit, Popkiss, transformed now from the pale, embarrassed cleric of the saloon bar, orated with the ease and energy shared by officers and men throughout the Battalion. His text was from Ezekiel. Popkiss read the passage at length:

"The hand of the Lord was upon me, and carried me out in the spirit of the Lord, and set me down in the midst of the valley which was full of bones, and caused me to pass them round about: and, behold, there were very many in the open valley: and, lo, they were very dry. And he said unto me, Son of man, can these bones live? And I answered, O Lord God thou knowest. Again he said unto me, Prophesy upon these bones, and say unto them, O ye dry bones, hear the word of the Lord. Thus saith the Lord God unto these bones; Behold, I will cause breath to enter into you, and ye shall live. And I will lay sinews upon you, and cover you with skin, and put breath into you, and ye shall live; and ye shall know that I am the Lord. So I prophesied as I was commanded; and as I prophesied there was a noise, and behold a shaking, and the bones came together, bone to bone. And when I beheld, lo, the sinews and the flesh came upon them, and the skin covered them above; and there was no breath in them. Then he said unto me, Prophesy unto the wind, prophesy, son of man, and say to the wind, Thus saith the Lord God; Come from the four winds, O breath, and breathe upon these slain that they may live. So I prophesied as he commanded me, and the breath came unto them and they lived, and stood up upon their feet, an exceeding great army . . ."

Popkiss paused, looked up from his Testament, stretched out his arms on either side. The men were very silent in the pitch-pine pews.

". . . Oh, my brethren, think on that open valley, think on it with me . . . a valley, do I picture it, by the shaft of a shut-down mine, where, under the dark mountain side, the slag heaps lift their heads to the sky, a valley such as those valleys in which you yourselves abide . . . Journey with me, my brethren, into that open valley, journey with me . . . Know you not those same dry bones? . . . You know them well. . . . Bones without flesh and sinew, bones without skin or breath . . . They are our bones, my brethren, the bones of you and of me, bones that await the noise and the mighty shaking, the gift of the four winds of which the prophet of old did tell . . . Must we not come together, my brethren, everyone of us, as did the bones of that ancient valley, quickened with breath, bone to bone, sinew to sinew, skin to skin . . . Unless I speak falsely, an exceeding great army . . ."

Two

THE movement order came not much more than a week afterwards, before I had properly awakened from the dream through the perspectives of which I ranged, London as remote from me as from Kedward, Isobel's letters the only residuum of a world occupied by other matters than platoon training or turning out the guard. As if by the intoxication of a drug, or compulsive hypnotic influences on the will, another world had been entered by artificial means, through which one travelled irresistibly, ominously, like Dr. Trelawney and his fellow magicians, borne by their spells out on to the Astral Plane. Now, at last, I was geared to the machine of war, no longer an extraneous organism existing separately in increasingly alien conditions. For the moment, routine duties scarcely allowed thought. There was a day frantically occupied with packing. Then the whole Battalion was on parade. Orders were shouted. We moved off in column of route, leaving behind us Sardis, one of the Seven Churches of Asia, where the garments were white of those few who remained undefiled. The men, although departing from their own neighbourhoods and country, were in a fairly buoyant mood. Something was beginning at last. They sang softly:

> "Guide me, O thou great Jehovah,
> Pilgrim through this barren land:
> I am weak, but though art mighty,
> Hold me with thy powerful hand,

> Bread of heaven,
> Bread of heaven
> Feed me till I want no more . . ."

This singing on the march, whatever form it took, always affirmed the vicissitudes of life, the changes, so often for the worse, that beset human existence, especially in the army, especially in time of war. After a while they abandoned the hymn, though not those accustomed themes of uncertainty, hardship, weariness, despondency, vain effort, contemplation of which gives such support to the soldier:

> "We had ter join,
> We had ter join,
> We had ter join Belisha's army:
>
> Ten bob a week,
> Bugger all to eat,
> Great big boots and blisters on yer feet.
>
> We had ter join,
> We had ter join,
> We had ter join Belisha's army:
>
> Sitting on the grass,
> Polishing up the brass,
> Great black spiders running up yer—back.
>
> We had ter join—we had ter join—
> We had ter join—we had ter join . . ."

Gwatkin was in a state of unconcealed excitement. He bawled out his commands, loud as if through a megaphone, perpetually checking Kedward, Breeze and myself about minor matters. I could just see Bithel plodding along with his platoon at the rear of the company immediately ahead of us. He had turned up on parade carrying a small green leather dressing-case, much battered, which he grasped while he marched.

"Didn't like to trust it with the heavy baggage," he said,

adjusting the worn waterproof cover, while we stood easy at the railway station. "The only piece of my mother's luggage I have left. She's gone to a Better Place now, you know."

The train set out towards the north. This was the beginning of a long journey to an unknown destination. Night fell. Hours later, we detrained in stygian darkness. Here was a port. Black craft floated on a pitchy, infernal lake. Beyond the mouth of the harbour, the wash of waves echoed. The boat on which the Battalion embarked was scarcely large enough to accommodate our strength. The men were fitted in at last, sitting or lying like the cargo of a slave ship. The old steamer chugged away from the jetty, and into open sea. Wind was up. We heaved about in choppy waters. There was not going to be much sleep for anyone that night. After much scurrying about on the part of officers and NCOs, Sergeant Pendry reported at last that all was correct. He was accompanied by Corporal Gwylt, one of the Company's several wits, tiny, almost a dwarf, with a huge head of black curly hair; no doubt a member of that primitive race of which the tall, fair Celt had become overlord. Not always to be relied upon to carry out purely military duties to perfection, Gwylt was acceptable as an NCO because he never stopped talking and singing, so that his personality, though obtrusive, helped the Platoon through some of the tedium inseparable from army life.

"Has everyone had their cocoa issue, Sergeant Pendry?"

"That they have, sir, very good it was."

"Some of the boys was too sick to drink their cocoa, sir," said Corporal Gwylt, who felt his comment always required.

"Are a lot of the Platoon sea-sick?"

"I told them to lie still and it would pass," said Sergeant Pendry. "They do make a lot of fuss, some of them."

"Oh, bloody sick, some of them," said Corporal Gwylt, like a Greek chorus. "That fair boy, Jones, D., bloody sick he has been."

The boat ploughed through wind and wave. Was this the night journey on the sea of a thousand dreams loaded with hidden meaning? Certainly our crossing was no less myste-

rious than those nocturnal voyages of sleep. Towards morning
I retired below to shave, feeling revived when I returned to
deck. The sky was getting lighter and land was in sight. An
easterly breeze was blowing when we went ashore, which
sprayed about a gentle drizzle. Beyond the harbour stretched
a small town, grey houses, factory chimneys. In the distance,
mountains were obscured by cloud. Everything looked mean
and down-at-heel. There was nothing to make one glad to
have arrived in this country.

"March your men ashore promptly when the order comes,
platoon commanders," said Gwatkin. "Show initiative. Don't
hang about. Get cracking."

He looked rather green in the face, as if, like Jones, D.,
he too had been sick during the crossing, himself far from
the condition required for "getting cracking." The companies
filed down the gangway, one by one, forming up later by a
railway line. There were the usual delays. The rain, borne
towards us on a driving wind, was increasing in volume. The
Battalion stood easy, waiting for word from the Embarkation
Staff. Girls with shawls over their heads were on their way
to work. Disregarding the rain, they stopped and watched us
from the side of the road, standing huddled together, talking
and laughing.

"Aigh-o, Mary," shouted Corporal Gwylt. "Have you come
to see the foreigners?"

The girls began to giggle purposefully.

"It's no brave day ye've brought with ye," one of them
called back.

"What was that you said, Mary, my love?"

"Why did ye not bring a braver day with ye, I'm asking.
'Tis that we've been wanting since Sunday, sure."

"What kind of a day, Mary, my own?"

"Why a brave day. 'Tis prosperous weather we're needing."

Corporal Gwylt turned to Sergeant Pendry and made a
gesture with his hand to convey absolute incredulity at such
misuse of language.

"*Brave* day?" he said. "Did you hear what she called it,
Sergeant Pendry?"

"I did that, Corporal Gwylt."

"So that's a funny way to talk."

"That it is."

"Now you can tell the way people speak we're far from home."

"You'll be getting many surprises in this country, my lad," said Sergeant Pendry. "You may be sure of that."

"Will some of them be nice surprises, Sergeant?"

"Ask not that of me."

"Oh, don't you think I'll be getting some nice surprises, Sergeant Pendry," said Corporal Gwylt in a soft wheedling tone, "like a plump little girl to keep me warm at night."

CSM Cadwallader was pottering about nearby, like a conscientious matron at a boys' school determined to make sure all was well. He had the compact professional feeling of the miner, which he combined with a rather unusual taste for responsibility, so that any company commander was lucky to claim his services.

"We'll be keeping you warm, Corporal Gwylt," he said. "Make no mistake. There'll be plenty of work for you, I'll tell you straight. Do not worry about the night-time. Then you will want your rest, not little girls, nor big ones neither."

"But a plump little girl, Sergeant-Major? Do not yourself wish to meet a plump little girl?"

"Put not such ideas into the Sergeant-Major's head, Corporal Gwylt," said Sergeant Pendry. "He does not wish your dirty things."

"Nor me, the *dirty* girls," said Corporal Gwylt. "I never said the dirty ones."

"Nor then the clean ones, understand."

"Oh, does he not?" said Corporal Gwylt, in feigned astonishment. "Not even the clean ones? Do you think that indeed, Sergeant Pendry?"

"I do think that, I tell you."

"And why, whatever?"

"The Sergeant-Major is a married man, you must know."

"So you think girls are just for young lads like me, Sergeant-Major? That is good for me, I'm sure."

"Never mind what I think, Corporal."

"He is a lucky man, the Sergeant-Major," said Sergeant Pendry sententiously. "You will be glad when you reach his age, no longer foolish and running after girls."

"Oh, dear me, is it true what Sergeant Pendry says, Sergeant-Major, that girls are for you no longer? I am that sorry to hear."

CSM Cadwallader allowed himself a dry smile.

"Have you never heard, Corporal Gwylt, there's those to find many a good tune played on old fiddles?" he said benevolently.

The Embarkation Staff Officer turned up at that moment with a sheaf of papers. The Battalion was on the move again. Corporal Gwylt had just time to blow a kiss to the girls, who waved frantically, redoubling their gigglings. The Company tramped off towards the train in a siding.

"Now then, there," shouted the Sergeant-Major, "pick up the step in the rear files. Left—left—left, right, left . . ."

We steamed through bare, dismal country, wide fields, white cabins, low walls of piled stones, stretches of heather, more mountains far away on the horizon.

"This will give us better training areas than back home," said Gwatkin.

He had recovered from his sea sickness and the tension brought on by the move. Now he was relatively calm.

"We shall be more like soldiers here," he said with satisfaction.

"What happens when we arrive, Rowland?" Breeze asked. "I hope there'll be something to eat."

Breeze's questions were usually aimed to score the textbook answer from Gwatkin.

"The second echelon of the supply column will have preceded us," said Gwatkin sharply.

"And what do they do?"

"They will have broken bulk and be ready to issue to units. You should spend more time on your *Field Service Pocket Book*, Yanto."

We arrived at a small, unalluring industrial town. Once

more the Battalion formed up. By now the men were tired. Singing was sombre as we marched in:

"My lips smile no more, my heart loses its
   lightness,
No dream of the future my spirit can cheer,
I only would brood on the past and its brightness,
The dead I have mourned are again gathered here.
From every dark nook they press forward to meet
   me,
I lift up my eyes to the broad leafy dome.
And others are there looking downward to greet me,
The ashgrove, the ashgrove, alone is my home . . ."

Gwatkin was right about being more like soldiers in these new surroundings. Barracks had been created from a disused linen factory, the long narrow sheds in which the flax had formerly been treated offering barrack-rooms stark as a Foreign Legion film set. Officers were billeted in a forlorn villa on the outskirts of the town, a house that had no doubt once belonged to some successful local businessman. It was a mile or more away from the barracks. There, I still shared a room with Kedward, Breeze and Pumphrey, the last of whom had not yet achieved his RAF transfer. Another subaltern, Craddock, was in with us too, brother of the girl to whom Kedward was engaged. Craddock, fat and energetic, was Messing Officer, which meant he returned to billets in the middle of the night several times a week, when he would either turn on the light, or blunder about the room in the dark, falling over other people's camp-beds in a fruitless effort to find his own. Both methods were disturbing. There was, in any case, not much room to manoeuvre round the beds, even when the light was on. Craddock's midnight arrivals were not the only inconvenience. Breeze left old razor blades about in profusion, causing Pumphrey to cut his foot one morning. Kedward talked in his sleep throughout the night, shouting commands, as if he were drilling a company: "At the halt—on the left— form close column of—platoons . . ."

Pumphrey, inclined to bicker, would throw towels about and sponges. A window pane was broken, which no one ever seemed responsible for mending, through which the night wind whistled, while cold struck up insistently from the floor, penetrating the canvas of a camp-bed. Snow had returned. I record these conditions not as particularly formidable in the circumstances, but to indicate they were sufficiently far from ideal to encourage a change, when, as it happened, opportunity arose. This came about through Gwatkin in an unexpected manner. During the weeks that followed our arrival in these new surroundings, I began to know him better. He was nearer my own age than the other subalterns, except Bithel. Even the captains tended to be younger than Gwatkin and myself, as time went on, some of the older ones being gradually shifted, as insufficiently proficient at their job, to Holding Battalions or the Infantry Training Centre.

"We're getting rid of the dead wood," said Gwatkin. "Just as well."

His own abrupt manner of speaking continued, and he loved to find fault for its own sake. At the same time, he evidently wanted to be friendly, while fearing that too easy a relationship with a subordinate, even one of similar age, might be unmilitary. There were unexpected sides to Gwatkin, sudden displays of uncertainty under a façade meant to be very certain. Some of his duties he carried out very well; for others, he had little or no natural talent.

"A company commander," said Dicky Umfraville, when we met later that year, "needs the qualifications of a ringmaster in a first-class circus, and a nanny in a large family."

Gwatkin aspired to this dazzling combination of gifts—to become (as Pennistone later said) a military saint. Somehow he always fell short of that coveted status. His imperfections never derived from any willingness to spare himself. On the contrary, inability to delegate authority, insistence that he must do everything himself, important or unimportant, was one of Gwatkin's chief handicaps in achieving his high aim. For example, he instituted a "Company Officer of the Day," one of whose duties was to make sure all was well at the men's dinners. This job, on the whole redundant, since the Orderly Officer of necessity visited all Mess Rooms to investigate "any complaints," was made additionally superfluous by Gwatkin himself appearing as often as not at dinners, in order to make sure the Company Officer of the Day was not shirking his rounds. In fact, he scarcely allowed himself any time off at all. He seemed half aware that this intense keenness was not, in final result, what was required; at least not without more understanding on his own part. Besides, Gwatkin had none of that faculty, so necessary in the army, of accepting rebuke—even unjust rebuke—and carrying on as if nothing had happened. Criticism from above left him dreadfully depressed.

"It's no good letting the army get you down," the Adjutant, Maelgwyn-Jones, used to say. "Just remember, when you're worrying about the Brigadier's inspection, that day will pass, as other days in the army pass."

Maelgwyn-Jones himself did not always act upon this teaching. He was an efficient, short-tempered Regular, whose slight impediment of speech became a positive stutter when he grew enraged. He wanted to get back to the battalion he came from, where there was more hope of immediate action and consequent promotion. Thoroughly reliable as an officer, hard working as an adjutant, Maelgwyn-Jones did not share— indeed was totally unapprehending of—Gwatkin's resplendent vision of army life. When he pulled up Gwatkin for some such lapse as unpunctual disposal of the Company's swill, Gwatkin would behave as if his personal honour had been called into question; then concentrate feverishly on more energetic training, smarter turn-out. In a sense, of course, that was correct enough, but the original cause of complaint was not always put right in the most expeditious manner. The fact was Gwatkin lacked in his own nature that grasp of "system" for which he possessed such admiration. This deficiency was perhaps connected in some way with a kind of poetry within him, a poetry which had somehow become a handicap in its efforts to find an outlet. Romantic ideas about the way life is lived are often to be found in persons themselves fairly coarse-grained. This was to some extent true of Gwatkin. His coarseness of texture took the form of having to find a scapegoat after he himself had been in trouble. The scapegoat was usually Breeze, though any of the rest of the Company might suffer. Bithel, usually in hot water of some kind, would have offered an ever available target for these punitive visitations of Gwatkin's, but Bithel was in another company. All the same, although no concern of his in the direct sense, Bithel's appearance and demeanour greatly irked Gwatkin in a general way. He spoke of this one afternoon, when Bithel, wearing one of his gaiters improperly adjusted, crossed our path on the way back from afternoon training.

"Did you ever see such an unsoldierly type?" Gwatkin said. "And his brother a VC too."

"Is it certain they're brothers, not just fairly distant relations?"

I was not sure whether Bithel's words to me on that earlier occasion had been spoken in confidence. The tone he had adopted suggested something of the sort. Besides, Bithel might suddenly decide to return to the earlier cycle of legends he had apparently disseminated about himself to facilitate his Reserve call-up; or at least he might not wish to have them specifically denied on his own authority. However, Gwatkin showed no wish to verify the truth, or otherwise, of Bithel's alleged kinships.

"Even if they are not brothers, Bithel is a disgrace for a man with a VC in the family," Gwatkin said severely. "He should be ashamed. That VC ought to give him a pride in himself. I wish a relative of mine had won the VC, won an MC even. And it is my belief, I am telling you, Nick, that all about Bithel's rugger is tommy-rot."

That last conviction was unanswerable by this time. No one who had seen Bithel proceeding at the double could possibly suppose his abilities in the football field had ever been more than moderate.

"Do you know when Idwal was Orderly Officer last week," said Gwatkin, "he found Bithel in his dressing-gown listening to the gramophone with the Mess waiters. Bithel said he was looking for Daniels, that servant of his I don't much like either. And then we are expected to keep discipline in the unit."

"That bloody gramophone makes a frightful row at all hours."

"So it does, too, and I'm not going to stay in those billets any longer. I have had enough. My camp-bed was taken down to the Company Officer this morning. That is the place for a company commander to be. Half the day is lost in this place walking backwards and forwards from billets to barracks. We are lucky enough to have an office next door to the Company Store. The bed can be folded up and go into the store for the day."

We had reached a fork in the road. One way led to barracks, the other to billets. Gwatkin seemed suddenly to come to a decision.

"Why don't you come down to the Company Office too?" he asked.

He spoke roughly, almost as if he were demanding why I had disobeyed an order.

"Would there be room?"

"Plenty."

"We're pretty thick on the ground where I am at present, even though Idwal is on the Anti-gas course at the moment."

"It won't be so lively sleeping in the office."

"I can stand that."

"The great thing is you're on the spot. Near the men. Where every officer should be."

I was flattered by the suggestion. Kedward was at the Corps School of Chemical Warfare at Castlemallock—usually known as the Anti-gas School—so that Breeze and I were Gwatkin's only subalterns at that moment, and there was a lot of work to do. As I have said, accommodation at the billets had little to recommend it. The Company Office was at least no worse a prospect. To be in barracks would be convenient, not least in its reduction of continual trudging backwards and forwards to the billets.

"I'll have my kit taken down this evening."

That was the beginning of my comparative intimacy with Gwatkin. Sharing with him the Company Office at night altered not only our mutual relationship, but also the whole tempo of night and morning. Instead of the turmoil of Kedward, Breeze, Pumphrey and Craddock getting dressed, talking, scuffling, singing, there was only the occasional harsh, serious, professional comment of Gwatkin; his tense silences. He slept heavily, often dropping off before the electric light was out and the blackout down; never, like myself, lying awake listening to the talk in the Company Store next door. The partition between the store and the office did not reach all the way to the ceiling, so that conversation held in the store after Lights Out, although usually carried out in comparatively low tones—in contrast with the normal speech of the unit—was often audible. Only the storeman, Lance-Corporal Gittins, was supposed to sleep in the store at night, but, in practice, the room usually housed several others; semi-official assistants of Gittins, friends, relations, Company personalities, like Corporal Gwylt. These would gather in the evening, if not on guard duties, and listen to the wireless; several of those assembled later staying the night among the crates and piles of blankets, to slumber in the peculiar, musty smell of the store, an odour somewhere between the Natural History Museum and an oil-and-colour shop. Lance-Corporal Gittins was CSM Cadwallader's brother-in-law. He was a man not always willing to recognise the artificial and temporary hierarchy imposed by military rank.

"Now, see it you must, Gareth," I heard the Sergeant-Major's voice once insisting on the other side of the partition. "In time of peace—in the mine—you are above me, Gareth, and above Sergeant Pendry. Here, that is not. No longer is it the mine. In the Company we are above you. It would be good you remember that, Gareth."

Gittins was a figure of some prestige in the Company, not only on account of dominion over valuable stock-in-trade, but also for his forcible character. Dark, stocky, another strongly pre-Celtic type, he could probably have become sergeant—even sergeant-major—without difficulty, had he wished for promotion. Like many others, he preferred to avoid such responsibilities, instead ruling the store, where he guarded every item as if it were his own personal property acquired only after long toil and self-denial. Nothing was more difficult than to extort from him the most insignificant replacement of kit.

"I tell you, not without the Skipper's direct order," was his usual answer to such requests. This circumspection was very generally respected. To coax anything from Gittins was considered a triumph. One of the attractions of the store was its wireless, which would sometimes be tuned in to Haw-Haw's propaganda broadcast from Germany. These came on just after midnight:

". . . This is *Chairmany* calling . . . *Chairmany* calling . . . These are the stations Köln, Hamburg and DJA . . . Here is the news in English . . . Fifty-three more British aircraft were shot down over Kiel last night making a total of one hundred and seventeen since Tuesday . . . One hundred and seventeen more British aircraft have been shot down in forty-eight hours . . . The British people are asking their Government why British pilots cannot stay in the air . . . They are asking why British aircraft is inferior to *Chairman* aircraft . . . The British people are asking themselves why they have lost the war in the air . . . They are asking, for example, what has happened to the Imperial Airways Liner *Ajax* . . . Why is the Imperial Liner *Ajax* three weeks overdue, they are asking . . . We can tell you . . . The Imperial Airways Liner *Ajax* is at the bottom of the sea . . . The fishes are swimming in and out of the wreckage of the Imperial Airways Liner *Ajax* . . . The Imperial Airways Liner *Ajax* and her escort were shot down by *Chairman* fighter planes . . . The British have lost the war in the air . . . They have lost the war in the air . . . It is the same on the water . . . The Admiralty is wondering about the *Resourceful* . . . They are worried at the Admiralty about the *Resourceful* . . . They need not worry about the *Resourceful* any more . . . We will tell them about the *Resourceful* . . . The *Resourceful* is at the bottom of the sea with the Imperial Airways Liner *Ajax* . . . The *Resourceful* was sunk by a *Chair-*

man submarine . . . The Admiralty is in despair at *Chairman* command of the sea . . . Britain has lost the war on the sea . . . One hundred and seventy-five thousand *gross registered* tons of British shipping was sent to the bottom last week . . . The British Government is in despair at these losses in the air and on the water . . . That is not the only thing that makes the British Government despair . . . Not by any means . . . The food shortage in Britain is becoming acute . . . The evacuated women and children are living in misery . . . Instead of food, they are being fed on lies . . . Government lies . . . Only *Chairmany* can tell you the truth . . . The *Chairman* radio speaks the truth . . . The *Chairman* radio gives the best and latest news . . . *Chairmany* is winning the war . . . Think it over, Britain, think it over . . . *Chairmany* is winning the war . . . Listen, Britain . . . Listen, Britain . . . We repeat to all listeners in the Far East . . . Listen, South America . . ."

Someone in the store turned the button. The nagging, sneering, obsessive accents died away with a jerk, as if a sack had been advantageously thrust over the speaker's head, bestowing an immediate sense of relief at his extinction. There was a long pause next door.

"I do wonder he can remember all that," said a voice, possibly that of Williams, W.H., one of the singers of Sardis, now runner in my platoon.

"Someone writes it down for him, don't you see," said another voice that could have been Corporal Gwylt's.

"And do they give him all those figures too?"

"Of course they do."

"So that is it."

"You must know that, lad."

"What a lot he do talk."

"That's for they pay him."

"Bloody sure he is Germany will win the war. Why does he call it like that—*Chairmany*—it's a funny way to speak to be sure."

"Maybe that's the way they say it there."

"If Hitler wins the war, I tell you, lad, we'll go down the mine for sixpence a day."

No one in the store attempted to deny this conclusion. There was another pause and some coughing. It was not easy to tell how many persons were collected there. Gittins himself appeared to have gone to sleep, only Gwylt and Williams, W. H., unable to bring the day to a close. I thought they too must have nodded off, when suddenly Williams's voice sounded again.

"How would you like to go up in an aircraft, Ivor?"

"I would not mind that so much."

"I hope I do not have to do that."

"We are not in the RAF, lad, what are you thinking?"

"I would not like it up there I am sure too."

"They will not put you up there, no worry."

"You do not know what they will do, look at those parachutists, indeed."

"You make me think of Dai and Shoni when they went up in a balloon."

"And what was that, I wonder."

"They took two women with them."

"Did they, then?"

"When the balloon was in the sky, the air began to leak something terrible out of it, it did, and Dai was frightened, so frightened Dai was, and Dai said to Shoni, Look you, Shoni, this balloon is not safe at all, and the air is leaking out of it terrible, we shall have to jump for it, and Shoni said to Dai, But, Dai, what about the women? and Dai said, Oh, fook the women, and Shoni said, But have we time?"

"We shall not have any time to sleep till morning break, I am telling you, if you will jaw all through the night," spoke another voice, certainly Lance-Corporal Gittins, the storeman, this time. "How many hundred and hundred of those Dai and Shoni stories have I in all my days had to hear, I should like to know, and most of them said by you, Ivor. Is tarts never out of your thought."

"Why, Gareth, you talk about tarts too," said Williams, W. H. "What was that you was telling my butty of Cath Pendry yesterday?"

"What about her?"

Gittins sounded more truculent this time.

"Her and Evans the checkweighman."

"You was not meant to hear that, I tell you, Williams, W. H."

"Come on, Gareth," said Gwylt.

"Never mind you, Ivor."

"Oh, that do sound something I would like to hear."

No one answered Gwylt. There was a lot more coughing, some throat clearing, then silence. They must all have gone to sleep. I was on the point of doing the same, had even reached a state of only semi-consciousness, when there was a sudden exclamation from the direction of Gwatkin's bed. He had woken with a start and was feeling for his electric torch. He found the torch at last and, clambering out of bed, began to put up the blackout boards on the window frame.

"What is it, Rowland?"

"Turn the light on," he said, "I've got this board fixed now."

I switched on the light, which was nearer my bed than his.

"I've just thought of something," Gwatkin said agitatedly. "Do you remember I said units had been issued with a new codeword for intercommunication within the Brigade?"

"Yes."

"What did I do with it?"

He seemed almost to be talking in his sleep.

"You put it in the box, didn't you?"

Gwatkin's usual treatment of the flow of paper that entered the Company Office daily was to mark each item with the date in the inked letters of the Company's rubber stamp, himself initialling the centre of its circular mauve impression. He would treat the most trivial printed matter in this way, often wryly smiling as he remarked: "This becomes a habit." The click of the instrument on an official document, together with his own endorsement "R. G."—written with a flourish—seemed to give him a feeling of having settled that matter once and for all, a faint but distinct sense of absolute power. If classified as "Secret" or "Confidential," the stuff was put in a large cashbox, of which Gwatkin himself kept the key. The Company's "Imprest Account" was locked away in this box, together with all sorts of other papers which had taken Gwatkin's fancy as important. The box itself was kept in a green steel cupboard, the shape of a wardrobe, also locked, though its key was considered less sacred than that of the cashbox.

"Are you sure I put it in the box?"

"Pretty sure."

"Codewords are vital."

"I know."

"I'd better make certain."

He put on a greatcoat over his pyjamas, because the nights were still fairly cold. Then he began fumbling about with the keys, opening the cupboard and bringing out the cashbox. There was not much room in the Company Office at the best of time, when both beds were erected, scarcely any space at all in which to operate, so that the foot of my own bed was the only convenient ledge on which to rest the box while Gwatkin went through its contents. He began to sort out the top layer of papers, arranging them in separate piles over the foot of my bed, all over my greatcoat, which was serving as eiderdown. I sat up in bed, watching him strew my legs with official forms and instructional leaflets of one kind or another. He dealt them out with great care, as if diverting himself with some elaborate form of Patience, military pamphlets doing duty for playing cards. The deeper he delved into the cashbox, the more meticulously he arranged the contents. Among other items, he turned out a small volume bound in faded red cloth. This book, much tattered, was within reach. I picked it up. Opening at the fly-leaf: I read: "R. Gwatkin, Capt.," together with the designation of the Regiment. The title-page was that of a pocket edition of *Puck of Pook's Hill.* Gwatkin gave a sudden grunt. He had found whatever he was seeking.

"Here it is," he said. "Thank God. I remember now. I put it in a envelope in a special place at the bottom of the box."

He began to replace the papers, one by one, in the elaborate sequence he had ordained for them. I handed him *Puck of Pook's Hill*. He took the book from me, still apparently pondering the fearful possibilities consequent on failure to trace the codeword. Then he suddenly became aware I had been looking at the Kipling stories. He took the little volume from me, and pushed it away under a *Glossary of Military Terms and Organization in the Field*. For a second he seemed a shade embarrassed.

"That's a book by Rudyard Kipling," he said defensively, as if the statement explained something.

"So I see."

"Ever read anything by him?"

"Yes."

"Read this one?"

"Ages ago."

"What did you think of it?"

"I liked it."

"You've read a lot of books, haven't you, Nick?"

"I have to in my profession."

Gwatkin locked the tin box and replaced it in the cupboard.

"Turn the light out," he said. "And I'll take the blackout down again."

I switched out the light. He removed the window boards. I heard him arranging the greatcoat over himself in the bed.

"I don't expect you remember," he said, "but there's a story in that book about a Roman centurion."

"Of course."

"That was the one I liked."

"It's about the best."

"I sometimes read it again."

He pulled the greatcoat higher over him.

"I've read it lots of times really," he said. "I like it. I don't like any of the others so much."

"The Norman knight isn't bad."

"Not so good as the centurion."

"Do you like his other books?"

"Whose?"

"Kipling's."

"Oh, yes, of course. I know he wrote a lot of other books. I did try one of them. I couldn't get on with it somehow."

"Which one did you try?"

"I can't remember the name. Can't remember much about it, to tell the truth. I just didn't like it. All written in a special sort of language I didn't understand. I don't read much. Got other things to do. It's not like you, reading more or less as a business."

He stopped speaking, was almost immediately asleep and breathing heavily. This was the first evidence come to light that anyone in the unit had ever read a book for pleasure, unless Bithel's "digests" might be thought to have brought him to a public library in search of some work on sexual psychology. This was an interesting discovery about Gwatkin. By now snores were sounding from the store. I rolled over towards the wall and slept too. The following day Gwatkin made no reference to this nocturnal conversation. Perhaps he had forgotten about it. Leaving barracks that evening there was a small incident to illustrate the way in which he took failure to heart. This happened when Gwatkin, Kedward and I were passing the vehicle park, where the bren-carriers stood.

"I'd like to try driving one of those buses," Kedward said.

"They're easy enough," said Gwatkin.

He scrambled into the nearest carrier and started up the engine. However, when he put the vehicle in gear, it refused to move, only rocking backwards and forwards on its tracks. Gwatkin's small head and black moustache bobbed up and down at the end of the carrier, so that he seemed part of the chassis, a kind of figurehead, even the front half of an armoured centaur. There was also something that recalled a knight in the game of chess, immensely large and suddenly animated by some inner, mysterious power. For a time Gwatkin heaved up and down there, as if riding one of the cars on a warlike merry-go-round; then completely defeated by the machinery, perhaps out of order, he climbed slowly to the ground and rejoined us.

"I shouldn't have done that," he said, humiliated.

All the same, this sort of thing did not at all impair his

confidence in himself when it came to dealing with the men. Gwatkin prided himself on his relationship with the "other ranks" in his company. He did not talk about it much, but the conviction was implicit in his behaviour. His attitude towards Sayce provided a good example. That was clear even before I witnessed their great scene together. Sayce was the Company bad character. He had turned up with another couple of throw-outs voided as unsuitable for employment from one of the regular battalions. His previous unit must have been thankful to get rid of him. Small and lean, with a yellow face and blackened teeth, his shortcomings were not to be numbered. Apart from such recurrent items as lateness on parade, deficiency of shaving kit, lack of clean socks, mislaid paybook, filthy rifle, generally unsatisfactory turnout, Sayce would produce some new, hitherto unthought-of crime most days. Dirty, disobliging, quarrelsome, little short of mutinous, he was heartily disliked by all ranks. Although a near criminal, he possessed none of the charm J. G. Quiggin, as a reviewer, used to attribute to criminals who wrote memoirs. On the contrary, Sayce, immoderately vain, was also stupid and unprepossessing. From time to time, in order to give him a chance to redeem himself from a series of disasters, he would be assigned some individual task, easy to undertake, but within range of conferring credit by its simple discharge. Sayce always made a hash of it; always, too, for the worst of reasons. He seemed preordained for detention.

"It will be the Glasshouse for that bugger Sayce," Sergeant Pendry, who got along pretty well with almost everyone, used often to remark.

In dealing with Sayce, therefore, it might be thought Gwatkin would assume his favoured role of martinet, imposing a series of punishments that would eventually bring Sayce before the Commanding Officer; and certainly Sayce took his share of CBs from Gwatkin in the Company Office. At the same time, their point of contact, at least on Gwatkin's side, was not entirely unsympathetic. The fact was, Sayce appealed to Gwatkin's imagination. Those stylized pictures of army life on which Gwatkin's mind loved to dwell did not exclude a soldier of Sayce's type. Indeed, a professional bad character was obviously a type from which no army could remain wholly free. Accordingly, Gwatkin was prepared to treat Sayce with what many company commanders would have considered excessive consideration, to tolerate him up to a point, even to make serious efforts to reform him. Gwatkin had spoken to me more than once about these projects for Sayce's reformation, before he finally announced that he had planned a direct appeal to Sayce's better feelings.

"I'm going to have a straight talk with Sayce," he said one day, when Sayce's affairs had reached some sort of climax. "I'd like you to be present, Nick, as he's in your platoon."

Gwatkin sat at the trestle table with the army blanket over it. I stood behind. Sayce, capless, was marched in by CSM Cadwallader and a corporal.

"You and the escort can leave the room, Sergeant-Major," said Gwatkin. "I want to have a word with this soldier in private—that is to say myself and his Platoon Commander, Mr. Jenkins."

The Sergeant-Major and other NCO withdrew.

"You can stand easy, Sayce," said Gwatkin.

Sayce stood easy. His yellow face showed distrust.

"I want to speak to you seriously, Sayce," said Gwatkin. 'To speak to you as man to man. Do you understand what I mean, Sayce?"

Sayce made some inaudible reply.

"It is not my wish, Sayce, to be always punishing you," said Gwatkin slowly. "Is that clear? I do not like doing that at all."

Sayce muttered again. It seemed very doubtful that he found Gwatkin's statement easy to credit. Gwatkin leant forward over the table. He was warming up. Within him were deep reserves of emotion. He spoke now with that strange cooing tone he used on the telephone.

"You can do better, Sayce. I say you can do better."

He fixed Sayce with his eye. Sayce's own eyes began to roll.

"You're a good fellow at heart, aren't you, Sayce?"

All this was now beginning to tell on Sayce. I had to admit to myself there was nothing I should have liked less than to be grilled by Gwatkin in this fashion. A week's CB would be infinitely preferable. Sayce began swallowing.

"You are, Sayce, aren't you?" Gwatkin repeated more pressingly, as if time were becoming short for Sayce to reveal that unexpected better side of himself, and gain salvation.

"Yes, sir," said Sayce, very low.

He spoke without much conviction. That could scarcely be because there was doubt in his mind of his own high qualifications. He probably suspected any such information, freely given, might be a dangerous admission, lead to more work.

"Well, Sayce," said Gwatkin, "that is what I am going to believe about you. Believe you are a good fellow. You know why we are all here?"

Sayce did not answer.

"You know why we are all here, Sayce," said Gwatkin again, louder this time, his voice shaking a little with his own depths of feeling. "Come on, Sayce, you know."

"Don't know, sir."

"Yes, you do."

"Don't, sir."

"Come on, man."

Sayce made a great effort.

"To give me CB for being on a charge," he offered wretchedly.

It was a reasonable hypothesis, but Gwatkin was greatly disturbed at being so utterly misunderstood.

"No, no," he said, "I don't mean why we are in the Company Office at this moment. I mean why we are all in the army. You must know that, Sayce. We are here for our country. We are here to repel Hitler. You know that as well as I do. You don't want Hitler to rule over you, Sayce, do you?"

Sayce gulped again, as if he were not sure.

"No, sir," he agreed, without much vigour.

"We must all, every one of us, do our best," said Gwatkin, now thoroughly worked up. "I try to do my best as Company

Commander. Mr. Jenkins and the other officers of the Company do their best. The NCOs and privates do their best. Are you going to be the only one, Sayce, who is not doing his best?"

Sayce was now in almost as emotional a state as Gwatkin himself. He continued to gulp from time to time, looking wildly round the room, as if for a path of escape.

"Will you do your best in future, Sayce?"

Sayce began sniffing frantically.

"I will, sir."

"Do you promise me, Sayce."

"All right, sir."

"And we're agreed you're a good chap, aren't we?"

"Yes, sir."

Indeed, Sayce seemed moved almost to tears by the thought of all his own hitherto unrevealed goodness.

"Never had a chance since I've been with the unit," he managed to articulate.

Gwatkin rose to his feet.

"We're going to shake hands, Sayce," he said.

He came round to the front of the table and held out his palm. Sayce took it gingerly, as if he still suspected a trick, a violent electric shock, perhaps, or just a terrific blow on the ear administered by Gwatkin's other hand. However, Gwatkin did no more than shake Sayce's own hand heartily. It was like the termination of some sporting event. Gwatkin continued to shake hands for several seconds. Then he returned to his seat behind the table.

"Now," he said, "I'm going to call in the escort again, so stand to attention, Sayce. All right? Get them in, Mr. Jenkins."

I opened the door and said the word. CSM Cadwallader and the corporal returned to their places, guarding Sayce.

"Prisoner admonished," said Gwatkin, in his military voice.

The Sergeant-Major was unable to conceal a faint tightening of the lips at the news of Sayce escaping all punishment. No doubt he had supposed it would be a matter for the Commanding Officer this time.

"Prisoner and escort—about turn—quick march—left wheel—"

They disappeared into the passage, like comedians retiring in good order from their act, only music lacking, CSM Cadwallader, with an agility perfected for such occasions, closing the door behind him without either pausing or turning.

Gwatkin sat back in his chair.

"How was that?" he asked.

"All right. Jolly good."

"You thought so?"

"Certainly."

"I think we shall see a change in Sayce," he said.

"I hope so."

This straight talk to Sayce on the part of Gwatkin had a stimulating effect, as it turned out, on Gwatkin, rather than Sayce. It cheered up Gwatkin greatly, made him easier to work with; Sayce, on the other hand, remained much what he had been before. The fact was Gwatkin needed drama in his life. For a brief moment drama had been supplied by Sayce. However, this love of the dramatic sent Gwatkin's spirits both up and down. Not only did his own defeats upset him, but also, vicariously, what he considered defeats for the Battalion. He felt, for example, deeply dishonoured by the case of Deafy Morgan, certainly an unfortunate incident.

"Somebody ought to have been shot for it," Gwatkin said at the time.

When we had arrived on this side of the water, Maelgwyn-Jones had given a talk to all ranks on the subject of internal security.

"This Command is very different from the Division's home ground," he said. "The whole population of this island is not waging war against Germany—only the North. A few miles away from here, over the Border, is a neutral state where German agents abound. There and on our side too elements exist hostile to Britain and her Allies. There have been cases of armed gangs holding up single soldiers separated from their main body, or trying to steal weapons by ruse. You may have noticed, even in this neighbourhood, that some of the corner boys look sullen when we pass and the children sing about hanging up washing on the Maginot—rather than the Siegfried—Line."

Accordingly, rifles were checked and re-checked, and Gwatkin was given additional opportunity for indulging in those harangues to the Company which he so greatly enjoyed delivering:

"Stand the men easy, Sergeant-Major," he would say. "No talking. Move up a little closer at the back so that you can hear me properly. Right. Now I want you all to attend very clearly to what I have to say. The Commanding Officer has ordered me to tell you once again you must all take care of your rifles, for a man's rifle is his best friend in time of war, and a soldier is no longer a soldier when his weapon is gone from him. He is like a man who has had that removed which makes him a man, something sadder, more useless, than a miner who has lost his lamp, or a farmer his plough. As you know, we are fighting Hitler and his hordes, so this Company must show the stuff she is made of, and you must all take care of your rifles or I will put you on a serious charge which will bring you before the Colonel. There are those not far from here who would steal rifles for their own beastly purpose. That is no funny matter, losing a rifle, not like long hair nor a dirty button. There is a place at Aldershot called the Glasshouse, where men who have not taken proper care of their rifles do not like to visit a second time. Nevertheless, I would not threaten you. That is not how I wish to lead you. It is for the honour of the Regiment that you should guard your rifles, like you would guard your wife or your little sister. Moreover, it may be some of the junior NCOs have not yet a proper sense of their own responsibilities in the matter of rifles and others. You Corporals, you Lance-Corporals, consider these things in your hearts. All rifles will be checked at Pay Parade each week, so that a man will bring his rifle to the table when he receives his due, and where you must remember to come smartly to attention and look straight in front of you without moving. That is the way we shall all pull together, and, as we heard the Rev. Popkiss, our Chaplain, read out at Church Parade last Sunday, so may it be said of this Company: Arise Barak, and lead thy captivity captive, thou son of Abinoam. So let your rifles be well guarded and be the smartest company of the Battalion both on parade and in the field. All right, Sergeant-Major . . ."

I was impressed by the speech, though there were moments when I thought Gwatkin's listeners might deride the images he conjured up, such as a man losing what made him a man, or little sisters who had to be protected. On the contrary, the Company listened spellbound, giving a low grunt of emphasis when the Glasshouse was mentioned, like a cinema audience gasping aloud in pleasurable appreciation of some peculiarly agonising sequence of horror film. I remembered Bracey, my father's soldier-servant, employing that very same phrase about his rifle being the soldier's best friend. After twenty-five years, that sentiment had stood up well to the test of time and the development of more scientific weapons of war.

"It does the lads good to be talked to like that," said CSM Cadwallader afterwards. "Captain does know how to speak. Very excellent would he have been to preach the Word."

Even Gittins, whose inherent strain of scepticism was as strong as any in the Battalion, had enjoyed Gwatkin's talk. He told me so when I came to the Store later, to check supplies of web equipment held there.

"A fine speech that was, the Skipper's," said Gittins. "That should make the boys take care of their rifles proper, it should. And the rest of their stuff, too, I hope, and not come round here scrounging what they've lost off me, like a present at Christmas, it was."

Kedward was less impressed.

"Rowland doesn't half love jawing," he said, "I should just say so. But what's he going to be like when we get into action, I wonder, he is so jumpy. Will he keep his head at that?"

The doubts Kedward felt about Gwatkin were to some extent echoed by Gwatkin himself in regard to Kedward.

"Idwal is a good reliable officer in many ways," he confided his opinion to me, "but I'm not sure he has just the quality for leading men."

"The men like him."

"The men can like an officer without feeling he inspires them. Yanto told me the other day he thought the men liked Bithel. You wouldn't say Bithel had the quality of leadership, would you?"

Gwatkin's dislike of Bithel was given new impetus by the Deafy Morgan affair, which followed close on the homily about rifles. Deafy Morgan, as his cognomen—it was far more than a mere nickname—implied, was hard of hearing. In fact, he was as deaf as a post. Only in his middle or late thirties, he gave the impression—as miners of that age often do—of being much older than his years. His infirmity, in any case, set him apart from the hurly-burly of the younger soldiers' life, giving him a mild, even beatific cast of countenance, an expression that seemed for ever untroubled by moral turmoil or disturbing thought. It was probably true to say that Deafy Morgan did not have many thoughts, disturbing or otherwise, because he was not outstandingly bright, although at the same time possessing all sorts of other good qualities. In short, Deafy Morgan was the precise antithesis of Sayce. Always spick and span, he was also prepared at all times to undertake boring or tedious duties without the least complaint—in what could only be called the most Christlike spirit. Even among good soldiers, that is a singular quality in the army. No doubt it was one of the reasons why Deafy Morgan had not been relegated to the Second Line before the Division moved. Not at all fit, he would obviously have to be transferred sooner or later to the rear echelons. However, his survival was mainly due not so much to this habit of working without complaint, rare as that might be, as to the fact that everyone liked him. Besides, he had served as a Territorial longer than any other soldier in the ranks, wanted to remain with his friends—he was alleged to possess at home a nagging wife—so that no one in authority had had the heart to put Deafy Morgan's name on whatever Army Form was required to effect his removal. He was in Bithel's platoon.

Bithel himself had recently been appointed Musketry Officer. This was not on account of any notable qualifications for that duty, simply because the Battalion was short of officers on the establishment, several being also absent on courses. By this time Bithel's individual status had become more clear to me. He was a small-town misfit, supporting himself in peacetime by odd jobs, preferably those on the outskirts of the theatrical world, living a life of solitude and toping, always on the verge of trouble, always somehow managing to extricate himself from anything serious. In the Battalion, there had been no repetition of the dance of love round the dummy, not anything comparable with that in exoticism. All the same, I suspected such expressions of Bithel's personality were dormant rather than totally suppressed. He was always humble, even subservient, in manner, but this demeanour seemed to cloak a good opinion of himself, perhaps even delusions of grandeur.

"Have you ever been interested in the Boy Scout movement?" he asked. "I was keen about it at one time. Wonderful thing for boys. Gives them a chance. I threw it up in the end. Some of them are little brutes, you know. You'd never guess the things they say. I was surprised they knew about such matters. And their language among themselves. You wouldn't credit it. I was told I was greatly missed after my resignation. They have a great deal of difficulty in getting *suitable* fellows to help. There are some nasty types about."

The army is at once the worst place for egoists, and the best. Thus it was in many ways the worst for Bithel, always being ordered about and reprimanded, the best for Gwatkin, granted—anyway up to a point—the power and rank he desired. Nevertheless, in the army, as elsewhere, nothing is for ever. Maelgwyn-Jones truly said: "That day will pass, like other days in the army." Gwatkin's ambition—the satisfaction of his "personal myth," as General Conyers would have called it—might be temporarily realized, but there was always the danger that a re-posting, promotion, minor adjustment of duties, might alter everything. Even the obstacles set in the way of Bithel indulging the pottering he loved, could, for the same reasons, be alleviated, if not removed entirely. For instance, Bithel was tremendously pleased at being appointed

Musketry Officer. There were several reasons for this. The job gave him a certain status, which he reasonably felt lacking, although there was probably less to do at the range than during the day by day training of a platoon. In addition, Bithel's soldier-servant, Daniels, was on permanent duty at the butts.

"I call him the priceless jewel," Bithel used to say. "You know how difficult it is to get a batman in this unit. They just don't want to do the job, in spite of its advantages. Well, Daniels is a little marvel. I don't say he's always on time, or never forgets things. He fails in both quite often. But what I like about him is that he's always got a cheerful word in all weathers. Besides, he's as clean as a whistle. A real pleasure to look at when he's doing PT, which is more than you can say for some of them in early morning. In any case, Daniels is not like all those young miners, nice boys as they are. He is more used to the world. You're not boots for three months at the Green Dragon in my home town without hearing some gossip."

Others took a less favourable view of Daniels, who, although skilled in juggling with dummy grenades, was in general regarded as light-fingered and sly. There was, I found in due course, nothing unusual in an officer being preoccupied—one might almost say obsessed—by the personality of his servant, though on the whole that was apt to occur in ranks senior to subaltern. The relationship seems to develop a curious state of intimacy in an unintimate society; one, I mean, far removed from anything to be thought of as overstepping established limits of propriety or everyday discipline. Indeed, so far from even approaching the boundaries of sexual aberration or military misconduct, the most normal of men, and conscientious of officers, often provided the most striking instances. Even my father, I remembered, had possessed an almost mystic bond with Bracey, certainly a man of remarkable qualities. It was a thing not easily explicable, perhaps demanded by the emotional conditions of an all-male society. Regular officers, for example, would sometimes go to great pains to prevent their servants suffering some deserved minor punishment for an infringement of routine. Such things made

Bithel's eulogies of Daniels no cause for comment. In any case, even if Bithel enjoyed the presence of Daniels at the range, it was not Daniels, but Deafy Morgan, who was source of all the trouble.

"Why on earth did Bith ever send Deafy back there and then?" said Kedward afterwards. "That bloody rifle could perfectly well have waited an hour or two before it was mended."

The question was never cleared up. Perhaps Bithel was thereby given opportunity for a longer hob-nob with Daniels. Even if that were the object, I am sure nothing dubious took place between them, while the "musketry details" were still at the butts. Anything of the sort would have been extremely difficult, even if Bithel had been prepared to take such a risk. Much more likely—Deafy Morgan being one of his own men—Bithel had some idea of avoiding, by immediate action, lack of a rifle in his platoon. Whatever the reason, Bithel sent Deafy Morgan back to barracks by himself with a rifle that had developed some defect requiring the attention of the Sergeant-Armourer. The range, where musketry instruction took place, was situated in a deserted stretch of country, two or three miles by road from the town. This distance could be reduced by taking a short cut across the fields. In wet weather the path across the fields was apt to be muddy, making the journey heavy going. Rain was not falling that day—something of a rarity—and Deafy Morgan chose the path through the fields.

"I suppose I ought to have ordered him to go by road," Bithel said later. "But it takes such a lot of shouting to explain anything to the man."

The incident occurred in a wood not far from the outskirts of the town. Deafy Morgan, by definition an easy victim to ambush, was surrounded by four young men, two of whom threatened him with pistols, while the other two possessed themselves of his rifle. Deafy Morgan struggled, but it was no good. The four of them made off at a run, disappearing behind a hedge, where, so the police reported later, a car had been waiting. There was nothing for Deafy Morgan to do but return to barracks and report the incident. Sergeant Pendry, as it happened, was Orderly Sergeant that day. He handled the trouble with notable competence. Contact was made with the Adjutant, who was touring the country in a truck in the course of preparing a "scheme": the Constabulary, who handled such matters of civil subversion, were at once informed. Deafy Morgan was, of course, put under arrest. There was a considerable to-do. This was just such an incident as Maelgwyn-Jones outlined in his "internal security" talk. The Constabulary, perfectly accustomed to ambuscades of this type, corroborated the presence of four suspects in the neighbourhood, who had later withdrawn over the Border. It was an unhappy episode, not least because Deafy Morgan was so popular a figure. Gwatkin, as I have said, was particularly disturbed by it. His mortification took the form of blaming all on Bithel.

"The CO will have to get rid of him," Gwatkin said. "It can't go on. He isn't fit to hold a commission."

"I don't see what old Bith could have done about it," said Breeze, "even though it was a bit irregular to send Deafy back on his own like that."

"It may not have been Bithel's fault directly," said Gwatkin sternly, "but when something goes wrong under an officer's command, the officer has to suffer. That may be unjust. He has to suffer all the same. In my opinion, there would be no injustice in this case. Why, I shouldn't wonder if the Colonel himself was not superseded for this."

That was true enough. Certainly the Commanding Officer was prepared for the worst, so far as his own appointment was concerned. He said so in the Mess more than once. However, in the end nothing so drastic took place. Deafy Morgan was courtmartialled, getting off with a reprimand, together with transfer to the Second Line and his nagging wife. He had put up some fight. In the circumstances, he could hardly be sent to detention for losing his weapon and failing to capture four youngish assailants for whom he had been wholly unprepared; having been certainly too deaf to hear either their approach, or, at an earlier stage, the substance of Maelgwyn-Jones's security talk. The findings of the courtmartial had just been promulgated, when the Battalion was ordered to prepare for a thirty-six-hour Divisional exercise, the first of its kind in which the unit had been concerned.

"This is the new Divisional Commander making himself felt," said Kedward. "They say he is going to shake us up, right and proper."

"What's he called?"

To those serving with a battalion, even brigadiers seem infinitely illustrious, the Divisional Commander, a remote, godlike figure.

"Major-General Liddament," said Gwatkin. "He's going to ginger things up, I hope."

It was at the start of this thirty-six-hour exercise—reveille at 4.30 a.m., and the first occasion we were to use the new containers for hot food—that I noticed all was not well with Sergeant Pendry. He did not get the Platoon on parade at the right time. That was very unlike him. Pendry had, in fact, shown no sign of breaking down after a few weeks' energetic work, in the manner of Breeze's warning about NCOs who could not perform their promise. On the contrary, he continued to work hard, and his good temper had something of Corporal Gwylt's liveliness about it. No one could be expected to look well at that hour of the morning, but Sergeant Pendry's face was unreasonably greenish at breakfast, like Gwatkin's after the crossing, something more than could be attributed to early rising. I thought he must have been drinking the night before, a foolish thing to do as he knew the early hour of reveille. On the whole, there was very little drinking throughout the Battalion—indeed, small opportunity for it with the pressure of training—but Pendry had some reputation in the Sergeants' Mess for capacity in sinking a pint or two. I thought perhaps the moment had come when Breeze's prediction was now going to be justified, that Pendry had suddenly reached the point when he could no longer sustain an earlier efficiency. The day therefore opened badly, Gwatkin justifiably angry that my Platoon's unpunctuality left him insufficient time to inspect the Company as thoroughly as he wished, before parading with the rest of the Battalion. We were to travel by bus to an area some way from our base, where the exercise was to take place.

"Oh, I do like to ride in a smart motor-car," said Corporal Gwylt. "A real pleasure it is to spin along."

Sergeant Pendry, usually as noisy as any of them, sat silent at the back of the bus, looking as if he might vomit at any moment. Outside, it was raining as usual. We drove across a desolate plain set against a background of vast grey skies, arriving at our destination an hour or two later. Gwatkin had gone ahead in his Company Commander's truck. He was waiting impatiently by the road when the platoons arrived.

"Get the men off the buses at once," he said, "and on to the other side of the road—and get some ack-ack defence out, and an anti-gas scout—and have the buses facing up the lane towards that tree, with No. 2 Platoon's vehicle at the head, not where it is now. Do that right away. Then send a runner to B Company to cancel the earlier message that we are going to recce the country on the left flank between us. That order has been changed to the right flank. Now, I want to say a word of warning to all Platoon Commanders before I attend the Commanding Officer's conference for Company Commanders. I wish to make clear that I am not at all satisfied so far today. You've none of you shown any drive up to date. It's a bad show. You've got to do better, or there will be trouble. Understand? Right. You can rejoin your platoons."

He had draped a rubber groundsheet round him like a cloak, which, with his flattish-brimmed steel helmet, transformed him into a figure from the later Middle Ages, a captain-of-arms of the Hundred Years' War, or the guerrilla campaigning of Owen Glendower. I suddenly saw that was where Gwatkin belonged, rather than to the soldiery of modern times, the period which captured his own fancy. Rain had wetted his moustache, causing it to droop over the corners of the mouth, like those belonging to effigies on tombs or church brasses. Persons at odds with their surroundings not infrequently suggest an earlier historical epoch. Gwatkin was not exactly at odds with the rest of the world. In many ways, he was the essence of conventional behaviour. At the same time, he never mixed with others on precisely their own terms. Perhaps people suspected—disapproved—his vaulting dreams. The platoons had by this time, after much shouting and commanding, unwillingly withdrawn from the comfort of the buses into the pouring rain, and were gloomily forming up.

"Rowland is in a bloody rotten temper this morning," said Breeze. "What did he want to bite our heads off for?"

"He's in a state," said Kedward. "He nearly left his maps behind. He would have done, if I had not reminded him. Why were you late, Nick? That started Rowland being browned off."

"Had some trouble with Sergeant Pendry. He doesn't seem well today."

"I heard the Sergeant-Major say something about Pendry last night," said Breeze. "Did you hear what it was, Idwal?"

"Something about his leave," said Kedward. "Just like old Cadwallader to tackle Rowland about an NCO's leave when he was in the middle of preparing for the exercise."

Gwatkin returned some minutes later, the transparent talc surface of his map-cover marked all over with troop dispositions shown in chinagraph pencil of different colours. "The Company is in support," he said. "Come over here, Platoon Commanders, and look at the map."

He started to explain what we had to do, beginning with a few general principles regarding a company "in support"; then moving on to the more specific technical requirements of the moment. These two aspects of the operation merged into an interwoven mass of instruction and disquisition, no doubt based, in the first instance, on sound military doctrine, but not a little confusing after being put through the filter of Gwatkin's own complex of ideas. He had obviously pondered the theory of being "in support," poring in his spare time over the pages of *Infantry Training*. In addition, Gwatkin had also memorized with care phrases used by the Commanding Officer in the course of his issue of orders . . . start-line . . . RVs

... forming-up areas ... B echelon ... These milestones in the efficiency of the manœuvre were certainly intended to be considered in relation to ground and other circumstances; in short, left largely to the discretion of the junior commander himself. However, that was not the way Gwatkin looked at things. Although he liked saying that he wanted freedom to make his own tactical arrangements, he always found it hard to disregard the words of the textbook, or those of a comparatively senior officer. By the time he had finished talking, it was clear the Company was to be put through every movement possible to associate with the state of being "in support."

"Right," said Gwatkin. "Any questions?"

There were no questions; chiefly because of the difficulty in disentangling one single item from the whole. We checked map references; synchronised watches. Rain had stopped falling. The day was still grey, but warmer. When I returned to my platoon trouble was in progress. Sayce, the near criminal, was having an altercation with Jones, D., who carried the anti-tank rifle. As usual, Sayce was morally in the wrong, though technically perhaps on this occasion in the right. That was if Sayce were telling the truth, in itself most improbable. The row was something to do with a case of ammunition. In ordinary circumstances, Sergeant Pendry would have cleared up in a moment anything of this sort. In his present state, higher authority had to be brought in. I adjudicated, leaving both contestants with a sense of grievance. We moved off across open country. At first I closely followed Gwatkin's instructions; then, finding my Platoon lagging behind Breeze and his men, took them on at greater speed. Even so, when we arrived, later in the morning, at the field where the Company was to reassemble, much time had been lost by the formality of the manœuvring. The men were "stood easy," then allowed to lie on the grass with groundsheets beneath them.

"Wait orders here," said Gwatkin.

He was still in that tense state which desire to excel always brought about in him. However, his temper was better than earlier in the day. He spoke of the ingenuity of the tactical system as laid down in the book, the manner in which the Company had put this into practice.

"It's all worked out to the nearest minute," he said.

Then he strolled away, and began to survey the country through field-glasses.

"That's bloody well wrong," said Kedward, under his breath. "We ought to be a mile further on at least, if we're going to be any use at the Foremost Defended Localities when the moment comes."

Holding no strong views on the subject myself, I was inclined to think Kedward right. All was confusion. I had only a very slight idea what was happening by now, and what role the Company should rightly play. I should have liked to lie on the ground and stretch my legs out like the men, instead of having to be on the alert for Gwatkin's next order and superintend a dozen small matters. Some minutes later a runner came up with a written message for Gwatkin.

"Good God," he said.

Something had evidently gone badly amiss. Gwatkin took off his helmet and shook the rain from it. He looked about him hopelessly.

"It hasn't worked out right," he said agitatedly.

"What hasn't?"

"Fall in your men at once," he said. "It's long past the time when we should have been in position. That's what the message says."

Instead of being close up behind the company we were supposed to support, here we were, in fact, hanging about miles away; still occupied, I suppose, with some more preliminary involution of Gwatkin's labyrinthine tactical performance. Kedward was right. We ought to have been advancing at greater speed. Gwatkin had done poorly. Now, he began to issue orders right and left. However, before anything much could happen, another runner appeared. This one carried an order instructing Gwatkin to halt his company for the time being, while we "let through" another company, by now close on our heels. Like golfers who have lost their ball, we allowed this company to pass between our deployed ranks. They were on their way to do the job assigned to ourselves. Bithel was one of their platoon commanders. He trotted by quite near me, red in the face, panting like a dog. As he came level, he paused for a moment.

"Haven't got an aspirin about you?" he asked.

"Afraid not."

"Forgot to bring mine."

"Sorry."

"That's all right," he said, loosening the helmet from his forehead for a moment, "just felt an aspirin might be the answer."

His teeth clicked metallically. He hurried on again to catch up his men, rejoining the platoon as they were already beginning to disappear from sight. We "stood by" for ages, awaiting an order.

"Can the men sit down again?" asked Breeze.

"No," said Gwatkin.

He was deeply humiliated by these circumstances, standing silent, fidgeting with his revolver holster. At last the order came. Gwatkin's company was to proceed by road to Battalion Headquarters in the field. He was himself to report to the Commanding Officer forthwith.

"I've let the whole Battalion down," he muttered, as he went off towards his Company Commander's truck.

Kedward thought the same.

"Did you ever see such frigging about," he said. "Why, even as it was, I was behindhand in bringing my platoon up level with the main body of the Company, and by then I'd cut out at least half the things Rowland had told me to do. If I'd done them all, it would have taken a week. We wouldn't even have got as far as that field where we had a breather."

We set off for Battalion HQ. By the time I brought my platoon in, it was late in the afternoon. Rain had begun to fall again. The place was a clearing in some woods where field kitchens had been set up. At last there was prospect of something to eat, a subject much on the men's minds, scarcely less on my own. I was very ready for a meal, breakfast soon after 5 a.m. by now a long way off. For some reason, probably because it was becoming hard to obtain, I carried no chocolate in my haversack. Gwatkin was waiting for us when we arrived. From his appearance it was clear he had been hauled pretty roughly over the coals by the Commanding Officer for failure to bring up the Company in time earlier that day. His face was white.

"You are to take your platoon out at once on patrol," he said.

"But they've had no dinner."

"The men just have time for a mouthful, if they're quick. You can't. I've got to go over the map with you. You are to make a recce, then act as a Standing Patrol. It can't be helped that you haven't eaten yourself."

He gave the impression of rather enjoying this opportunity for working off his feelings. There seemed no necessity to underline the fact that I was to starve until further notice. Whatever the Commanding Officer had said had certainly not improved Gwatkin's state of mind. He was thoroughly upset. His hand shook when he pointed his pencil at names on the map. He was in a vile temper.

"You will take your men up to this point," he said. "There you will establish an HQ. Here is the canal. At this map reference the Pioneers have thrown a rope bridge across. You will personally cross by the rope bridge and make a recce of the far bank from here to here. Then return to your platoon and carry out the duties of a Standing Patrol as laid down in *Infantry Training,* having reported the map reference of your HQ by runner to me at this point here. In due course I shall come and inspect the position and receive your report. All right?"

"Yes."

He handed over some map references.

"Any questions?"

"None."

Gwatkin strode off. I returned to my platoon, far from pleased. The fact that missing a meal or two in the army must be regarded—certainly by an officer—as all in the day's work, makes these occasions no more acceptable. Sergeant

Pendry was falling in the men when I returned to the area of the wood that had been allotted to the Platoon. They were grumbling at the hurried nature of dinner, complaining the stew had "tasted" from being kept in the new containers. The only bright spot was that we were to be transported by truck some of the distance towards the place where we were to undertake these duties. Thirty men take an age to get on, or off, a vehicle of any kind. Jones, D., slipped while climbing over the wheel, dropping the anti-tank rifle—that inordinately heavy, already obsolete weapon—on the foot of Williams, W. H., the platoon runner, putting him temporarily out of action. Sayce now began a long story about feeling faint, perhaps as a result of eating the stew, and what the MO had said about some disease he, Sayce, was suffering from. These troubles were unwillingly presented to me through the sceptical medium of Corporal Gwylt. I was in no mood for pity. If the meal had made Sayce feel queasy, that was better than having no meal at all. Such was my answer. All these things obstructed progress for about ten minutes. I feared Gwatkin might return to find reasonable cause for complaint of this delay, but Gwatkin had disappeared, bent on making life uncomfortable for someone else, or perhaps anxious only to find a quiet place where he could himself mope for a short period, while recovering his own morale. Sergeant Pendry was still showing less than his usual vigour in keeping things on the move. There could be no doubt Breeze had been right about Pendry, I thought, unless he turned out to be merely unwell, sickening for some illness, rather than suffering from a hangover. He dragged his feet when he walked, hardly able to shout out a command. I took him aside as the last man settled into the truck.

"Are you feeling all right, Sergeant?"

He looked at me as if he did not understand.

"All right, sir?"

"You got something to eat with the others just now?"

"Oh, yes, sir."

"Enough?"

"Plenty there, sir. Didn't feel much like food, it was."

"Are you sick?"

"Not too good, sir."

"What's wrong?"

"Don't know just what, sir."

"But you must know if you're feeling ill."

"Had a bit of a shock back home, it was."

This was no time to go into the home affairs of the platoon's personnel, now that at last we were ready and I wanted to give the driver the order to move off.

"Have a word with me when we get back to barracks."

"All right, sir."

I climbed into the truck beside the driver. We travelled several miles as far as some crossroads. There we left the truck, which returned to its base. Platoon HQ was set up in a dilapidated cowshed, part of the buildings of a small farm that lay not far away across the fields. When everything was pretty well established in the cowshed, including the siting of the imaginary 2-inch mortar which travelled round with us, I went off to look for the rope bridge over the canal. This was found without much difficulty. A corporal was in charge. I explained my mission, and enquired about the bridge's capacity.

"It do wobble a fair trifle, sir."

"Stand by while I cross."

"That I will, sir."

I started to make the transit, falling in after about three or four yards. The water might have been colder for the time of year. I swam the rest of the way, reaching the far bank not greatly wetter than the rain had left me. There I wandered about for a time, making notes of matters to be regarded as important in the circumstances. After that, I came back to the canal, and, disillusioned as to the potentialities of the rope bridge, swam across again. The canal banks were fairly steep, but the corporal helped me out of the water. He did not seem in the least surprised to find that I had chosen this method of return in preference to his bridge.

"Very shaky, those rope bridges," was all he said.

By now it was dark, rain still falling. I returned to the

cowshed. There a wonderful surprise was waiting. It appeared that Corporal Gwylt, accompanied by Williams, W. H., had visited the neighbouring farm and managed to wheedle from the owners a jug of tea.

"We saved a mug for you, sir. Wet you are, by Christ, too."

I could have embraced him. The tea was of the kind Uncle Giles used to call "a good sergeant-major's brew." It tasted like the best champagne. I felt immediately ten years younger, hardly wet at all.

"She was a big woman that gave us that jug of tea, she was," said Corporal Gwylt.

He addressed Williams, W. H.

"Ah, she was," agreed Williams, W. H.

He looked thoughtful. Good at running and singing, he was otherwise not greatly gifted.

"She made me afraid, she did," said Corporal Gwylt. "I would have been afraid of that big woman in a little bed."

"Indeed, I would too that," said Williams, W. H., looking as if he were sincere in the opinion.

"Would you not have been afraid of her, Sergeant Pendry, a great big woman twice your size?"

"Shut your mouth," said Sergeant Pendry, with unexpected force. "Must you ever be talking of women?"

Corporal Gwylt was not at all put out.

"I would be even more afeared of her in a *big* bed," he said reflectively.

We finished our tea. A runner came in, brought by a sentry, with a message from Gwatkin. It contained an order to report to him at a map reference in half an hour's time. The place of meeting turned out to be the crossroads not far from the cowshed.

"Shall I take the jug back, Corporal?" asked Williams, W. H.

"No, lad, I'll return that jug," said Corporal Gwylt. "If I have your permission, sir?"

"Off you go, but don't stay all night."

"I won't take long, sir."

Gwylt disappeared with the jug. The weather was clearing

up now. There was a moon. The air was fresh. When the time came, I went off to meet Gwatkin. Water dripped from the trees, but a little wetness, more or less, was by then a matter of indifference. I stood just off the road while I waited, expecting Gwatkin would be late. However, the truck appeared on time. The vehicle drew up in the moonlight just beside me. Gwatkin stepped out. He gave the driver instructions about a message he was to take and the time he was to return to this same spot. The truck drove off. Gwatkin began to stride slowly up the road. I walked beside him.

"Everything all right, Nick?"

I told him what we had been doing, giving the results of the reconnaissance on the far side of the canal.

"Why are you so wet?"

"Fell off the rope bridge into the canal."

"And swam?"

"Yes."

"That was good," he said, as if it had been a brilliant idea to swim.

"How are things going in the battle?"

"The fog of war has descended."

That was a favourite phrase of Gwatkin's. He seemed to derive support from it. There was a pause. Gwatkin began to fumble in his haversack. After a moment he brought out quite a sizeable bar of chocolate.

"I brought this for you," he said.

"Thanks awfully, Rowland."

I broke off a fairly large portion and handed the rest back to him.

"No," he said. "It's all for you."

"All this?"

"Yes."

"Can you really spare it?"

"It's meant for you. I thought you might not have any chocolate with you."

"I hadn't."

He returned to the subject of the exercise, explaining, so far as possible, the stage things had reached, what our immediate movements were to be. I gnawed the chocolate. I had forgotten how good chocolate could be, wondering why I had never eaten more of it before the war. It was like a drug, entirely altering one's point of view. I felt suddenly almost as warmly towards Gwatkin as to Corporal Gwylt, though nothing would ever beat that first sip of tea. Gwatkin and I had stopped by the side of the road to look at his map in the moonlight. Now he closed the case, buttoning down its flap.

"I'm sorry I sent you off like that without any lunch," he said.

"That was the order."

"No," said Gwatkin. "It wasn't."

"How do you mean?"

"There would have been lots of time for you to have had something to eat," he said.

I did not know what to answer.

"I had to work off on someone that rocket the CO gave me," he said. "You were the only person I could get at — any way the first one I saw when I came back from the Colonel. He absolutely took the hide off me. I'd have liked to order the men off, too, right away, without their dinner, but I knew I'd only get another rocket — an even bigger one — if it came out they'd missed a meal unnecessarily through an order of mine."

I felt this a handsome apology, a confession that did Gwatkin credit. Even so, his words were nothing to the chocolate. There were still a few remains clinging to my mouth. I licked them from the back of my teeth.

"Of course you've got to go," said Gwatkin vehemently. "Lunch or no lunch, if it's an order. Go and get caught up on a lot of barbed wire and be riddled by machine-gun fire, stabbed to death with bayonets against a wall, walk into a cloud of poison gas without a mask, face a flame-thrower in a narrow street. Anything. I don't mean that."

I agreed, at the same time feeling no immediate necessity to dwell at length on such undoubtedly valid aspects of military duty. It seemed best to change the subject. Gwatkin had made amends — one of the rarest things for anyone to attempt in life—now he must be distracted from cataloguing further disagreeable potentialities to be encountered in the course of a soldier's life.

"Sergeant Pendry hasn't been very bright today," I said. "I think he must be sick."

"I wanted to talk to you about Pendry," said Gwatkin.

"You noticed he was in poor shape?"

"He came to me last night. There wasn't time to tell you before, with all the preparations going on for the exercise— or at least I forgot to tell you."

"What's wrong with Pendry?"

"His wife, Nick."

"What about her?"

"Pendry had a letter from a neighbour saying she was carrying on with another man."

"I see."

"You keep on reading in the newspapers that the women of this country are making a splendid war effort," said Gwatkin, speaking with all that passion which would well up in him at certain moments. "If you ask me, I think they are making a splendid effort to sleep with as many other men as possible while their husbands are away."

Even if that were an exaggeration, as expressed by Gwatkin, it had to be admitted letters of this kind were common enough. I remembered my brother-in-law, Chips Lovell, once saying: "The popular Press always talk as if only the rich committed adultery. One really can't imagine a more snobbish assumption." Certainly no one who administered the Company's affairs for a week or two would make any mistake on that score. I asked Gwatkin if details were known about Pendry's case. None seemed available.

"It makes you sick," Gwatkin said.

"I suppose the men have some fun too. It isn't only the women. Not that any of us are given much time for it here— except perhaps Corporal Gwylt."

"It's different for a man," said Gwatkin. "Unless he gets mixed up with a woman who makes him forget his duty."

These words recalled a film Moreland and I had seen together in days before the war. A Russian officer—the story had been set in Tsarist times—had reprimanded an unpunctual subordinate with just that phrase: "A woman who causes a man to neglect his duty is not worth a moment's consideration." The young lieutenant in the film, so far as I could remember, had arrived late on parade because he had been spending the night with the Colonel's mistress. Afterwards, Moreland and I had often quoted to each other that stern conclusion.

"It's just the way you look at it," Moreland had said. "I know Matilda, for instance, would take the line that no woman was worth a moment's consideration unless she were capable of making a man neglect his duty. Barnby, on the other hand, would say no duty was worth a moment's consideration if it forced you to neglect women. These things depend so much on the subjective approach."

I wondered if Gwatkin had seen the film too, and memorized that scrap of dialogue as a sentiment which appealed to him. On the whole it was unlikely that the picture, comparatively highbrow, had penetrated so deep in provincial distribution. Probably Gwatkin had simply elaborated the idea for himself. It was a high-minded, but not specially original one. Widmerpool, for example, when involved with Gypsy Jones, had spoken of never again committing himself with a woman who took his mind from his work. Gwatkin rarely spoke of his own wife. He had once mentioned that her father was in bad health, and, if he died, his mother-in-law would have to come and live with them.

"What are you going to do about Pendry?" I asked.

"Arrange for him to have some leave as soon as possible. I'm afraid that will deprive you of a platoon sergeant."

"Pendry will have to go on leave sooner or later in any case. Besides, he's not much use in his present state."

"The sooner Pendry goes, the sooner he will bring all this trouble to a stop."

"If he can."

Gwatkin looked at me with surprise.

"Everything will come right when he gets back home," he said.

"Let's hope so."

"Don't you think Pendry will be able to deal with his wife?"

"I don't know anything about her."

"You mean she might want to go off with this other man?"

"Anything might happen. Pendry might do her in. You can't tell."

Gwatkin hesitated a moment.

"You know that Rudyard Kipling book the other night?"

"Yes."

"There are sort of poems at the beginning of the stories."

"Yes?"

"One of them always stuck in my head—at least bits of it. I can never remember all the words of anything like that."

Gwatkin stopped again. I feared he thought he had already said too much, and was not going to admit the verse of his preference.

"Which one?"

"It was about—was it some Roman god?"

"Oh, Mithras."

"You remember it?"

"Of course."

"Extraordinary."

Gwatkin looked as if he could scarcely credit such a mental feat.

"As you said, Rowland, it's my profession to read a lot. But what about Mithras?"

"Where it says 'Mithras also a soldier—'"

Gwatkin seemed to think that sufficient clue, that I must be able to guess by now all he hoped to convey. He did not finish the line.

"Something about helmets scorching the forehead and sandals burning the feet. I can't imagine anything worse than marching in sandals, especially on those cobbled Roman roads."

Gwatkin disregarded the logistic problem of sandal-shod infantry. He was very serious.

"'—keep us pure till the dawn,'" he said.

"Oh, yes."

"What do you make of that?"

"Probably a very necessary prayer for a Roman legionary."

Again, Gwatkin did not laugh.

"Does that mean women?" he asked, as if the notion had only just struck him.

"I suppose so."

I controlled temptation to make flippant suggestions about other, more recondite vices, for which, with troops of such mixed origin as Rome's legions, the god's hasty moral intervention might be required. That sort of banter did not at all fit in with Gwatkin's mood. Equally pointless, even hopelessly pedantic, would be a brief exegesis explaining that the Roman occupation of Britain, historically speaking, was rather different from the picture in the book. At best one would end up in an appalling verbal tangle about the relationship of fact and poetry.

"Those lines make you think," said Gwatkin slowly.

"About toeing the line?"

"Make you glad you're married," he said. "Don't have to bother any more about women."

He turned back towards the place where we had first met. There was the sound of a car further up the road. The truck came into sight again. Gwatkin abandoned further speculations about Mithras. He became once more the Company Commander.

"We've talked so much I haven't inspected your platoon position," he said. "There's nothing special I ought to see there?"

"Nothing."

"Bring your men right away to the place I showed you on the map. We've got some farm buildings for a billet tonight. It's not far from here. Everyone will have a bit of a rest. Nothing much expected of us until midday tomorrow. All right?"

"All right."

He climbed into the truck. It drove off again. I returned

to the platoon. Sergeant Pendry came forward to report. He looked just as he had looked that morning; no better, no worse.

"Captain Gwatkin just had a word with me about your leave, Sergeant. We'll arrange that as soon as the exercise is over."

"Thank you very much, sir."

He spoke tonelessly, as if the question of leave did not interest him in the least.

"Fall the platoon in now. We're billeted in a farm near here. There's prospect of some sleep."

"Right, sir."

As usual, the distance to march turned out further than expected. Rain came on again. However, the farm buildings were pretty comfortable when we arrived. The platoon was accommodated in a thatched barn where there was plenty of straw. Corporal Gwylt, as always, was unwilling to believe that agricultural surroundings could ever be tolerable.

"Oh, what nasty smells there are here," he said. "I do not like all these cows."

I slept like a log that night. It must have been soon after breakfast the following morning, when I was checking sentry duties with Sergeant Pendry, that Breeze hurried into the barn to issue a warning.

"A staff car flying the Divisional Commander's pennon has just stopped by the road," Breeze said. "It must be a snap inspection by the General. Rowland says get all the men cleaning weapons or otherwise usefully occupied forthwith."

He rushed off to warn Kedward. I set about generating activity in the barn. Some of the platoon were at work re-moving mud from their equipment. Those not so obviously engaged on useful task were found other commendable oc-cupations. All was in order within a few minutes. This was not a moment too soon. There was the sound of a party of people approaching the barn. I looked out, and saw the Gen-eral, his ADC and Gwatkin slopping through the mud of the farmyard.

"They're coming, Sergeant Pendry."

They entered the barn. Sergeant Pendry called those assembled to attention. It was at once obvious that General Liddament was not in the best of tempers. He was a serious looking man, young for his rank, cleanshaven, with the air of a scholar rather than a soldier. His recent taking over of the Division's command was already to be noticed in small matters of routine. Though regarded by regular soldiers as something of a military pedant—so Maelgwyn-Jones had told Gwatkin—General Liddament was said to be an officer with ideas of his own. Possibly in order to counteract this reputation for an excessive precision in approach to his duties, an imperfection of which he was probably aware and hoped to correct, the General allowed himself certain informalities of dress and turn-out. For example, he carried a long stick, like the wand of a verger in a cathedral, and wore a black-and-brown check scarf thrown carelessly about his neck. A hunting horn was thrust between the buttons of his battle-dress blouse. Maelgwyn-Jones also reported that two small dogs on a lead sometimes accompanied General Liddament, causing great disturbance when they squabbled with each other. Today must have been too serious an occasion for these animals to be with him. The presence of dogs would have increased his air of being a shepherd or huntsman, timeless in conception, depicted in the idealized pastoral scene of some engraving. However, General Liddament's manner of speaking had none of this mild, bucolic tone.

"Tell them to carry on," he said, pointing his long stick at me. "What's the name of this officer?"

"Second-lieutenant Jenkins, sir," said Gwatkin, who was under great strain.

"How long have you been with this unit, Jenkins?"

I told the General, who nodded. He asked some further questions. Then he turned away, as if he had lost all interest in me, all interest in human beings at all, and began rummaging furiously about the place with his stick. After exploring the corners of the barn, he set about poking at the roof.

"Have your men been dry here?"

"Yes, sir."

"Are you sure?"

"Yes, sir."

"There is a leak in the thatch here."

"There is a leak in that corner, sir, but the men slept the other end."

The General, deep in thought, continued his prodding for some seconds without visible effect. Then, as he put renewed energy into the thrusts of his stick, which penetrated far into the roofing, a large piece of under-thatch all at once descended from above, narrowly missing General Liddament himself, completely overwhelming his ADC with debris of dust, twigs and loam. At that, the General abandoned his activities, as if at last satisfied. Neither he nor anyone else made any comment, nor was any amusement expressed. The ADC, a pink-faced young man, blushed hotly and set about cleaning himself up. The General turned to me again.

"What did your men have for breakfast, Jenkins?"

"Liver, sir."

I was impressed by his retention of my name.

"What else?"

"Jam, sir."

"What else?"

"Bread, sir—and margarine."

"Porridge?"

"No, sir."

"Why not?"

"No issue, sir."

The General turned savagely on Gwatkin, who had fallen into a kind of trance, but now started agonisingly to life again.

"No porridge?"

"No porridge, sir."

General Liddament pondered this assertion for some seconds in resentful silence. He seemed to be considering porridge in all its aspects, bad as well as good. At last he came out with an unequivocal moral judgment.

"There ought to be porridge," he said.

He glared round at the platoon, hard at work with their

polishing, oiling, pulling-through, whatever they were doing. Suddenly he pointed his stick at Williams, W. H., the platoon runner.

"Would you have liked porridge?"

Williams, W.H., came to attention. As I have said, Williams, W.H., was good on his feet and sang well. Otherwise, he was not particularly bright.

"No, sir," he said instantly, as if that must be the right answer.

The General was taken aback. It would not be too much to say he was absolutely staggered.

"Why not?"

General Liddament spoke sharply, but seriously, as if some excuse like religious scruple about eating porridge would certainly be accepted as valid.

"Don't like it, sir."

"You don't like porridge?"

"No, sir."

"Then you're a foolish fellow—a very foolish fellow."

After saying that, the General stood in silence, as if in great distress of mind, holding his long staff at arm's length from him, while he ground it deep into the earthy surface of the barnhouse floor. He appeared to be trying to contemplate as objectively as possible the concept of being so totally excluded from the human family as to dislike porridge. His physical attitude suggested a holy man doing penance vicariously for the sin of those in his spiritual care. All at once he turned to the man next to Williams, W. H., who happened to be Sayce.

"Do *you* like porridge?" he almost shouted.

Sayce's face, obstinate, dishonest, covered with pockmarks, showed determination to make trouble if possible, at the same time uncertainty as how best to achieve that object. For about half a minute Sayce turned over in his mind the pros and cons of porridge eating, just as he might reflect on the particular excuse most effective in extenuation of a dirty rifle barrel. Then he spoke.

"Well, sir—" he began.

General Liddament abandoned Sayce immediately for Jones, D.

"—and you?"

"No, sir," said Jones, D., also speaking with absolute assurance that a negative answer was expected of him.

"—and you?"

"No, sir," said Rees.

Moving the long stick with feverish speed, as if he were smelling out witches, the General pointed successively at Davies, J., Davies, E., Ellis, Clements, Williams, G.

No one had time to answer. There was a long pause at the end of the line. Corporal Gwylt stood there. He had been supervising the cleaning of the bren. General Liddament, whose features had taken on an expression of resignation, stood now leaning forward, resting his chin on the top of the stick, his head looking like a strange, rather malignant totem at the apex of a pole. He fixed his eyes on Gwylt's cap badge, as if ruminating on the history of the Regiment symbolized in the emblems of its design.

"And you, Corporal," he asked, this time quite quietly. "Do you like porridge?"

An enormous smile spread over Corporal Gwylt's face.

"Oh, yes, yes, sir," he said, "I do like porridge. I did just wish we had had porridge this morning."

Slowly General Liddament straightened himself. He raised the stick so that its sharp metal point almost touched the face of Corporal Gwylt.

"Look," he said, "look, all of you. He may not be the biggest man in the Division, but he is a sturdy fellow, a good type. There is a man who eats porridge. Some of you would do well to follow his example."

With these words, the Divisional Commander strode out of the barn. He was followed by Gwatkin and the ADC, the last still covered from head to foot with thatch. They picked their way through the mud towards the General's car. A minute later, the pennon disappeared from sight. The inspection was over.

"The General is a funny-looking chap," said Breeze afterwards. "But there's not much he misses. He asked where the latrines were constructed. When I showed him, he told me dig them downwind next time."

"Just the same with me," said Kedward. "He made some of the platoon turn up the soles of their boots to see if they wanted mending. I was glad I had checked them last week."

We returned from the exercise to find Germany had invaded Norway and Denmark.

"The war's beginning now," said Gwatkin. "It won't be long before we're in it."

His depression about failing to provide "support" in the field was to some extent mitigated by the Company tying for first place in a practice march across country. In fact, at the time when Sergeant Pendry returned from his leave, Gwatkin certainly felt his prestige as a Company Commander in the ascendant. Pendry on the other hand—who had left for home almost immediately after the termination of the thirty-six-hour exercise—came back looking almost as gloomy as before. He returned, however, far more capable of carrying out his duties. No one knew how, if at all, he had settled his domestic troubles. I had never seen a man so greatly changed in the course of a few weeks. From being broad and heavily built, Pendry had become thin and haggard, his formerly glittering blue eyes sunken and glassy. All the same, he could be relied upon once more as Platoon Sergeant. His energy was renewed, though now all the cheerfulness that had once made him such a good NCO was gone. There was no more lateness on parade or forgetting of orders: there was also no more good-natured bustling along of the platoon. Pendry nowadays lost his temper easily, was morose when things went wrong. In spite of this change, there was little to complain of in his work. I told Gwatkin of this improvement.

"I expect Pendry put his foot down," Gwatkin said. "It's the only way with women. There should be no more difficulty with him now."

I felt less certain. However, Pendry's troubles were forgotten. There were other things to think about. He simply settled down as a different sort of person. That happened long before the incident at the road-blocks, by which time everyone was used to Pendry in his new character.

"When Cadwallader goes, which he'll have to, sooner or later," Gwatkin said, "Pendry will have to be considered for CSM."

The road-blocks were concrete pill-boxes constructed throughout the Command to impede an enemy, should the Germans decide to invade this island in the first instance. In addition to normal guard routines, road-blocks were manned after dark, the Orderly Officer inspecting them in turn throughout the night. This inspection continued until dawn, when there was time for him to have a couple of hours' sleep before coming on parade. Breeze had been Orderly Officer that day: Sergeant Pendry, NCO in charge of road-blocks. By one of the anomalies of Battalion arrangements, Pendry had been on quarter-guard, followed by a Brigade night exercise, so that "road-blocks" made his third night running with little or no sleep. It was bad luck, but for some reason—probably chronic shortage of sergeants—there was no avoiding this situation. I spoke a word of condolence on the subject.

"Do not worry, sir," Pendry said. "I do not seem to want much sleep now, it is."

That was a surprising answer. In the army, sleep is prized more than anything else; beyond food, beyond even tea. I decided to speak again to Gwatkin about Pendry, find out whether, as Company Commander, he thought all was well. I felt guilty about having allowed Pendry's situation to slip from my mind. He might be on the verge of a breakdown. Disregard for sleep certainly suggested something of the sort. Trouble could be avoided by looking into matters. However, such precautions, even if they had proved effective, were planned too late in the day. The rest of the story came out at the Court of Inquiry. Its main outlines were fairly clear. Breeze had made his inspection of the pill-box where Pendry was on duty, found all correct, moved on in the Orderly Officer's truck to the next post. About ten minutes after Breeze's departure, the sentry on duty in the pill-box noticed suspicious movements by some tumbledown sheds and fences further up the road. That is, the sentry thought he saw suspicious movements. This may have been his imagination. The Deafy Morgan affair had shown the possibility of hostility from other than German sources. What was going on in the shadows might indicate preparations for some similar aggression. Sergeant Pendry said he would investigate these activities himself. His rifle was loaded. He approached the sheds, where he disappeared from sight. Nothing was seen in that direction for some minutes; then a dog ran across the road. This dog, it was said afterwards, could have been the cause of the original disturbance. Sergeant Pendry could still not be seen. Then there was the echo of a shot; some said two shots. Pendry did not return. After a while, two men from the pill-box went to look for him. His body was found in a pit or ditch among the shacks. Pendry was dead. His rifle had been fired. It was never cleared up for certain whether an assailant caused his death; whether, in tripping and falling into the pit, his own weapon killed him; whether, alone in that dark gloomy place, oppressed with misery, strung up with lack of sleep, Pendry decided to put an end to himself.

"He always meant to do it," Breeze said.

"It was murder," said Gwatkin, "Pendry's the first. There'll be others in due course."

The Court of Inquiry expressed the opinion that Pendry would have acted more correctly in taking a man with him to conduct the investigation. It was doubtful, too, whether he should have loaded his rifle without direct order from an officer. In this respect, standing instructions for road-block NCOs showed a certain ambiguity. The whole question of ammunition supervision in relation to road-block guards was re-examined, the system later overhauled. Breeze had a trying time while the Court was taking evidence. He was exonerated from all blame, but when opportunity arose, he volunteered for service with one of the anti-tank companies which were being organized on a Divisional basis. Breeze understandably wanted to get away from the Battalion and disagreeable associations. Perhaps he wanted to get away from Gwatkin too.

Gwatkin himself, just as he had blamed Bithel for the Deafy Morgan affair, was unwilling to accept the findings of the Court of Inquiry in its complete clearing of Breeze.

"Yanto was just as responsible for Sergeant Pendry's death as if he had shot him down from the German trenches," Gwatkin said.

"What could Yanto have done?"

"Yanto knew, as we all did, that Pendry had talked of such a thing."

"I never knew, and Pendry was my own Platoon Sergeant."

"CSM Cadwallader knows more than he will say."

"What does the Sergeant-Major think?"

"He just spoke about Pendry once or twice," said Gwatkin moodily. "It's only now I see what he meant. I blame myself too. I should have foreseen it."

This was another of Gwatkin's ritual sufferings for the ills of the Battalion. Maelgwyn-Jones took a more robust, more objective view, when I went to see him about arrangements for Pendry's funeral.

"These things happen from time to time," he said. "It's just the army. Surprising there aren't more cases. Here's the bumph about the firing party to give Rowland."

"Almost every man in the Company volunteered for it."

"They love this sort of thing," said Maelgwyn-Jones. "By the way, you're going to Aldershot on a course next week. Tell Rowland that too."

"What sort of a course?"

"General training."

I remarked to Gwatkin, when we were turning in that night, how the men had almost fought to be included in the firing party.

"Nothing brings a company together like death," he said sombrely. "It looks as though there might be one in my family too. My wife's father isn't at all well."

"What does he do?"

"In a bank, like the rest of us," said Gwatkin.

He had been thoroughly upset by the Pendry incident. Over the partition, in the store, Lance-Corporal Gittins was still awake. When last seen, he had been sorting huge piles of Army Form "ten-ninety-eight," and was probably still thus engaged. He, too, seemed preoccupied with thoughts of mortality, for, while he sorted, he sang quietly to himself:

"When I tread the verge of Jordan,
Bid my anxious fears subside,
Death of Death and hell's destruction,
Land me safe on Canaan's side:
        Songs of praises,
        Songs of praises
I will ever give to thee . . ."

Three

THE train, long, grimy, closely packed, subject to many delays *en route,* pushed south towards London. Within the carriage cold fug stiflingly prevailed, dimmed bulbs, just luminious, like phosphorescent molluscs in the eddying backwaters of an aquarium, hovering above photographic views of Blackpool and Morecambe Bay: one of those interiors endemic to wartime. At a halt in the Midlands, night without still dark as the pit, the Lancashire Fusilier next to me, who had remarked earlier he was going on leave in this neighbourhood, at once guessed the name of the totally blacked-out station, collected his kit and quitted the compartment hurriedly. His departure was welcome, even the more crowded seat now enjoying improved leg-room. The grey-moustached captain, whose leathery skin and several medal ribbons suggested a quartermaster, eased himself nearer to where I occupied a corner seat, while he grunted irritably under his breath, transferring from one pocket to another thick sheaves of indents classified into packets secured by rubber bands. Additional space offered hope of less fitful sleep, but, when the engine was getting up steam again, the carriage door slid open. A figure wearing uniform looked in.

"Any room?"

There was no definite denial of the existence of a spare place, but the reception could not be called welcoming. The light grudgingly conceded by the fishy globules flickering in the shallows was too slight to distinguish more than a tall man wearing a British Warm, the shoulder straps of which displayed no badges of rank. The voice was authoritative, precise, rather musical, a voice to be associated with more agreeable, even more frivolous circumstances than those now on offer. One might even have heard it against the thrumming of a band a thousand years before. If so, the occasion was long forgotten. While he shook himself out of his overcoat, the new passenger made a certain amount of disturbance before he settled down, among other things causing the quartermaster to move his kit a few necessary inches along the rack, where it was certainly taking up more than a fair share of room. The quartermaster made some demur at this. His reluctance was confronted with absolute firmness. The man in the British Warm had his way in the end. The kit was moved. Having disposed of his own baggage, he took the place next to me.

"Last seat on the train," he said.

He laughed; then apparently passed into sleep. We rumbled on for hours through the night. I slept too, beset with disturbing dreams of administrative anxieties. The quartermaster left his seat at five, returning after an age away, still muttering and grumbling to himself. Morning came, a sad, pale light gently penetrating the curtains. Some hidden agency extinguished the blue lamps. It grew warmer. People began to stretch, blow noses, clear throats, light cigarettes, move along the corridor to shave or relieve themselves. I examined the other occupants of the carriage. Except for the middle-aged captain, all had one pip, including the new arrival next to me. I took a look at him while he was still asleep. His face was thin, rather distinguished, with a hook nose and fairish hair. The collar badges were "Fortnum & Mason" General Service. The rest of the compartment was filled by two officers of the Royal Corps of Signals, a Gunner, a Green Howard (Ted Jeavons's first regiment in the previous war, I remembered) and a Durham Light Infantryman. The thin man next to me began to wake up, rubbing his eyes and gently groaning.

"I think I shall wait till London for a shave," he said.

"Me too."

"No point in making a fetish of elegance."

"None."

We both dozed again. When it was light enough to read, he took a book from his pocket. I saw it was in French, but could not distinguish the title. Again, his manner struck me as familiar; again, I could not place him.

"Is there a breakfast car on this train?" asked the Green Howard.

"God, no," said the Durham Light Infantryman. "Where do you think you are—the Ritz?"

One of the Signals said there was hope of a cup of tea, possibly food in some form, at the next stop, a junction where the train was alleged to remain for ten minutes or more. This turned out to be true. On arrival at this station, in a concerted move from the carriage, I found myself walking along the platform with the man in General Service badges. We entered the buffet together.

"Sitting up all night catches one across the back," he said.

"It certainly does."

"I once sat up from Prague to the Hook and swore I'd never do it again. I little knew one was in for a lifetime of journeys of that sort."

"Budapest to Vienna by Danube can be gruelling at night too," I said, not wishing to seem unused to continental discomforts. "Do you think we are in a very strategic position for getting cups of tea?"

"Perhaps not. Let's try the far end of the counter. One might engage the attention of the lady on the second urn."

"Also stand a chance of buying one of those faded, but still beautiful, sausage rolls, before they are all consumed by Other Ranks."

We changed our position with hopeful effect.

"Talking of Vienna," he said, "did you ever have the extraordinary experience of entering that gallery in the Kunsthistorisches Museum with the screen across the end of it? On the other side of the screen, quite unexpectedly, you find those four staggering Bruegels."

"The *Hunters in the Snow* is almost my favourite picture."

"I am also very fond of the *Two Monkeys* in the Kaiser Friedrich in Berlin. I've just been sharing a room with a man in the Essex Regiment who looked exactly like the ape on the left, the same shrewd expression. I say, we're not making much headway with the tea."

There were further struggles at the counter, eventually successful. The reward was a sausage roll apiece.

"Should we return to the train now? I don't feel absolutely confident about that corner seat."

"In that case I shall take this sausage roll with me."

Back in the carriage, the quartermaster went to sleep again; so did the two Signals and the Gunner. Both the Durham Light Infantryman and the Green Howard brought out button-sticks, tins of polish, cloths, brushes. Taking off their tunics, they set to work energetically shining themselves up, while they discussed allowances.

"Haven't we met before somewhere?" I asked.

"My name is Pennistone—David Pennistone."

I knew no one called that. I told him my own name, but we did not establish a connexion sufficiently firm to suggest a previous encounter. Pennistone said he liked Moreland's music, but did not know Moreland personally.

"Are you going on leave?"

"To a course—and you?"

"I've just come from a course," he said. "I'm on leave until required."

"That sounds all right."

"I'm an odd kind of soldier in any case. Certain specific qualifications are my only excuse. It will be rather nice to be on one's own for a week or two. I'm trying to get something finished. A case of earn while you learn."

"What sort of thing?"

"Oh, something awfully boring about Descartes. Really not worth discussing. *Cogito ergo sum*, and all that. I feel quite ashamed about it. By the way, have you ever read this work? I thought one might profit by it in one's new career."

He held out to me the book he had been reading. I took

it from his hand and read the title on the spine: *Servitude et Grandeur Militaire: Alfred de Vigny.*

"I thought Vigny was just a poet—*Dieu! que le son du Cor est triste au fond des bois! . . .*"

"He also spent fourteen years of his life as a regular soldier. He ended as a captain, so there is hope for all of us."

"In the Napoleonic wars?"

"Too young. Vigny never saw action. Only the most irksome sort of garrison duty, spiced with a little civil disturbance— having to stand quietly in the ranks while demonstrators threw bricks. That kind of thing."

"I see."

"In some ways the best viewpoint for investigating army life. Action might have confused the issue by proving too exciting. Action is, after all, exciting rather than interesting. Anyway, this book says what Vigny thought about soldiering."

"What were his conclusions?"

"That the soldier is a dedicated person, a sort of monk of war. Of course he was speaking of the professional armies of his day. However, Vigny saw that in due course the armed forces of every country would be identified with the nation, as in the armies of antiquity."

"When the bombing begins here, clearly civilians will play as dangerous a role as soldiers, if not more dangerous."

"Of course. Even so, Vigny would say those in uniform have made the greater sacrifice by losing the man in the soldier—what he calls the warrior's abnegation, his renunciation of thought and action. Vigny says a soldier's crown is a crown of thorns, amongst its spikes none more painful than passive obedience."

"True enough."

"He sees the role of authority as essentially artificial, the army a way of life in which there is as little room for uncontrolled fervour as for sullen indifference. The impetuous volunteer has as much to learn as the unwilling conscript."

I thought of Gwatkin and his keenness; of Sayce, and his recalcitrance. There was something to be said for this view of the army. By this time, Pennistone and I were the only ones awake in the compartment. The button cleaners had abandoned their paraphernalia, resumed their tunics and nodded off like the rest. The quartermaster began to snore. He did not look particularly saintly, nor even dedicated, though one never could tell. Probably Vigny knew what he was talking about after fourteen years of it.

"All the same," I said, "it's a misapprehension to suppose, as most people do, that the army is inherently different from all other communities. The hierarchy and discipline give an outward illusion of difference, but there are personalities of every sort in the army, as much as out of it. On the whole, the man who is successful in civilian life, all things being equal, is successful in the army."

"Certainly—and there can be weak-willed generals and strong-willed privates."

"Look, for example, at the way you yourself compelled my neighbour to move his kit last night."

Pennistone laughed.

"One can just imagine Vigny romanticising that fat sod," he said, "but that is by the way. Probably Vigny, while emphasising that we are back with the citizen army of classical times which he himself envisaged, would agree with what you say. He was certainly aware that nothing is absolute in the army—least of all obeying orders. Take my own case. I was instructed to wait until this morning for a train, as there had been local complaints of army personnel overcrowding the railways over weekends to the detriment of civilian travel facilities. I made careful enquiries, found chances of retribution remote and started the night before, thus saving a day of my journey."

"In other words, the individual still counts, even in the army."

"Although consigned to circumstances in which, theoretically, no individuality—though much will-power—exists."

"What would Vigny have thought of your disobeying that order?"

"I could have pleaded that the army was not my chosen profession, that my ill-conduct was a revulsion from uniform, drum, drill, the ritual of the parade ground, the act of an unworthy, amateur neophyte of war."

We both went to sleep after that. When the train reached London, I said goodbye to Pennistone, who was making his way to the country and his home, there to stay until recalled to duty.

"Perhaps we'll meet again."

"Let's decide to anyway," he said. "As we've agreed, these things are largely a matter of will."

He waved, and disappeared into the crowds of the railway station. Later in the morning, while attending to the many odd jobs to be done during my few hours in London, I was struck by a thought as to where I might have seen Pennistone before. Was it at Mrs. Andriadis's party in Hill Street ten or twelve years ago? His identity was revealed. He was the young man with the orchid in his buttonhole with whom I had struck up a conversation in the small hours. This seemed our characteristic relationship. Stringham had taken me to the party, Pennistone informed me that the house itself belonged to the Duports. Pennistone had told me, too, that Bob Duport had married Peter Templer's sister, Jean. It was Pennistone, that same evening—when all was confusion owing to Milly Andriadis's row with Stringham—whom she had pushed into an armchair when he had tried to tell her an anecdote about Prince Theodoric and the Prince of Wales. By then Pennistone was rather tight. It all seemed centuries ago: the Prince of Wales now Duke of Windsor, Prince Theodoric, buttress of pro-Allied sentiment in a country threatened by German invasion, Pennistone and myself second-lieutenants in our middle thirties. I wondered what had happened to Stringham, Mrs. Andriadis and the rest. However, there was no time to ponder long about all that. Other matters required attention. I was glad—overjoyed—to be back in England even for a month or so. There would be weekend leaves from the course, when it should be possible to get as far as my sister-in-law Frederica Budd's house, where Isobel was staying until the child was born. The London streets, empty of traffic, looked incredibly bright and sophisticated, the tarts in Piccadilly dazzling nymphs. This was before the blitz. I knew how Persephone must have felt on the first day of her annual release from the underworld. An RAF officer of unconventional appearance advancing up the street turned out to be Barnby. He recognised me at the same moment.

"I thought you were a war artist."

"I was for a time," he said. "Then I got sick of it and took a job doing camouflage for this outfit."

"Disguising aerodromes as Tudor cottages?"

"That sort of thing."

"What's it like?"

"Not bad. If I'm not able to paint in the way I want, I'd as soon do this as anything else."

"I thought war artists were allowed to paint whatever they wanted."

"They are in a way," said Barnby, "I don't know. I prefer this for some reason, while there's a war on. They let me go on an occasional operational flight."

I felt a pang. Barnby was a few years older than myself. I had nothing so lively to report. He looked rather odd in his uniform, thick, square, almost as if he were still wearing the blue overalls in which he was accustomed to paint.

"Where are you, Nick?" he asked.

I gave him some account of my life.

"It doesn't sound very exciting."

"It isn't."

"I've got a wonderful new girl," he said.

I thought how, war or peace, nothing ever really changes in such aspects.

"How long are you in London?" he said. "I'd like to tell you about her. She's got one extraordinary trait. It would amuse you to hear about it. Can't we dine together tonight?"

"I've got to report to Aldershot this afternoon. I've been sent there on a course. Are you stationed in London?"

"Up for the night only. I have to see a man in the Air Ministry about some special camouflage equipment. How's Isobel?"

"Having a baby soon."

"Give her my love. What happened to the rest of the Tolland family?"

"George is in France with a Guards battalion. He was on the Regular Reserve, of course, now a captain. Robert, always a mysterious figure, is a lance-corporal in Field Security, believed to be on his way to getting a commission. Hugo doesn't want to be an officer. He prefers to stay where he is as a gunner on the South Coast—bombardier now, I believe. He says you meet such awful types in the Officers' Mess."

"What about those chaps Isobel's sisters married?"

"Roddy Cutts—as an MP—had no difficulty about getting into something. His own county Yeomanry, I think. I don't know his rank, probably colonel by now. Susan is with him. Chips Lovell has joined the Marines."

"That's an unexpected arm. Is Priscilla with him?"

"So far as I know."

We spoke of other matters, then parted. Talking to Barnby increased the feeling that I had been released from prison, at the same time inducing a new sensation, that prison life was all I was fit for. Barnby's conversation, everything round about, seemed hopelessly unreal. There was boundless relief in being free, even briefly free, from the eternal presence of Gwatkin, Kedward, Cadwallader, Gwylt and the rest of them; not to have to worry whether the platoon was better occupied digging themselves in or attacking a hill; whether Davies, G., should have a stripe or Davies, L., lose one; yet, by comparison, the shapes of Barnby and Pennistone were little more than figments of the imagination, shadows flickering on the slides of an old-fashioned magic-lantern. I had scarcely arrived in London, in any case, before it was time to leave for Aldershot. In the train on the way there, I reflected on the ideas Pennistone had put forward: the "occasional operational flights" of Barnby. How would one feel on such aerial voyages? It might be like Dai and Shoni in their balloon. In the army, as up to now experienced, danger, although it might in due course make appearance, at present skulked out of sight in the background; the foreground for ever cluttered with those moral obligations outlined by Vigny. I envied Pennistone, who could turn from war to Descartes, and back again, without perceptible effort. I knew myself incapable of writing a line of a novel—by then I had written three or four—however long released from duty. Whatever inner processes are required for writing novels, so far as I myself was concerned, war now utterly inhibited. That was one of the many disagreeable aspects of war. It was not only physically inescapable, but morally inescapable too. Why did one envy Barnby his operational flights? That was an absorbing question. Certainly not because one wanted to be killed, nor yet because the qualities of those who excel in violent action were the qualities to which one had any claim. For that matter, such qualities were not specially Barnby's. There was perhaps the point. Yet it was absurd to regard war as a kind of competition of just that sort between individuals. If that was the aim in war, why not in peace? No doubt there were plenty of individuals who felt that sort of emulation in peacetime too, but their preoccupations were not one's own. Looked at calmly, war created a situation in which the individual—if he wished to be on the winning side—was of importance only in so much as he contributed to the requirements of the machine, not according to the picturesque figure he cut in the eyes of himself and others. It was no more reasonable, if you were not that sort of person, to aspire to lead a cavalry charge, than, without financial gifts, to dream of cornering the pepper market; without scientific training, split the atom. All the same, as Pennistone had said, these things are largely a matter of the will. I thought of Dr. Trelawney, the magician, the night Duport and I had helped him to bed after his asthma attack, when he had quoted as all that was necessary: "To know, to dare, to will, to be silent." Armed with those emblems of strength, one might, however out of character, lead a cavalry charge, perhaps even corner the pepper market and split the atom too. Anyway, I thought, it would be a dull world if no one ever had dreams of glory. Moreland was fond of quoting Nietzsche's opinion that there is no action without illusion. Arrival at Aldershot brought an end to these reflections. Most of the train's passengers turned out to be officers on their way to the same course as myself. After reporting to the Orderly Room, we were shown the lines where we were to sleep, a row of small redbrick houses built round a sort of square. Their interiors were uninviting.

"Former married quarters," said the gloomy C.3 lance-corporal guiding my group. "Condemned in 1914, don't half wonder."

I did not wonder either. 1914 was, in fact, the year when, as a child, I had last set eyes on these weary red cantonments, my father's regiment stationed at a hutted camp between here and Stonehurst, the remote and haunted bungalow where my parents lived at that time. I remembered how the Battalion, polished and blancoed, in scarlet and spiked helmets, had marched into Aldershot for some ceremonial parade, drums beating, colours cased, down dusty summer roads. Afterwards, my father had complained of a sore heel caused by the rub of his wellington boot, an abrasion scarcely cured before it was time to go to war. That war, too, had been no doubt the reason why these ramshackle married quarters had never been demolished and replaced. When peace came, there were other matters to think about. Here we were accommodated on the ground floor, a back and front room. Of the five others who were to share this billet, four—two from the Loyals, two from the Manchesters—were in their late twenties. They did their unpacking and went off to find the Mess. The remaining subaltern, from a Midland regiment, was much younger. He was short and square, with dark skin, grey eyes and very fair curly hair.

"Those Lancashire lads in here with us are a dumb crowd," he remarked to me.

"What makes you think so?"

"Do you know they thought I talked so broad I must come from Burton-on-Trent," he said.

He spoke as if he had been mistaken for a Chinese or Ethiopian. There was something of Kedward about him; something, too, which I could not define, of my brother-in-law, Chips Lovell. He did not have a smudgy moustache like Kedward's, and his personality was more forceful, more attractive too.

"We're going to be right cooped up in here," he said. "Would you be satisfied if I took over this area of floor space, and left you as far as the wall?"

"Perfectly."

"My name is Stevens," he said, "Odo Stevens."

I told him my own name. He spoke with a North Country or Midland intonation, not unlike that Quiggin used to assume in his earlier days, when, for social or literary reasons, he chose to emphasize his provincial origins and unvarnished, forthright nature. Indeed, I could see nothing inherently absurd in the mistake the "Lancashire lads" had made in supposing Stevens a native of Burton-on-Trent. However, I laughed and agreed it was a ludicrous error. I was flattered that he considered me a person to take into his confidence on the subject; glad, too, that I was housed next to someone who appeared agreeable. In the army, the comparative assurance of your own unit, whatever its failings, is at once dissipated by changed circumstances, which threaten fresh conflicts and induce that terrible, recurrent army dejection, the sensation that no one cares a halfpenny whether you live or die.

"Where *do* you come from?"

"Brum, of course."

"Birmingham?"

"What do you think," he said, as if it were almost insulting to suppose the matter in the smallest doubt. "Can't you tell the way I say it? But I've managed to keep out of my home town for quite a while, thank God."

"Don't you like it there?"

"Finest city in the world," he said, laughing again, "but something livelier suits me. As a matter of fact, I was on the continent for the best part of six months before I joined the army."

"Whereabouts?"

"Holland, Belgium. Even got as far afield as Austria."

"Doing what?"

"There was an exchange of apprentices for learning languages. I pick up languages pretty easily for some reason. They were beginning to think I'd better come home and do some work just at the moment war broke out."

"What's your job?"

"Imitation jewellery."

"You sell it?"

"My pa's in a firm that makes it. Got me into it too. A business with a lot of foreign connexions. That's how I fixed up getting abroad."

"Sounds all right."

"Not bad, as jobs go, but I don't want to spend a lifetime at it. That's why I wasn't sorry to make a change. Shall we push along to the Mess?"

We sat next to each other at dinner that night. Stevens asked me what I did for a living.

"You're lucky to have a writing job," he said, "I've tried writing myself. Sometimes think I might take it up, even though peddling costume jewellery is a good trade for putting yourself over with the girls."

"What sort of writing?"

"Spot of journalism in the local paper—'Spring comes to the Black Country'—'Sunset on Armistice Day'—that sort of thing. I knock it off easily, just as I can pick up languages."

I saw Stevens would go far, if he did not get killed. He was aware of his own taste for self-applause and prepared to laugh at it. The journalistic streak was perhaps what recalled Chips Lovell, whom he did not resemble physically.

"Did you volunteer for the Independent Companies?" he asked.

"I didn't think I'd be much good at them."

The Independent Companies—later called Commandos—were small guerilla units, copiously officered. They had been employed with some success in Norway. Raising them had skimmed off the best young officers from many battalions, so that they were not popular with some Commanding Officers for that reason.

"I was in trouble with my CO the time they were recruiting them," said Stevens. "He bitched up my application. It was really because he thought me useful to him where I was. All the same, I'll get away into something. My unit are a lot of louts. They're not going to prevent me from having what fun the army has to offer."

Here were dreams of military glory very different from Gwatkin's. After all this talk, it was time to go to bed. The following morning there was drill on the square. We were squadded by a stagey cluster of glengarry-capped staff-sergeants left over from the Matabele campaign, with Harry Lauder accents and eyes like poached eggs. Amongst a couple of hundred students on the course, there was hope of an acquaintance, but no familiar face showed in the Mess the previous night. Then, slow-marching across the asphalt I recognised Jimmy Brent in another squad moving at right-angles to our own, a tallish, fat, bespectacled figure, forgotten since Peter Templer had brought him to see Stringham and myself when we were undergraduates. Brent looked much the same. I had not greatly liked him at the time. Nothing heard about him since caused me, in a general way, to want to see more of him. Here, however, any face from the past was welcome, especially so veteran a relic as Brent. After the parade was dismissed, I tackled him.

"We met years ago, when you came over in Peter Templer's second-hand Vauxhall, and he drove us all into the ditch."

I told him my name. Brent clearly did not recognise me. There was little or no reason why he should. However, he remembered the circumstances of Templer's car accident, and seemed pleased to find someone on the course who had known him in the outside world.

"There were some girls in the car, weren't there," he said, his face lighting up at that happy memory, "and Bob Duport too. I knew Peter took us to see a couple of friends he'd been at school with, but I wouldn't be able to place them at this distance of time. So you were one of them? What a memory you've got. Well, it's nice to find a pal in this god-forsaken spot."

"Do you ever see Peter now? I'd like to hear what's happened to him."

"Peter's all right," said Brent, speaking rather cautiously, "wise enough not to have mixed himself up with the army like you and me. Got some Government advisory job. Financial side. I think Sir Magnus Donners had a hand—Donners hasn't got office yet, I'm surprised to see—Peter always did a spot of prudent sucking-up in that direction. Peter knows which side his bread is buttered. He's been quite useful to Donners on more than one occasion."

"I met Peter once there—at Stourwater, I mean."

"You know Donners too, do you. I've done a little business with him myself. I'm an oil man, you know. I was in the South American office before the war. Did you ever meet Peter's sister, Jean? I used to see quite a bit of her there."

"I knew her ages ago."

"She married Bob Duport," said Brent, "who was with us on the famous occasion when the Vauxhall heeled over."

There was a perverse inner pleasure in knowing that Brent had had a love affair with Jean Duport, which he could scarcely guess had been described to me by her own husband. Even though I had once loved her myself—to that extent the thought was painful, however long past—there was an odd sense of power in possessing this secret information.

"I ran into Duport just before war broke out. I never knew him well. I gather they are divorced now."

"Quite right," said Brent.

He did not allow the smallest suggestion of personal interest to colour the tone of his voice.

"I heard Bob was in some business balls-up," he said. "Chromite, was it? He got across that fellow Widmerpool, another of Donners's henchmen. Widmerpool is an able fellow, not a man to offend. Bob managed to rub him up the wrong way. Somebody said Bob was connected with the Board of Trade now. Don't know whether that is true. The Board of Trade wanted me to stay in Latin America, as a matter of fact."

"You'd have had a safe billet there."

"Glad to leave the place as it happened, though I was doing pretty well."

"How do you find yourself here?"

"Managed to get into this mob through the good offices of our Military Attaché where I was. His own regiment. Never heard of them before."

I supposed that Brent had been relieved to find this opportunity of moving to another continent after Jean had abandoned him. That disappointment, too, might explain his decision to join the army as a change of occupation. He was several years older than myself, in fact entering an age group to be reasonably considered beyond the range of unfriendly criticism for remaining out of uniform; especially if, as he suggested, his work in South America was officially regarded as of some national importance. I remembered Duport's story clearly now. After reconciliation with Jean, they had sailed for South America. Brent had sailed with them. At that time Jean's affair with Brent had apparently been in full swing. Indeed, from what Duport said, there was every reason to suppose that affair had begun before she told me of her own decision to return to her husband. So far as that went, Jean had deceived me as much as she had deceived Duport. Fortunately Brent was unaware of that.

"How do you like the army?"

"Bloody awful," he said, "but I'd rather be in than out."

"Me, too."

The remaining students of the course were an unexceptional crowd, most of the usual army types represented. We drilled on the square, listened to lectures about the German army, erected barbed wire entanglements, drove 3-ton lorries, map read. One evening, preceding a night exercise in which one half of the course was arrayed in battle against the other half, Stevens showed a different side of himself. The force in which we were both included lay on the ground in a large semi-circle, waiting for the operation to begin. The place was a clearing among the pine woods of heathery, Stonehurst-like country. Stevens and I were on the extreme right flank of the semi-circle. On the extreme left, exactly opposite us, whoever was disposed there continually threw handfuls of gravel across the area between, which landed chiefly on Stevens and myself.

"It must be Croxton," Stevens said.

Croxton was a muscular neurotic of a kind, fairly common, who cannot stop talking or creating a noise. He sang or ragged joylessly all the time, without possessing any of those inner qualities—like Corporal Gwylt's, for example—required for making such behaviour acceptable to others. He was always starting a row, playing tricks, causing trouble. There could be little doubt that Croxton was responsible for the hail of small stones that continued to spatter over us. The moon had disappeared behind clouds, rain threatening. There seemed no prospect of the exercise beginning.

"I think I'll deal with this," Stevens said.

He crawled back into the cover of the trees behind us, disappearing in darkness. Some minutes elapsed. Then I heard a sudden exclamation from the direction of the gravel thrower. It was a cry of pain. More time went by. Then Stevens returned.

"It was Croxton," he said.

"What did you do?"

"Gave him a couple in the ribs with my rifle butt."

"What did he think about that?"

"He didn't seem to like it."

"Did he put up any fight?"

"Not much. He's gasping a bit now."

The following day, during a lecture on the German Division, I saw Croxton, who was sitting a few rows in front, rub his back more than once. Stevens had evidently struck fairly hard. This incident showed he could be disagreeable, if so disposed. He also possessed the gift of isolating himself from his surroundings. These lectures on the German army admittedly lacked light relief—after listening to many of them, I had preserved only the ornamental detail that the German Reconnaissance Corps carried a sabre squadron on its establishment—and one easily dozed through the lecturer's dronings. On the other hand, to remain, as Stevens could, slumbering like a child, upright on a hard wooden chair, while everyone else was clattering from the lecture room, suggested considerable powers of self-seclusion. Another source of preservation to Stevens—unlike Gwatkin—was an imperviousness to harsh words. He and I had been digging a weapon pit together one afternoon without much success. An instructor came up to grumble at our efforts.

"That's not a damned bit of use," he said. "Wouldn't give protection to a cat."

"We've just reached a surface of rock, sir," said Stevens, "but I think I can say we've demonstrated the dignity of labour."

The instructor sniggered and moved on, without examining the soil. Not everyone liked this self-confident manner of Stevens. Among those who disapproved was Brent.

"That young fellow will get sent back to his unit," Brent said. "Mark my words. He's too big for his boots."

When the whole course was divided into syndicates of three for the purpose of a "tactical exercise without troops," Brent and I managed to be included in the same trio. To act with an acquaintance on such occasions is an advantage, but it was at the price of having Macfaddean as the third partner. However, although Macfaddean, a schoolmaster in civilian life, was feverishly anxious to make a good impression on the Directing Staff, this also meant that he was prepared to do most of the work. In his middle to late thirties, Macfaddean would always volunteer for a "demonstration," no matter how uncomfortable the prospect of crawling for miles through mud, for instance, or exemplifying the difficulty of penetrating dannert wire. When the task was written work, Macfaddean would pile up mountains of paper, or laboriously summarize, whichever method he judged best set him apart from the other students. He was so tireless in his energies that towards the end of the day, when we had all agreed on the situation report to be presented and there was some time to spare, Macfaddean could not bear these minutes to be wasted.

"Look here, laddies," he said, "why don't we go back into the woods and produce an alternative version? I'm not happy, for instance, about concentration areas. It would look good if we handed in two plans for the commander to choose from, both first-rate."

There could be no doubt that the anonymity of the syndicate system irked Macfaddean. He felt that if another report were made, the second one might be fairly attributed to his own unaided afforts, a matter that could be made clear when the time came. That was plain enough to both Brent and myself. We told Macfaddean that, for our part, we were going to adhere to the plan already agreed upon; if he wished to make another one, that was up to him.

"Off you go, Mac, if you want to," said Brent. "We'll wait for you here. I've done enough for today."

When Macfaddean was gone, we found a place to lie under some withered trees, blasted, no doubt, to their crumbling state by frequent military experiment. We were operating over the dismal tundra of Laffan's Plain, battlefield of a million mock engagements. The sky above was filled with low-flying aircraft, of outlandish colour and design, camouflaged perhaps by Barnby in a playful mood. Lumbering army reconnaissance planes buzzed placidly backwards and forwards through grey puffs of cloud, ancient machines garnered in from goodness knows what forgotten repository of written-off Governmental stores, now sent aloft again to meet a desperate situation. The heavens looked like one of those pictures of an imagined Future to be found in old-fashioned magazines for boys. Brent rolled over on his back and watched this rococo aerial pageant.

"You know Bob Duport is not a chap like you and me," he said suddenly.

He spoke as if he had given much thought to Duport's character; as if, too, my own presence allowed him at last to reach certain serious conclusions on that subject. Regarded by Templer, and Duport himself, as something of a butt—certainly a butt where women were concerned—Brent possessed a curious resilience in everyday life, which his exterior did not reveal. This was noticeable on the course, where, unlike Macfaddean, he was adept at avoiding work that might carry with it the risk of blame.

"What about Duport?"

"Bob's *really* intelligent," said Brent earnestly. "No intention of minimising your qualifications in that line, or even my own, but Bob's a real wonder-boy."

"Never knew him well enough to penetrate that far."

"Terrific gifts."

"Tell me more about him."

"Bob can do anything he turns his hand to. Wizard at business. Pick up any job in five minutes. If he were on this course, he'd be the star-turn. Then, girls. They simply lie down in front of him."

"I see."

"But he's not just interested in business and women."

"What else?"

"You wouldn't believe what he knows about art and all that."

"He never gave the impression of being that sort."

"You've got to know him well before he lets on. Have to keep your eyes open. Did you ever go to that house the Duports had in Hill Street?"

"Years ago, when they'd let it to someone else. I was taken to a party there."

"That place was marvellously done up," said Brent. "Absolute perfection in my humble opinion. Bob's got taste. That's what I mean. All the same, he isn't one of those who go round gushing about art. He keeps it to himself."

I did not immediately grasp the point of this great build up of Duport. It certainly shed a new light on him. I did not disbelieve the picture. On the contrary, in its illumination, many things became plainer. Duport's professional brutality of manner, thus interpreted in Brent's rough and ready style, might indeed conceal behind its façade sensibilities he was unwilling to reveal to the world at large. There was nothing unreasonable about that supposition. It might to some extent explain Duport's relationship with Jean, even if Brent's own connexion with her were thereby made less easy to understand. I thought of the views of my recent travelling companion, Pennistone, so plainly expressed at Mrs. Andriadis's party:

"... these appalling Italianate fittings—and the pictures—my God, the pictures ..."

However, such things were a matter of opinion. The point at issue was Duport's character: was he, in principle, regardless of personal idiosyncrasy, what Sir Gavin Walpole-Wilson used to call a "man of taste"? It was an interesting question. Jean herself had always been rather apologetic about that side of her married life, so that presumably Brent was right: Duport, rather than Jean, had been responsible for the Hill Street decorations and pictures. This was a new angle on Duport. I saw there were important sides of him I had missed.

"When you last met Bob," said Brent, using the tone of one about to make a confidence, "did he mention my name to you?"

"He said you and he had been in South America together."

"Did he add anything about me and Jean?"

"He did, as a matter of fact. I gather there was an involved situation."

Brent laughed.

"There was," he said. "I thought Bob would go round shooting his mouth off. Just like him. It's Bob's one weakness. He can't hold his tongue."

He sighed, as if Duport's heartless chatter about his own matrimonial situation had aroused in Brent himself a despair for human nature. He gave the impression that he thought it too bad of Duport. I was reminded of Barnby, exasperated at some woman's behaviour, saying: "It's enough to stop you ever committing adultery again." The deafening vibrations of an insect-like Lysander just above us, which seemed unable to decide whether or not to make a landing, put a stop to conversation for a minute or two. When it sheered off, Brent spoke once more.

"You said you knew Jean, didn't you?"

"Yes."

"Wonderful girl in her way."

"Very nice to look at."

"For a while we were lovers," said Brent.

He spoke in that reminiscent, unctuous voice men use when they tell you that sort of thing more to savour an enjoyable past situation, than to impart information which might be of interest. It must have been already clear to him that Duport had already revealed that fact.

"Oh, yes."

"Bob said that?"

"He put it more bluntly."

Brent laughed again, very good-naturedly. The way he set about telling the story emphasised his least tolerable side. I tried to feel objective about the whole matter by recalling one of Moreland's favourite themes, the attraction exercised over women by men to whom they can safely feel complete superiority.

"Are you hideous, stunted, mentally arrested, sexually maladjusted, marked with warts, gross in manner, with a cleft palate and an evil smell?" Moreland used to say. "Then, oh boy, there's a treat ahead of you. You're all set for a promising career as a lover. There's an absolutely ravishing girl round the corner who'll find you irresistible. In fact her knickers are bursting into flame at this very moment at the mere thought of you."

"But your description does not fit in with most of the lady-killers one knows. I should have thought they tended to be decidedly good-looking, as often as not, together with a lot of other useful qualities as well."

"What about Henri Quatre?"

"What about him?"

"He was impotent and he stank. It's in the histories. Yet he is remembered as one of the great lovers of all time."

"He was a king—and a good talker at that. Besides, we don't know him personally, so it's hard to argue about him."

"Think of some of the ones we do know."

"But it would be an awful world if no one but an Adonis, who was also an intellectual paragon and an international athlete, had a chance. It always seems to me, on the contrary, that women's often expressed statement, that male good looks don't interest them, is quite untrue. All things being equal, the man who looks like a tailor's dummy stands a better chance than the man who doesn't."

"All things never are equal," said Moreland, always impossible to shake in his theories, "though I agree that to be no intellectual strain is an advantage where the opposite sex is concerned. But you look into the matter. Remember Bottom and Titania. The Bard knew."

Brent, so far as he had been a success with Jean, seemed to strengthen Moreland's argument. I wondered whether I wanted to hear more. The Jean business was long over, but even when you have ceased to love someone, that does not necessarily bring an indifference to a past shared together. Besides, though love may die, vanity lives on timelessly. I knew that I must be prepared to hear things I should not like. Yet, although where unfaithfulness reigns, ignorance may be preferable to knowledge, at the same time, once knowledge is brutally born, exactitude is preferable to uncertainty. To learn at what precise moment Jean had decided to take on Brent, in preference to myself, would be more acceptable than to allow the imagination continually to range unhindered through boundless fields of disagreeable supposition. Even so, I half hoped Macfaddean would return, full of new ideas about terrain and lines of communication. However, the choice did not lie with me. The narrative rested in Brent's own hands. Whether I wanted to listen or not, he was determined to tell his story.

"You'd never guess," he said apologetically, "but Jean fell for me first."

"Talk about girls lying down for Bob Duport."

"Shall I tell you how it happened?"

"Go ahead."

"Peter Templer asked me to dine with him to meet a couple called Taylor or Porter. He could never remember which. Peter subsequently went off with Mrs. Taylor, whoever she was, but that was later. He also invited his sister, Jean, to the party, and a woman called Lady McReith. I didn't much take to the latter. We dined at the Carlton Grill."

Brent paused. I remembered perfectly the occasion of which he spoke. One evening when we were out together, Jean had remarked she was dining with her brother the following night. The fact that the dinner party was to be at the Carlton Grill pinpointed the incident in my mind. I had noted at the time, without soreness, that Peter Templer, as a result of his exertions in the City, could afford to entertain at restaurants of that sort, while I frequented Foppa's and the Strasbourg. It was one of several differences that had taken shape between us. I remembered thinking that. Then the whole matter had passed from my mind until Jean and I next met, when she had made rather a point of emphasising what a boring evening she had had to endure with her brother and his friends. In fact the party at the Carlton Grill appeared to have been so tedious she could not keep off the subject.

"Who was there?"

"Two business men you'd never have heard of, one of them married to a very pretty, silly girl, whom Peter obviously has his eye on. Then there was a rather older woman I've met before, who might be a lesbian."

"What was she called?"

"You wouldn't know her either."

"What made you think she was a lesbian?"

"Something about her."

Jean knew perfectly well I had met Lady McReith when, as a boy, I had stayed at the Templers' house. Even had she forgotten that fact, Lady McReith was an old friend of the Templer family, especially of Jean's sister, Babs. It was absurd to speak of her in that distant way. By that time, too, Jean must have made up her mind whether or not Gwen McReith was a lesbian. All this mystification was impossible to ascribe to any rational form of behaviour. Possibly the emphasis on an unknown lesbian was to distract attention from the unmarried business man—Brent. Jean wanted to talk about the party simply because Brent had interested her, yet instinct told her this fact must be concealed. It was rather surprising that she had never before met Brent with her brother. Certainly, if she had named him, I should have had no suspicion of what was to follow. If that were the reason—a desire to talk about the party, but at the same time not to mention Brent by name—she could have stated quite simply that Lady McReith was present, gossiped in a straightforward way about Lady McReith's past, present and future. In short, this utterly unnecessary, irrational lie was a kind of veiled attack on our own relationship, a deliberate deceiving of me for no logical reason, except that, by telling a lie of that kind, truth was suddenly undermined between us; thus even though I was unaware of it, moving us inexorably apart. It was a preliminary thrust that must have satisfied some strange inner urge.

"Poor Peter," Jean had said, "he really sees the most dreary people. One of the men at dinner had never heard of Chaliapin."

That musical ignoramus was no doubt Brent too. I made up my mind to confirm later his inexperience of opera, even if it meant singing the "Song of the Volga Boatmen" to him to prove that point. At the moment, however, I did no more than ask for his own version of the dinner party at the Carlton Grill.

"Well, I thought Mrs. Duport an attractive piece," Brent said, "but I'd never have dreamt of carrying things further, if she hadn't rung me up the next day. You see, it was obvious Peter had just given the dinner because he wanted to talk to the other lady—the one he ran away with. The rest of us had been got there for that sole purpose. Peter's an old friend of mine, so I just did the polite as required, chatted about this and that. Talked business mostly, which Mrs. Duport seemed to find interesting."

"What did she say when she rang up?"

"Asked my opinion about Amparos."

"Who is Amparos?"

"An oil share."

"Just that?"

"We talked for a while on the phone. Then she suggested I should give her lunch and discuss oil investments. She knows something about the market. I could tell at once. In her blood, I suppose."

"And you gave her lunch?"

"I couldn't that week," said Brent, "too full of business. But I did the following week. That was how it all started. Extraordinary how things always happen at the same time. That was just the moment when the question opened up of my transfer to the South American office."

I saw the whole affair now. From the day of that luncheon with Brent, Jean had begun to speak with ever increasing seriousness of joining up again with her husband; chiefly, she said, for the sake of their child. That seemed reasonable enough. Duport might have behaved badly; that did not mean I never suffered any sensations of guilt.

"How did it end?"

Brent pulled up a large tuft of grass and threw it from him.

"Rather hard to answer that one," he said.

He spoke as if the conclusion of this relationship with Jean required much further reflection than he had at present been able to allow the subject.

"The fact is," he said, "I liked Jean all right, and naturally I was pretty flattered that she preferred me to a chap like Bob. All the same, I always felt what you might call uneasy with her, know what I mean. You must have come across that with girls. Feel they're a bit too good for you. Jean was too superior a wench for a chap of my simple tastes. That was what it came to. Talked all sorts of stuff I couldn't follow. Did you ever go to that coloured night-club called the Old Plantation?"

"Never, but I know it by name."

" A little coloured girl sold cigarettes there. She was more in my line, though it cost me a small fortune to get her."

"So the thing with Jean Duport just petered out?"

"With a good deal of grumbling on her side, believe me, before it did. I think she'd have run away with me if I'd asked her. Didn't quite see my way to oblige in that respect. Then one day she told me she didn't want to see me again. As a matter of fact we hadn't met for quite a time when she said that."

"Why not?"

"Don't know. Suppose I hadn't done much about it. There'd been some trouble at one of our places up the river. Production dropped from forty or fifty, to twenty-five barrels a day. I had to go along there and take a look at things. That was one of the reasons why she hadn't heard from me for some time."

"Fact was you were tired of it."

"Jean seemed to think so, the way she carried on. She was bloody rude when we parted. Anyway, she had the consolation of feeling she broke it off herself. Women like that."

So it appeared, after all, the love affair had been brought to an end by Brent's apathy, rather than Jean's fickleness. Even Duport had not known that. He had supposed Brent to have been, in his own words, "ditched." It had certainly never occurred to Duport, as a husband, that Brent, his own despised hanger-on, had actually been pursued by Jean, had himself done the "ditching." I, too, had little cause for self-congratulation, if it came to that.

"How did Duport find out about yourself and his wife?"

"Through their dear little daughter."

"Good God—Polly? I suppose she must be twelve or thirteen by now."

"Quite that," said Brent. "Fancy your remembering. I expect Bob spoke of her when you saw him. He's mad about that kid. Not surprising. She's a very pretty little girl. Will need keeping an eye on soon—perhaps even now."

"Did Bob find out while it was still going on?"

"Just before the end. Polly let out something about a meeting between Jean and me. Bob remarked that if it had been anyone else he'd have been suspicious. Then Jean flew off the handle and told him everything. Bob couldn't believe it at first. Didn't think I was up to it. He always regarded me as an absolute flop where women were concerned. It was quite a blow to him in a way. To his pride, I mean."

In this scene between the Duports, I saw a parallel to the occasion when I had myself made a slighting remark about

Jimmy Stripling, and Jean, immediately furious, had told me
of her former affair with him. The pattern was, as ever,
endlessly repeated. There was something to be admired in
Brent's lack of vanity in so absolutely accepting Duport's low
estimate of his own attractions, even after causing Duport's
wife to fall in love with him. Whatever other reason Brent
might have had for embarking on the matter, a cheap desire
to score off Jean's husband had played no part whatever. That
was certain. Duport, cuckolded or no, remained Brent's ideal
of manhood.

   "I think it's just as well Bob finally got rid of her," Brent
said. "Now he'll probably find a wife who suits him better.
Work Jean out of his system. Anyway he'll have a freer hand
to live the sort of life he likes."

   The tramp of men and sound of singing interrupted us. A
detachment of Sappers were marching by, chanting their song,
voices harsh and tuneless after those of my own Regiment:

> "You make fast, I make fast, make fast the dinghy,
> Make fast the dinghy, make fast the dinghy,
> You make fast, I make fast, make fast the dinghy,
> Make fast the dinghy pontoon.
> For we're marching on to Laffan's Plain,
> To Laffan's Plain, to Laffan's Plain,
> Yes we're marching on to Laffan's Plain,
> Where they don't know mud from shit . . ."

The powerful rhythms, primitive, incantatory, hypnotic,
seemed not only the battle hymn of warring tribes, but also a
refrain with obscure bearing on what Brent had just told me,
a general lament for the emotional conflict of men and women.
The Sappers disappeared over the horizon, their song dying away
with them. From the other direction, Macfaddean approached
at the double. He was breathless when he arrived beside us.

   "Sorry to keep you laddies waiting," he said, still panting,
"but I've found a wizard alternative concentration area. Here,
look at the map. We won't revise our earlier plan, just show

up this as a second choice. It means doing the odd spot of collating. Give me the coloured pencils. Now, take down these map references. Look sharp, old man."

Meanwhile, the problem of how best to reach Frederica's house when leave was granted remained an unsolved one. I asked Stevens whether he were going to spend the weekend in Birmingham.

"Much too far," he said, "I'm getting an aunt and uncle to put me up. It won't be very exciting, but it's somewhere to go."

He named a country town not many miles from Frederica's village.

"That's the part of the world I'm trying to reach myself. It's not going to be too easy to get there and back in a weekend. Trains are rotten."

"Trains are hopeless," said Stevens. "You'll spend the whole bloody time going backwards and forwards. Look here, I've got a broken-down old car I bought with the proceeds of my writing activities. It cost a tenner, but it should get us there and back. I can put my hand on some black market petrol too. Where exactly do you want to go?"

I named the place.

"I've heard of it," said Stevens. "My uncle is an estate agent in those parts. I've probably heard him talk of some house he's done a deal with in the neighborhood—your sister-in-law's perhaps. I can drop you there easily, if you like. Then pick you up on Sunday night, when we're due back here."

So it was arranged. The day came. Stevens's car, a Morris two-seater, started all right. We set off. It was invigorating to leave Aldershot. We drove along, while Stevens talked about his family, his girls, his ambitions. I heard how his mother was the daughter of a detective-inspector who had had to leave the force on account of drink; why he thought his sister's husband, a master in a secondary school, was rather too keen on the boys; what a relief it had been when he had heard, just before taking leave of his unit for the Aldershot course, that he had not got a local girl in the family way. Such confidences are rare in the army. Narcissistic, Stevens was at the same time—if the distinction can be made—not narrowly egotistical. He was interested in everything round him, even though everything must eventually lead back to himself. He asked about Isobel. It is hard to describe your wife. Instead I tried to give some account of Frederica's household. He seemed to absorb it all pretty well.

"Good name, 'Frederica'," he said, "I was christened 'Herbert,' but a hieroglyphic like 'Odo' was put on an envelope addressed to me when I was abroad, and I saw at once that was the thing to be called. I was getting fed up with being 'Bert' as it was."

Apart from the unexpected circumstance that Stevens and I should be driving across country together, the war seemed far away. Frederica had lived in her house, a former vicarage, for a year or two. A widow, she had moved to the country for her children's sake. Not large, the structure was splayed out and rambling, so that the building looked as if its owners had at some period taken the place to pieces, section by section, then put it together again, not always in correct proportions. A white gate led up a short drive with rose bushes on either side. The place had that same air of intense respectability Frederica's own personality conveyed. In spite of war conditions, there was no sign of untidiness about the garden, only an immediate sense of having entered a precinct where one must be on one's best behaviour. Stevens stopped in front of the porch. Before I could ring or knock, Frederica herself opened the door.

"I saw you coming up the drive," she said.

She wore trousers. Her head was tied up in a handkerchief. I kissed her, and introduced Stevens.

"Do come in for a moment and have a drink," she said. "Or have you got to push on? I'm sure not at once."

Frederica was not usually so cordial in manner to persons she did not already know; often, not particularly cordial to those she knew well. I had not seen her since the outbreak of war. The war must have shaken her up. That was the most obvious explanation of this new demeanour. The trousers and handkerchief were uncharacteristic. It was not so much style of dress that altered her, as something within herself. Robin Budd her husband had been killed in a fall from his horse nine or ten years before. By now not far from forty, she had never—so far as her own family knew—considered remarriage, still less indulged in any casual love affair; though those rather deliberately formidable, armour-plated good looks of hers were of the sort to attract quite a lot of men. Her sister, Priscilla, had some story about Jack Udney, an elderly courtier whose wife had died not long before, getting rather tight at Ascot after a notable win, and proposing to Frederica, while the Gold Cup was actually being run, but the allegation had never been substantiated. It was true Frederica had snapped out total disagreement once, when Isobel met Jack Udney somewhere and said she thought him a bore. In short, Frederica's most notable characteristic was what Molly Jeavons called her "dreadful correctness." Now, total war seemed slightly to have dislodged this approach to life. Frederica's reception of Stevens showed that. Stevens himself did not need further pressing to come in for a drink.

"Nothing I'd like better," he said. "It'll help me to face Aunt Doris's woes about shortages and ration cards. Half a sec, I'll back the car to a place where I'm not blocking your front door."

He started up the car again.

"How's Isobel?"

"Pretty well," said Frederica. "She's resting. She'll be down in a moment. We're rather full here. Absolutely packed to the ceiling, as a matter of fact."

"Who have you got?"

"Priscilla is here—with Caroline."

"Who is Caroline?"

"Priscilla's daughter, our niece. You ought to know that."

"Ah, yes, I'd forgotten her name."

"Then Robert turned up unexpectedly on leave."

"I'll be glad to see Robert."

Frederica laughed.

"Robert has brought a lady with him."

"No?"

"But *yes.* One of my own contemporaries, as a matter of fact, though I never knew her well."

"What's she called?"

"She married an American, now deceased, and has the unusual name of Mrs. Wisebite. She was *née* Stringham. I used to see her at dances."

"Charles Stringham's sister, in fact."

"Yes, you knew him, didn't you. I remember now. Well, Robert has brought her along. What do you think of that? Then the boys are home for the holidays—and there's someone else you know."

"Who is that?"

"Wait and see."

Frederica laughed shrilly again, almost hysterically. That was most unlike her. I could not make out what was happening. Usually calm to the point of iciness, rigidly controlled except when she quarrelled with her sister, Norah, Frederica seemed now half excited, half anxious about something. It could hardly be Robert's morals she was worrying about, although she took family matters very seriously, and the fact that Robert had a woman in tow was certainly a matter for curiosity. That Robert should be associated with Stringham's sister was of special interest to myself. I had never met this sister, who was called Flavia, though I had seen her years before at Stringham's wedding. Chips Lovell, our brother-in-law, Priscilla's husband, had always alleged that Robert had a taste for "night-club hostesses old enough to be his mother." Mrs. Wisebite, though not a night-club hostess, was certainly appreciably older than Robert. By this time, after several changes of position, Stevens had parked the car to his own satisfaction. As he joined us, another possible explanation of Frederica's jumpiness suddenly occurred to me.

"Isobel hasn't had the baby yet without anyone telling me?"

"Oh, no, no, no."

However, something about the way I asked the question must have indicated to Frederica herself that her manner struck me as unaccustomed. While we followed her through the hall, she spoke more quietly.

"It's only that I'm looking forward to your meeting an old friend, Nick," she said.

Evidently Robert was not the point at issue. We entered a sitting-room full of people, including a lot of children. These younger persons became reduced, in due course, to four only; Frederica's two sons, Edward and Christopher, aged about ten and twelve respectively, together with a couple of quite little ones, who played with bricks on the floor. One of these latter was presumably Priscilla's daughter, Caroline. Priscilla herself, blonde and leggy, quite a beauty in her way, was also lying on the floor, helping to build a tower with the bricks. Her brother, Robert Tolland, wearing battle-dress, sat on the sofa beside a tall, good-looking woman of about forty. Robert had removed his gaiters, but still wore army boots. The woman was Flavia Wisebite. Not noticeably like her brother in feature, she had some of Stringham's air of liveliness weighed down with melancholy. In her, too, the melancholy predominated. There was something greyhound-like about her nose and mouth. These two, Robert and Mrs. Wisebite, seemed to have arrived in the house only a very short time before Stevens and myself. Tall, angular, Robert wore Intelligence Corps shoulder titles, corporal's stripes on his arm. The army had increased his hungry, even rather wolfish appearance. He jumped up at once with his usual manner of conveying that the last person to enter the room was the one he most wanted to see, an engaging social gesture that often caused people to exaggerate Robert's personal interest in his fellow human beings, regarding whom, in fact, he was inclined to feel little concern.

"Nick," he said, "it's marvellous we should have struck just the moment when you've been able to get away for a weekend. I don't think you've ever met Flavia, but she knows all about you from her brother."

I introduced Odo Stevens to them.

"How do you do, sir," said Robert.

"Oh, blow the sir, chum," said Stevens. "You can keep that for when we're on duty. I'm rather thick with the lance-corporal in your racket who functions with my Battalion. I've borrowed his motor bike before now. Where are you stationed?"

"Mytchett," said Robert, "but I hope to move soon."

"My God, so do I," said Stevens. "They train your I. Corps personnel at Mytchett, don't they?"

He seemed perfectly at ease in this rather odd gathering. Before I had time to say much to Mrs. Wisebite, a middle-aged man rose from an armchair. He had a tanned face, deep blue eyes, a very neat grey moustache. The sweater worn over a pair of khaki trousers seemed natural clothes for him, giving somehow the impression of horsy elegance. It was Dicky Umfraville. Frederica was right. His presence was certainly a surprise.

"You didn't expect to find me here, old boy, did you?" said Umfraville. "You thought I could only draw breath in night-clubs, a purely nocturnal animal."

I had to agree that night-clubs seemed the characteristic background for our past encounters. There had been two of these at least. Umfraville had turned up at Foppa's that night, ages before, when I had taken Jean Duport there to play Russian billiards; then, a year or two later, Ted Jeavons had brought me to the club Umfraville himself had been running, where Max Pilgrim had sung his songs, Heather Hopkins played the piano:

"Di, Di, in her collar and tie . . ."

I had not set eyes on Umfraville since that occasion, but he seemed determined that we were the oldest of friends. I tried to recall what I knew of him: service in the earlier war with the Foot Guards, I could not remember which; some considerable reputation as gentleman-rider; four wives. Like many men who have enjoyed a career of more than usual dissipation, he had come to look notably distinguished in middle years, figure slim, eyes bright, face brown with Kenya sun. This bronzed skin, well brushed greying hair emphasised the blue of his eyes, which glistened like Peter Templer's, as Sergeant Pendry's had done before his disasters. I could not recall whether or not Umfraville's moustache was an addition. If so, it scarcely altered him at all. His face, in repose, possessed that look of innate sadness which often marks the features of those habituated to the boundless unreliability of horses. I asked him how he was employed in the army.

"On the staff of London District, old boy."

He spoke with an exaggerated dignity, squaring his chest and coming to attention. Frederica, who was handing round drinks, now joined us. Once more she began to laugh helplessly.

"Dicky's got a very grand job," she said, "haven't you?"

She slipped her arm through Umfraville's. This was unheard-of licence for Frederica, something to be regarded as indicating decay of all the moral and social standards she had defended so long.

"It's certainly one of the bigger stations," Umfraville agreed modestly.

"Of course it is, darling."

"And should lead to promotion," he said.

"Without doubt."

"Collecting the tickets perhaps."

"Dicky is an RTO," said Frederica.

She was quite unable to control her laughter, which seemed not so much attributable to the thought of Umfraville being a Railway Transport Officer, as to the sheer delight she took in him for himself.

"He's got a cosy little office at one of those North London stations," she said. "I can never remember which, but I've visited him there. I say, Dicky, we'd better tell Nick, hadn't we?"

"About us?"

"Yes."

"The fact is," said Umfraville speaking slowly and with gravity, "the fact is Frederica and I are engaged."

Isobel came through the door at that moment, so the impact of this unexpected piece of news was to some extent lessened by other considerations immediately presenting themselves. Then and there, no more was said than a few routine congratulations, with further gigglings from Frederica. Isobel looked pale, though pretty well. I had not seen her for months, it seemed years. We went off to a corner together.

"How have you been?"

"All right. There was a false alarm about ten days ago, but it didn't get far enough to inform you."

"And you're feeling all right?"

"Most of the time—but rather longing for the little brute to appear."

We talked for a while.

"Who is the character on the floor playing bricks with the children and Priscilla?"

"He's called Odo Stevens. He's on the course and brought me over in his car. Come and meet him."

We went across the room. Stevens got to his feet and shook hands.

"Look here," he said, "I must go. Otherwise Aunt Doris will be upset thinking something's happened to me."

"Don't rush off, Mr. Stevens," said Priscilla, still prone on the carpet, "hullo, Nick, I've only had a wave from you so far. How are you?"

Frederica joined us.

"Another drink," she said.

"No, thank you, really," said Stevens, "I must be moving on."

He turned to say goodbye to Priscilla.

"I say," he said, "you'll lose your brooch, if you're not careful."

She looked down. The brooch hung from its pin. It was a little mandoline in silver-gilt, ornamented with musical symbols on either side, early Victorian keepsake in style, pretty, though of no special value. Priscilla used to wear it before she married Chips. I had always supposed it a present from Moreland in their days together, that the reason for the musical theme of its design. While she glanced down, the brooch fell to the ground. Stevens stooped to pick it up.

"The clasp is broken," he said. "Look, if I can take it with me now, I'll put it right in a couple of ticks. I can bring it back on Sunday night, when I turn up with the car."

"But that would be wonderful," she said. "Do you know about brooches?"

"All about costume jewellery. In the business."

"Oh, do tell me about it."

"I must be off now," he said. "Some other time."

He turned to me, and we checked the hour he would bring the car for our return to Aldershot. Then Stevens said goodbye all round.

"I'll come to the door with you," said Priscilla. "I want to hear more about costume jewellery, my favourite subject."

They went off together.

"What a nice young man," said Frederica. "He really made one feel as if one were his own age."

"Take care," said Umfraville. "That's just what I was like when I was young."

"But that's in his favour," she said, "surely it is."

"Barely twenty," said Umfraville, in reminiscence. "Blind with enthusiasm. Fighting like a hero on Flanders fields."

"Oh, rot," said Frederica. "You said you were nearly twenty-four when you went to the war."

"Well, anyway, look at me now," said Umfraville. "A lot of good my patriotism did me, a broken-down old RTO."

"Cheer up, my pet."

"Ah," said Umfraville, "the heroes of yesterday, they're the *maquereaux* of tomorrow."

"Well, you're my *maquereau* anyway," said Frederica, "so shut up and have another drink."

Later, when we were alone together upstairs, Isobel gave a fuller account of herself. There was a lot to talk about. The doctor thought everything all right, the baby likely to arrive in a couple of weeks' time. There were, indeed, far more things to discuss than could be spoken of at once. They would have to come out gradually. Instead of dealing with myriad problems in a businesslike manner, settling all kind of points that had to be settled, making arrangements about the future—if it could be assumed there was to be a future

—we talked of more immediate, more amusing matters.

"What do you think about Frederica?" Isobel asked.

"Not a bad idea."

"I think so too."

"When did she break the news?"

"Only yesterday, when he arrived on leave. I was a bit staggered when told. She's mad about him. I've never seen Frederica like that before. The boys get on well with him too, and seem to approve of the prospect."

Frederica and Dicky Umfraville getting married was something to open up hitherto unexplored fields of possibility. The first thought, that the engagement was grotesque, bizarre, changed shape after a time, developing until one saw their associating as one of those emotional hook-ups of the very near and the very far, which make human relationships easier to accept than to rationalize or disentangle. I remembered that if Frederica's husband, Robin Budd, had lived, his age would not have been far short of Umfraville's. I asked Isobel if the two of them had ever met.

"Just saw each other, I think. Rob looked a little like Dicky too."

"Where did Frederica pick him up?"

"With Robert. Dicky Umfraville knew Flavia Wisebite in Kenya. Her father farms there—or did, he died the other day—but of course you know that."

"Do you suppose Flavia and Dicky—"

"I shouldn't wonder. Anyway, it was an instantaneous click so far as Frederica was concerned."

"Frederica is aware, I suppose, that the past is faintly murky."

"One wife committed suicide, another married a jockey. Then there was the wife no one knows about—and finally Anne Stepney, who lasted scarcely more than a year, and is now, I hear, living with J. G. Quiggin."

"That's as many as are recorded. But where did Robert contract Mrs. Wisebite? That is even more extraordinary."

"One never knows with Robert. Tell me about her. She is sister of your old school pal, Charles Stringham. What else?"

"Charles never saw much of her after they were grown up. She first married a notorious character called Flitton, who lost an arm in the war before this one. A great gambler, also a Kenya figure. Dicky must know him well. Flitton ran away with Baby Wentworth, but refused to marry her after the divorce. Flavia had a daughter by Flitton who must be eighteen or nineteen by now."

"Flavia told me the late Mr. Wisebite, her second husband, came from Minneapolis, and died of drink in Miami."

"Is she sharing a room with Robert?"

"Not here. There isn't one to share. The beds are too narrow. But, in principle, they seem to be living together. How did you think Priscilla was looking?"

"All right. She was being a bit standoffish, except to Stevens. Who was the other child playing bricks? The Lovells have only Caroline, haven't they?"

"That's Barry."

"Who is Barry?"

"A slip-up of Frederica's maid, Audrey. Audrey had to bring him along with her, owing to war circumstances. Barry comes in very useful as an escort for Caroline. You know how difficult it always is to find a spare man, especially in the country."

"Does Barry's mother do the cooking?"

"No, Frederica. She found herself without a cook and no prospect of getting one. She's always been rather keen on cooking, you know. Now she could get a job in any but the very best houses."

I had an idea, from the way she spoke, that all this talk about Barry, and Frederica's cooking, was, on Isobel's part, a means of temporarily evading the subject of Priscilla. I could tell, from the way she had mentioned her sister, that, for some reason, Priscilla was on Isobel's mind. She was worried about her.

"Any news of Chips?"

"Priscilla isn't very communicative. Where do Marines go? Is he on a ship? She seems to hold it against him that he hasn't been able to arrange for them to have a house or a flat somewhere. I don't think that's Chip's fault. It's all this bloody war. That's why Priscilla is here. She is very restless."

"Is she having a baby too?"

"Not that I know of. Audrey is, though."

"Audrey sounds a positive Messalina."

"Not in appearance. She is a good-natured, dumpy little thing with spectacles."

"A bit too good-natured, or her lenses need adjusting. Is it Barry's father again?"

"On the contrary, but we understand it may lead to marriage this time."

"I suppose Frederica will be the next with a baby. What about Robert and Mrs. Wisebite?"

"No doubt doing their best. Robert, by the way, is on embarkation leave. He's only spending some of it here. He arrived with Flavia just before you did."

"Where is he going?"

"He doesn't know—or won't say for security reasons— but he thinks France."

"How on earth has he managed that?"

"He decided to withdraw his name from those in for a commission, as there was otherwise no immediate hope of a posting overseas."

"I see."

"Hardly what one would expect of Robert," Isobel said.

His own family regarded Robert as one of those quietly self-indulgent people who live rather secret lives because they find themselves thereby less burdened by having to think of others. No one knew much, for example, about his work in an export house dealing with the Far East. The general idea was that Robert was doing pretty well there, though not because he himself propagated any such picture. He would naturally be enigmatic about a situation such as that which involved him with Mrs. Wisebite. It was fitting that he should find himself in Field Security. Enterprise must have been required to place himself there too. I wondered what the steps leading to the Intelligence Corps had been. At one moment he had contemplated the navy. No less interesting was this attempt on Robert's part to move closer to a theatre of war at the price of immediately postponing the chance of becoming an officer.

"The war seems to have altered some people out of recognition and made others more than ever like themselves," said Isobel.

"Have you ever heard of someone called David Pennistone? He was a man in the army I talked to on a train. He said he was writing an article on Descartes."

"Haven't I seen the name at the end of reviews?"

"That's what I thought. We didn't manage to find anyone we knew in common, but I believe I met him years ago for a minute or two at a party."

"Didn't the Lovells talk about someone called Pennistone when they came back from Venice? I remember Chips explaining that he was no relation to the Huntercombes, because the name was spelt with a double-n. I have an idea Pennistone lives in Venice — some story of a *contessa*, beautiful but not very young. That's how I'm beginning to feel myself."

"Anyway, it's nice to meet again, darling."

"It's been a long time."

"A bloody long time."

"It certainly has."

Later that weekend, when I found him pacing the lawn, Umfraville himself supplied some of the background wanting in his own story.

"Look here, old boy," he said, when I joined him, "how do you think you and the others are going to stand up to having me as a brother-in-law?"

"A splendid prospect."

"Not everyone would think so," he said. "You know I must be insane to embrace matrimony again. Stark, staring mad. But not half as mad as Frederica to take me on. Do you realize she'll be my fifth? Something wrong with a man who keeps marrying like that. Must be. But I really couldn't resist Frederica. That prim look of hers. All the same, fancy her accepting me. You'd never expect it, would you? All that business of her emptying the royal slops. She'll have to give up that occupation of course. No good trying to be an Extra Woman of the Bedchamber with me in the offing. Not a bloody bit of use. You can just picture H.M. saying: 'Why's that fellow turned up again? I remember him. He used to be a captain in my Brigade of Guards. I had to get rid of him. He's a no-gooder. What does he mean by showing his ugly face again at Buck House? I won't stand it. Off with his head.' You agree, don't you?"

"I see what you mean."

Umfraville stared at me with bloodshot eyes. When we had first met at Foppa's, I had wondered whether he was not a little mad. The way he spoke now, even though it made me laugh, created the same disquieting impression. He nodded his head, smiling to himself, still contemplating his own characteristics with absolute absorption. I suddenly saw that Umfraville had been quite right when he said he was like Odo Stevens. Here again was an almost perfect narcissism, joined in much the same manner to a great acuteness of observation and relish for life.

"You're going to have a professional cad for a brother-in-law, old boy," he said, "make no mistake about that. Just to show you I know what I'm talking about when I apply that label to myself, I'll confide a secret. I was the one who took our little friend Flavia's virginity in Kenya years ago. Still, if that were the worst thing that ever happened to poor Flavia, she wouldn't have had much to complain about. Fancy being married to Cosmo Flitton and Harrison F. Wisebite in one lifetime."

"Isobel and I had already discussed whether you and Mrs. Wisebite had ever been in bed together."

"You had? That shows you're a discerning couple. She's a bright girl, your wife. Well, the answer is in the affirmative. You knew Flavia's brother Charles, didn't you?"

"I used to know him well. I haven't seen him for years."

"Met Charles Stringham in Kenya too. Came out for a month or two when he was quite a boy. I liked him very much. Then he took to drink, like so many other good chaps. Flavia says he has recovered now, and is in the army. Charles used to talk a lot about that bastard, Buster Foxe, whom their mother married when she and Boffles Stringham parted company. Charles hated Buster's guts."

"I haven't seen Commander Foxe for ages."

"Neither have I, thank God, but I hear he's in the neighbourhood. At your brother-in-law, Lord Warminster's home, in fact. He'll soon be my brother-in-law, too. Then there'll be hell to pay."

"But what on earth is Buster, a sailor, doing at Thrubworth? I thought it was a Corps Headquarters."

"Thrubworth isn't an army set-up any longer. It's still requisitioned, but they turned the place into one of those frightfully secret inter-service organizations. Buster has dug himself in there."

"Are they still letting Erry and Blanche inhabit their end of the house?"

"Don't object, so far as I hear."

No very considerable adjustment had been necessary when Thrubworth had been taken over by the Government at the beginning of the war. Erridge, in any case, had been living in only a small part of the mansion (seventeenth-century brick, fronted in the eighteenth century with stone), his sister, Blanche, housekeeping for him. Although the place was only twenty or thirty miles from Frederica's village, there was little or no communication between Erridge and the rest of his family. Since the outbreak of war he had become, so Isobel told me, less occupied than formerly with the practical side of politics, increasingly devoting himself to books about the Anabaptists and revolutionary movements of the Middle Ages.

"Buster's a contemporary of mine," said Umfraville, "a son-of-a-bitch in the top class. I've never told you my life story, have I?"

"Not yet."

"You'll hear it often enough when we become brothers-in-law," he said, "so I'll start by revealing only a little now."

Once more I thought of Odo Stevens.

"My father bred horses for a living," said Umfraville. "It was a precarious vocation and his ways were improvident.

However, he had the presence of mind to marry the daughter of a fairly well-to-do manufacturer of machinery for the production of elastic webbing. That allowed for a margin of unprofitable deals in bloodstock. If I hadn't learnt to ride as a boy, I don't know where I should have been. There was some crazy idea of turning me into a land-agent. Then the war came in 1914 and I got off on my own. Found my way into one of the newly formed Guards battalions. There had been terrific expansion and they didn't turn up their noses at me and many another like me. In fact some of my brother officers were heels such as you've never set eyes on. I never looked back after that. Not until I fell foul of Buster Foxe. If it hadn't been for Buster, I might have been major-general now, commanding London District, instead of counting myself lucky to be a humble member of its Movement Control staff."

"You remained on after the war with a regular commission?"

"That was it," said Umfraville. "I expect you've heard of a French marshal called Lyautey. Pacified North Africa and all that. Do you know what Lyautey said was the first essential of an officer? Gaiety. That was what Lyautey thought, and he knew his business. His own ideas of gaiety may not have included the charms of the fair sex, but that's another matter. Well, how much gaiety do you find among most of the palsied crackpots you serve under? Precious little, you can take it from me. It was my intention to master a military career by taking a leaf out of Lyautey's book—not as regards neglecting the ladies, but in other respects. First of all it worked pretty well."

"But what has Buster Foxe to do with Marshal Lyautey?"

"I'm coming to that," said Umfraville. "Ever heard of a girl called Dolly Braybrook?"

"No."

"Dolly was my first wife. Absolute stunner. Daughter of a fellow who'd formerly commanded the Regiment. Bloody Braybrook, her father was universally termed throughout the army, and with reason. She wouldn't have me at first, and who should blame her. Asked her again and again. The answer was always no. Then one day she changed her mind, the way women do. That pertinacity of mine has gone now. All the same, its loss has confirmed my opinion that the older I get, the more attractive I am to women."

"It certainly looks like it."

"Formerly, there was all that business of 'Not tonight, darling, because I don't love you enough,' then 'Not tonight, darling, because I love you too much'—Christ, I've been through the whole range of it. The nearest some women get to being faithful to their husband is making it unpleasant for their lover. However, that's by the way. The point is that Dolly married me in the end."

"How long did it last?"

"A year or two. Happy as the day's long, at least I was. I'd been appointed adjutant too. Then Buster Foxe appeared on the horizon. He was stationed at Greenwich at the time— the Naval College. I used to play an occasional game of cards with him and other convivial souls when he came up west. What should happen but under my very nose Dolly fell in love with Buster."

The exaggerated dramatic force employed by Umfraville in presenting his narrative made it hard to know what demeanour best to adopt in listening to the story. Tragedy might at any moment give way to farce, so that the listener had always to keep his wits about him. When I first met Umfraville I had noticed some resemblance to Buster Foxe, now revealed as that similarity companionship in early life confers on people.

"It was just the moment when the Battalion was moving from Buckingham Gate to Windsor," Umfraville said. "I had to go with them, of course, while Dolly stayed in London, until we could find somewhere to live. I went up to see her one day. Arrived home. The atmosphere was a shade chilly. The next thing was Dolly told me she wanted a divorce."

"A complete surprise?"

"Old boy, you could have knocked me down with a swizzle-stick. Always the way, of course. Nothing I could say was any good. Dolly was set on marriage to Buster. In the end I

agreed. There was no way out. I suppose I might have shot
Buster through the head, if I'd got close enough to him, even
though it is only the size of a nut. What the hell good would
that have done? Besides, I'd have run quite a chance of swing-
ing in this country. It's not like France, where they expect
you to react strongly. So I settled down to do the gentlemanly
thing, and provide evidence for Dolly to divorce me. I was
quite well ahead with that when Buster found Amy Stringham,
Flavia's mama, was just as anxious to marry him as Dolly
was. Now it didn't take Buster long to work out that marriage
to a lady with some very warm South African gold holdings,
not to mention a life interest in her first husband Lord
Warrington's estate, stud and country mansion, would be
more profitable than a wife like Dolly, one of a large family
without a halfpenny to bless herself with. Mrs. Stringham
was a few years older than Buster, it's true, but she was none
the less a beauty. We all had to admit that."

Umfraville paused.

"Next thing I heard," he said, "was that Dolly had taken
an overdose of sleeping pills."

"Divorce proceedings had started?"

"Not so far as that they couldn't have been put in reverse
gear. I suppose Dolly thought it too late in the day to suggest
return, though there's nothing I'd have liked better."

"But why did that prevent you from Commanding London
District?"

"That's a sensible question, old boy. The reason was this.
I had to leave the service—abandon my gallant and glorious
Regiment. I'll explain. You see I wasn't feeling too good after
my poor wife Dolly decided to join the angels, and naturally
I looked about for someone to console me. Found several, as
a matter of fact. The one I liked best was a girl I met one
night at the Cavendish called Joy Grant—at least that was
her professional name, and a very suitable one too—so I
thought I might as well marry her. Of course, there couldn't
be any question of staying in the Regiment, if I married Joy.
To begin with, I should have been hard put to it to name a

brother officer who hadn't shared the same idyllic experiences as myself in that respect. I sent in my papers and made up my mind to up stumps and emigrate with my blushing bride. Thought I'd try Kenya, the great open spaces where men are men, as Charles Stringham used to say. Well, Joy and I had scarcely arrived in the hotel at Nairobi when it became abundantly clear we had made a mistake in becoming man and wife. We were already living what's called a cat-and-dog life. In short, it wasn't long before she went off with a fellow called Castlemallock, twice her age, who looked like an ostler suffering from a dose of clap."

"The Corps School of Chemical Warfare is at a house called Castlemallock."

"That's the family. They used to live there until they lost all their money a generation or two ago. Castlemallock himself, marquess or not, was a common little fellow, but what was much worse, so far as he himself was concerned, was the fact that he found he couldn't perform with Joy in Kenya. He thought it might have something to do with the climate, the altitude, so he took her back to England to see if he could make better going there, or at least consult a competent medical man about getting a shot of something to liven him up occasionally. However, he took too long to find the right specialist, and meanwhile Joy went off with Jo Breen, the jockey, the chap who was suspended one year at Cheltenham for pulling Middlemarch. They keep a pub together now in one of those little places in the Thames Valley, and overcharge you most infamously if you ever drop in for a talk about old times."

Umfraville paused again. He took out a cigarette case and offered it to me.

"Now this business of wives departing was beginning to get me down," he said. "It seemed to be becoming a positive habit. This time, I thought, I'll be the one to do the cattle rustling, so I removed from him the wife of a District Commissioner. There was no end of trouble about that. When I previously found myself in that undignified position, I'd behaved like a gent. This fellow, the husband, didn't see things in that light at all. I found myself in a perfect rough-house."

He lit a cigarette and sighed.

"How did it end?"

"We got married," he said, "but she died of enteric six months later. You see I don't have much luck with wives. Then you were present yourself when I met little Anne Stepney at Foppa's. You know the end of the story. That was a crazy thing to do, to marry Anne, if ever there was. Anyway, it didn't last long. Least said, soonest mended. But now I've turned over a new leaf. Frederica is going to be my salvation. The model married couple. I'm going to find my way out of Movement Control, and once more set about becoming a general, just as I was before being framed by Buster. Frederica is going to make a first-class general's wife. Don't you agree? My God, I never dreamed I'd marry one of Hugo Warminster's daughters, and I don't expect he did either."

By then, it was time for luncheon. I found myself sitting next to Flavia Wisebite. She had a quiet, rather sad manner, suggesting one of those reserved, well behaved, fairly peevish women, usually of determined character, often to be found as wives, or ex-wives, of notably dissipated men like Flitton or Wisebite. Their peevishness appears to derive not so much from a husband's ill behaviour, as to be a trait natural to them, which attracts men of that kind. Such was mere conjecture, since I knew little or nothing of Flavia's private life, except that Stringham had more than once implied that his sister's matrimonial troubles were largely of her own choosing. In that she would have been, after all, not unlike himself. I asked for news of her brother.

"Charles?" she said. "He's in a branch of the army called the RAOC—Royal Army Ordnance Corps. I expect you know about it. According to Charles, they look after clothes and boots and blankets, all that sort of thing. Is it true?"

"Perfectly true. What rank?"

"Private."

"I see."

"And likely to remain so, he says."

"He's—all right now?"

"Oh, yes," she said. "Hardly touches a drop. In fact, so cured he can even drink a glass of beer from time to time. That's a great step. I always said it was just nerves, not real addiction."

Familiar herself with alcoholics, she took her brother's former state in a very matter-of-fact way; also his circumstances in the army, which did not sound very enviable. Stringham as a private in the RAOC required an effort of imagination even to picture.

"How does Charles like it?"

"Not much."

"I'm not surprised."

"He says it's rather hell, in fact, but he was bent on getting into something. For some reason, the RAOC were the only people who seemed to want him. I think Charles is having a more uncomfortable time than Robert. You rather enjoy the I. Corps, don't you, dear?"

"Enjoy is rather a strong word," said Robert. "Things might be worse at Mytchett. I always like prying into other people's business, and that's what Field Security is for."

Flavia Wisebite's manner towards Robert was almost maternal. She was nearer in age to Robert than to Umfraville, but gave the impression, although so different an example of it, of belonging much more to Umfraville's generation. Both she and Umfraville might be said to represent forms of revolt, and nothing dates people more than the standards from which they have chosen to react. Robert and Flavia's love affair, if love affair it were, took a very different shape from Frederica's and Umfraville's. Robert and Flavia gave no impression that, for the moment at least, they were having the time of their lives. On the contrary, they seemed very subdued. By producing Flavia at his sister's house, Robert was at last to some extent showing his hand, emotionally speaking, something he had never done before. Perhaps he was in love. The pressures of war were forcing action on everyone. Were his efforts to get to France part of this will to action, or an attempt to escape? The last might also be true. The telephone bell rang as we were rising from the table. Frederica went to answer it. She returned to the room.

"It's for you, Priscilla."

"Who is it?"

"Nick's friend, Mr. Stevens."

"Oh, yes, of course," said Priscilla. "About the brooch." She went rather pink.

"Priscilla's made a hit," said Umfraville.

I asked Flavia whether she ever saw her mother's former secretary, Miss Weedon, who had married my parents' old acquaintance, General Conyers.

"Oh, Tuffy," she said. "She used to be my governess, you know. Yes, I visited her only the other day. It is all going very well. The General read aloud to us an article he had written about heightened bi-sexuality in relation to early religiosity. He is now much more interested in psychoanalysis than in his 'cello playing."

"What does he think about the war?"

"He believed a German offensive would start any moment then, probably in several places at once."

"In fact this Norwegian and Danish business was the beginning."

"I suppose so."

"It doesn't sound as if things are going too well," Umfraville said, "I think we've taken some knocks."

Priscilla returned.

"It was about the brooch," she said. "Mr. Stevens can't do it himself, as one of the stones has come out, but he has arranged for someone he knows to mend it. He just wanted to warn me that he wouldn't have it for me when he came to pick up Nick in the car."

"I said he was a very polite young man," remarked Frederica, giving her sister rather a cold look.

The rest of the weekend passed with the appalling rapidity of wartime leave, melting away so quickly that one seemed scarcely to have arrived before it was time to go. Dinner was a trifle gloomy on that account, conversation fragmentary, for the most part about the news that evening.

"I wonder whether this heavy bombing is a prelude to a move in France," said Robert. "What do you think, Dicky?"

"That will be the next thing."

Towards the end of the meal, the telephone bell sounded.

"Do answer it, Nick," said Frederica. "You're nearest the door."

She spoke from the kitchen, where she was making coffee. The telephone was installed in a lobby off the hall. I went out to it. A man's voice asked if he were speaking to Frederica's number.

"Yes."

"Is Lance-Corporal Tolland there?"

"Who is speaking?"

He named some army unit. As I returned to the dining-room, a knocking came from the front door. I told Robert he was wanted on the telephone.

"Shall I answer the door, Frederica?"

"It's probably the vicar about a light showing," she said. "He's an air-raid warden and frightfully fussy. Bring him in, if it is. He might like a cup of coffee."

However, a tall naval officer was on the step when I opened the door. He had just driven up in a car.

"This is Lady Frederica Budd's house?"

"Yes."

"I must apologize for calling at this hour of the night, but I believe my step-daughter, Mrs. Wisebite, is staying here."

"She is."

"There are some rather urgent business matters to talk over with her. I heard she was here for a day or two, and thought Lady Frederica would not mind if I dropped in for a moment. I am stationed in the neighbourhood—at her brother, Lord Warminster's house, as a matter of fact."

"Come in. You're Commander Foxe, aren't you. I'm Nicholas Jenkins. We've met once or twice in the past."

"Good God, of course we have," said Buster. "This is your sister-in-law's house?"

"Yes."

"You were a friend of Charles's, weren't you. This is splendid."

Commander Foxe did not sound as if he thought finding me at Frederica's was as splendid as all that, even though he seemed relieved that his arrival would be cushioned by an introduction. Another sponsor would certainly be preferable, since any old friend of Stringham's was bound to have heard many stories to his own discredit. However, Buster, although he had that chronic air some men possess of appearing to consider all other men potential rivals, put a reasonably good face on it. For my own part, I suddenly thought of what Dicky Umfraville had told me. He would hardly welcome this arrival. There was nothing to be done about that. I took Buster along to the sitting-room, where the rest of the party were now sitting. Buster had evidently planned a fairly dramatic entry.

"I really must apologize, Lady Frederica—" he began to say, as he came through the door.

Following him into the room, I saw at once something disagreeable had happened. Robert appeared to be the centre of attention. He had evidently just announced news consequent on his telephone call. Everyone looked disturbed. Flavia Wisebite seemed near tears. When she saw Commander Foxe, her distress turned to furious annoyance.

"Buster," she said sharply, "where on earth have you come from?"

She sounded very cross, so cross that for a moment she forgot how upset she was. Commander Foxe must have grasped that his arrival was not altogether welcome at the moment. He was plainly taken aback by that. Smiling uneasily, he glanced round the room, as if to recover himself by finding some friendly face. His eyes rested first on Dicky Umfraville. Umfraville held out his hand.

"Hullo, Buster," he said, "a long time since we met."

When people really hate one another, the tension within them can sometimes make itself felt throughout a room, like atmospheric waves, first hot, then cold, wafted backwards and forwards, as if in an invisible process of air conditioning, creating a pervasive physical disturbance. Buster Foxe and Dicky Umfraville, between them, brought about that state. Their really overpowering mutual detestation dominated for a moment all other local agitations. The fact that neither party was going to come out in the open at this stage made the currents of nervous electricity generated by suppressed emotion even more powerful. At the same time, to anyone who did not know what horrors linked them together, they might have appeared a pair of old friends, met after an age apart. Their distinct, though imprecise, physical similarity increased this last impression. Before Buster could do more than make a gesture of acknowledgment in Umfraville's direction, Frederica came forward. Buster began once more to apologize, to explain he wanted only a brief word with Flavia, then be gone. Frederica listened to him.

"We're all in rather a stew here at the moment," she said. "My brother Robert has just heard his leave is cancelled. He has to go back as soon as possible."

Buster was obviously put out at finding himself in the disadvantageous position of having to listen to someone else's troubles, when he had come with the express object of stating his own. It had to be admitted he looked immensely distinguished, more so even than Umfraville. I had never before seen Commander Foxe in naval uniform. It suited him. His iron-grey hair, of which he still possessed plenty, was kept short on a head almost preternaturally small, as Umfraville had pointed out. Good looks, formerly of a near film-star quality, had settled down in middle-age to an appearance at once solid and forcible, a bust of the better type of Roman senator. A DSC was among his medal ribbons. I thought of Umfraville's lament that the heroes of yesterday are the *maquereaux* of tomorrow. Something had undoubtedly vexed Commander Foxe a great deal. He attempted, without much success, to assume a sympathetic expression about the subject of Robert's leave cancellation. Clearly ignorant of any connexion between Flavia and Robert, he was at a loss to understand why Flavia was so disturbed. After her first outburst, she had forgotten about Buster again, and was gazing at Robert, her eyes full of tears.

"Surely you can take a train tomorrow," she said. "You don't have to leave tonight, darling. What trains are there, Frederica?"

"Not very good ones," said Frederica. "But they'll get you there sooner or later. Why don't you do that, Robert?"

"Aren't you taking the army too seriously, Robert?" said Umfraville. "Having just sent you on leave, they can't expect you to go back at a moment's notice. Your unit doesn't know Nick is going back by car tonight. Even if you are a bit late, there's nothing the authorities can do to you, if they countermand their own orders in this way."

"That's not the point," said Robert.

This was the only time I had ever seen Robert fairly near to what might be called a state of excitement. He was knocking his closed fists together gently.

"If I don't get back before tomorrow night," he said, "I may miss the overseas draft. My name is only included in the list on sufferance anyway. If they've got an excuse, they'll remove it. That was the Orderly Room Sergeant on the line. He's rather a friend of mine, and was giving me warning about that. Of course he couldn't say it straight out, but he made his meaning quite clear to me. There are rows of other corporals they can send, if a party has been ordered to move forthwith. That's what it looks like. Besides, I don't want to have to make all my arrangements about packing and so on at the very last moment. That was why I thought your friend Stevens might be able to fit me into his car, Nick. You could then disgorge me somewhere in the neighbourhood of Mytchett. I could walk the last lap, if you landed me reasonably near."

"It won't be very comfortable in the car, but I don't see why you shouldn't come with us."

"When is Stevens arriving?"

"Any time now."

"I'll go and get my things ready," said Robert.

He went off upstairs. Flavia began to dab her eyes with a rolled-up handkerchief. Buster must have remembered he had met Priscilla before—at the party his wife had given for Moreland's symphony—and he filled in the time during this discussion about Robert's affairs by talking to her. That was also perhaps a method of avoiding Dicky Umfraville's eye. Buster was accompanying this conversation with a great display of middle-aged masculine charm. From time to time, he glanced in Flavia's direction to see if she were sufficiently calm to be tackled about whatever he hoped to speak. Now, Flavia, making an effort to recover herself, moved towards Buster of her own volition.

"What's happened?" she said. "I was going to ring you up, but I've been dreadfully entangled with other things. Besides, I've only just arrived here. Now all this has upset everything."

If Buster did not already know about Robert, that was not very enlightening, but he was probably sharp enough to have grasped the situation by this time.

"It's about your mother," he said. "It's all damned awkward. I thought the sooner you knew the better. There was a lot of difficulty in getting hold of your address. When I found by a lucky chance you were in the neighbourhood of Thrubworth, I decided to try and see you, in case I lost the opportunity for months."

"But what is it?"

"Your mother is behaving in a very extraordinary way. There are serious money difficulties for one thing. They may affect you and Charles. Your settlements, I mean."

"She's always quite reckless about money. You must have learnt that by now."

"She has been unwise about all kind of matters. I had no idea what was going on."

"Where is she now?"

"That's one of the points. She has closed both houses and gone to live in a workman's cottage to be near Norman."

"Norman Chandler?"

"Of course."

"But I thought Norman had joined the army."

"He has. He has been sent to a camp in Essex. That's why your mother has gone there. What's more, she wants to divorce me."

This news certainly surprised Flavia a lot.

"But—"

"I've nowhere to go," said Buster, speaking with great bitterness. "When I was last in London, I had to stay at my club. Now this news about a divorce is sprung on me. Your mother went off without a word. All kinds of arrangements have to be made about things. It is too bad."

"But does she want to marry Norman?"

"How do I know what she wants to do?" said Buster. "I'm the last person she ever considered. I think Norman, too, has behaved very badly to allow her to act in this way. I always liked Norman. I did not in the least mind his being what he is. I often told him so. I thought we were friends. Many men in my position would have objected to having someone like Norman about the house, doing the flowers and dancing attendance upon their wife. Norman pleased your mother. That was enough for me. What thanks do I get for being so tolerant? Your mother goes off to Essex with Norman, taking the keys with her, so that I can't even get at my own suits and shirts. On top of all that, I'm told I'm going to be divorced."

At that point there was another loud knock on the front door. This must be Stevens. I went to let him in. Umfraville followed me into the hall.

"Look here," he said, "tell me quickly what's happened to Buster to upset him so."

"Mrs. Foxe had a friend called Norman Chandler—a little dancer she adored, who was always about her house. He was quite a good actor too. It looks as if she has got fed up at last and kicked Buster out."

"Buster is going to get me into this secret set-up at Thrubworth. I've decided that."

"How's it going to be managed?"

"I once took a monkey off Buster at poker. Apart from his other misdemeanours, I've never seen my money. I know where I can make things unpleasant, if Buster doesn't jump to it and get me fixed up. Boffles Stringham once said: 'Mark my words, Dicky, the day will come when Amy will have to get rid of that damned polo-playing sailor.' That day has come. There are some other reckonings for Buster to pay too."

Another knock came on the door. Umfraville went back to the sitting-room. I admitted Stevens.

"I'm a bit late," he said, "we'll have to bustle back."

"There's rather a commotion going on here. My brother-in-law, Robert Tolland, has just had his leave cancelled. He wants to get back to Mytchett tonight. Will it be all right if he comes with us? We pass near his unit and can drop him on the way."

"Of course. If he doesn't mind having his balls crushed in the back of the car. Is he ready?"

"He's just gone off to pack. Then there's a naval officer making a scene with his step-daughter."

"Bring 'em all on," said Stevens. "We oughtn't to delay too long. I'd just like to have word with that lady about her brooch."

We went into the sitting-room. By that time things had quietened down. Buster, especially, had recovered his poise. He was now talking to Frederica, having presumably settled with Flavia whatever he had hoped to arrange. Flavia and Robert had retired to a sofa and were embracing. Stevens said a word of greeting to Frederica, then made at once for Priscilla. Frederica turned again to Buster.

"I'm glad to hear Erry is behaving himself," she said.

"I agree we were all prepared to find your brother rather difficult," said Buster, "but on the contrary—anyway so far as I am personally concerned—he has done everything in his power to make my life agreeable. He has, if I may say so, the charm of all your family, though in a different manner to the rest of you."

Umfraville interrupted them.

"Come and talk shop with me for a moment, Buster," he said.

They went into a corner of the room together. Isobel and I went into another one. It was clearly time to get under way.

If we did not set out without further delay, we should not be back by the required hour. Then Isobel went rather white.

"Look here," she said, "I'm sorry to have to call attention to myself at this moment, but I'm feeling awfully funny. I think perhaps I'd better go to my room—and Frederica or someone can ring up the doctor."

That was the final touch. In a state of the utmost confusion and disquiet we left them at last, arriving in Aldershot just in time, having dropped Robert on the way.

"Not feeling much like going on the square tomorrow, are you?" said Stevens. "Still it was the hell of a good weekend's leave. I had one of the local girls under a hedge."

Four

WHEN, during those rare, intoxicating moments of solitude, I used to sit in a window seat at Castlemallock, reading *Esmond*, or watching the sun go down over the immense brick rampart of the walled garden, the Byronic associations of the place made me think of *Don Juan*:

> I pass my evenings in long galleries solely,
> And that's the reason I'm so melancholy . . .

The long gallery at Castlemallock, uncarpeted, empty of furniture except for a few trestle tables and wooden chairs, had these built-in seats all along one side. Here one could be alone during the intervals between arrival and departure of Anti-Gas students, when Kedward and I would be Duty Officer on alternate days. That meant little more than remaining within the precincts of the castle in the evening, parading "details"—usually a couple of hundred men—at Retreat, sleeping at night by the telephone. We were Gwatkin's only subalterns now, for this was the period of experiment, later abandoned as unsatisfactory, when one platoon in each company was led by a warrant-officer. If an Anti-Gas course were in progress, we slept alternate nights in the Company Office, in case there was a call from Battalion. I often undertook Kedward's tour of duty, as he liked to "improve his eye," when training was over for the day, by exploring the neighbouring country with a view to marking down suitable sites for machine-gun nests and anti-tank emplacements. Lying in the window-seat, I would think how it felt to be a father, of the times during the latter part of the Aldershot course when I had been able to see Isobel and the child. She and the baby, a boy, were "doing well," but there had been difficulty in visiting them, Stevens's car by then no longer available. Stevens, as Brent prophesied, had been "Returned to Unit."

"I shan't be seeing you lads after tomorrow," he said one afternoon.

"Why not?"

"I've been RTU-ed."

"Whatever for?"

"I cut one of those bloody lectures and got caught."

"Sorry about this."

"I don't give a damn," he said. "All I want is to get abroad. This may start me on the move. I'll bring it off sooner or later. Look here, give me your sister-in-law's address, so I can keep in touch with her about that brooch."

There was a certain bravado about all this. To get in the army's black books is something always to be avoided; as a rule, no help to advancement in any direction. I gave Stevens the address of Frederica's house, so that he could send Priscilla back her brooch. We said goodbye.

"We'll meet again."

"We will, indeed."

The course ended without further incident of any note. On its last day, I had a word with Brent, before our ways, too, parted.

"Pleased we ran into each other," he said. "To tell the truth, I was glad to spill all that stuff about the Duports for some reason. Don't quite know why. You won't breathe a word, will you?"

"Of course not. Where are you off to now?"

"The ITC—for a posting."

I sailed back across the water. Return, like the war news, was cheerless. The Battalion had been re-deployed further south, in a new area nearer the border, where companies were on detachment. Gwatkin's, as it turned out, was quartered at the Corps School of Chemical Warfare, the keeps, turrets and castellations of which also enclosed certain Ordnance stores of some importance, which came under Command. For these stores, Gwatkin's company provided security guards, also furnishing men, if required, for Anti-Gas demonstrations. When the Battalion operated as a unit, we operated with the rest, otherwise lived a life apart, occupied with our own training or the occasional demands of the School.

Isobel wrote that her aunt, Molly Jeavons — as a rule far from an authority on such matters — had lent her a book about Castlemallock, its original owner, a Lord Chief Justice (whose earldom had been raised to a marquisate for supporting the Union), having been a distant connexion of the Ardglass family. His heir — better known as Hercules Mallock, friend of d'Orsay and Lady Blessington — had sold the place to a rich linen manufacturer, who had pulled down the palladian mansion and built this neo-gothic castle. The second Lord Castlemallock died unmarried, at a great age, in Lisbon, leaving little or nothing to the great-nephew who inherited the title, father or grandfather of the Castlemallock who had run away with Dicky Umfraville's second wife. Like other houses of similar size throughout this region, Castlemallock, too large and inconvenient, had lain untenanted for twenty or thirty years before its requisitioning. The book also quoted Byron's letter (a fragment only, said to be of doubtful authenticity) written to Caroline Lamb who had visited the house when exiled from England by her family on his account. Isobel had copied this out for me:

". . . even though the diversions of Castlemallock may exceed those of Lismore, I perceive you are ignorant of one matter — that he to whose *Labours* you appear not insensible was once known to your humble servant by the chaste waters of the Cam. Moderate, therefore, your talent for novel writing, My dear Caro, or at least spare me an account of his protestations of affection & recollect that your host's namesake

preferred *Hylas* to the *Nymphs*. Learn, too, that the theme of
assignations in romantick groves palls on a man with a cold
& quinsy & a digestion that lately suffered the torment of
supper at Lᵈ Sleaford's . . ."

This glade in the park at Castlemallock was still known
as "Lady Caro's Dingle," and thought of a Byronic interlude
here certainly added charm to grounds not greatly altered at
the time of the rebuilding of the house. An air of thwarted
passion could be well imagined to haunt these grass-grown
paths, weedy lawns and ornamental pools, where moss-covered
fountains no longer played. Such memories were not in themselves sufficient to make the place an acceptable billet. At
Castlemallock I knew despair. The proliferating responsibilities of an infantry officer, simple in themselves, yet, if properly carried out, formidable in their minutiae, impose a strain
in wartime even on those to whom they are a lifelong professional habit; the excruciating boredom of exclusively male
society is particularly irksome in areas at once remote from
war, yet oppressed by war conditions. Like a million others,
I missed my wife, wearied of the officers and men round me,
grew to loathe a post wanting even the consolation that one
was required to be brave. Castlemallock lacked the warmth
of a regiment, gave none of the sense of belonging to an army
that exists in any properly commanded unit or formation.
Here was only cursing, quarrelling, complaining; inglorious
officers of the instructional and administrative staff, Other
Ranks—except for Gwatkin's company—of low medical cat-
egory. Here, indeed, was the negation of Lyautey's ideal, though
food enough for the military resignation of Vigny.

Nevertheless, there was an undoubted aptness in this sham
fortress, monument to a tasteless, half-baked romanticism,
becoming now, in truth, a military stronghold, its stone walls
and vaulted ceilings echoing at last to the clatter of arms and
oaths of soldiery. It was as if its perpetrators had re-created
the tedium, as well as the architecture of mediaeval times.
At fourteenth-century Stourwater (which had once caused
Isobel to recall the *Morte d'Arthur*), Sir Magnus Donners was

far less a castellan than the Castlemallock commandant, a grey-faced Regular, recovering from appendicitis; Sir Magnus's guests certainly less like feudatories than the seedy Anti-Gas instructors, sloughed off at this golden opportunity by their regiments. The Ordnance officers, drab seneschals, fitted well into this gothic world, most of all Pinkus, Adjutant-Quartermaster, one of those misshapen dwarfs who peer from the battlements of Dolorous Garde, bent on doing disservice to whomsoever may cross the drawbridge. This impression—that one had slipped back into a nightmare of the Middle Ages—was not dispelled by the Castlemallock "details" on parade. There were warm summer nights at Retreat when I could scarcely proceed between the ranks of these cohorts of gargoyles drawn up for inspection for fear of bursting into fits of uncontrollable demoniac laughter.

"Indeed, they are the maimed, the halt and the blind," CSM Cadwallader remarked more than once.

In short, the atmosphere of Castlemallock told on the nerves of all ranks. Once, alone in the Company Office, a former pantry set in a labyrinth of stone passages at the back of the house, I heard a great clatter of boots and a frightful wailing like that of a very small child. I opened the door to see what was happening. A young soldier was standing there, red faced and burly, tears streaming down his cheeks, his hair dishevelled, his nose running. He looked at the end of his tether. I knew him by sight as one of the Mess waiters. He swayed there limply, as if he might fall down at any moment. A sergeant, also young, followed him quickly up the passage, and stood over him, if that could be said of an NCO half the private's size.

"What the hell is all this row?"

"He's always on at me," said the private, sobbing convulsively.

The sergeant looked uncomfortable. They were neither of them Gwatkin's men.

"Come along," he said.

"What's the trouble?"

"He's a defaulter, sir," said the sergeant. "Come along now, and finish that job."

"I can't do it, my back hurts," said the private, mopping his eyes with a clenched hand.

"Then you should report sick," said the sergeant severely, "see the MO. That's what you want to do, if your back hurts."

"Seen him."

"See him again then."

"The Adjutant-Quartermaster said if I did any more malingering he'd give me more CB."

The sergeant's face was almost as unhappy as the private's. He looked at me as if he thought I might be able to offer some brilliant solution to their problems. He was wrong about that. I saw no way out. Anyway, they were neither of them within my province.

"Well, go away, and don't make a disturbance outside here again."

"Sorry, sir."

The two of them went off quietly, but, as they reached the far end of the stone passage, I heard it all starting up again. They were not our men, of course, amongst whom such a scene would have been inconceivable, even when emotions were allowed full rein, which sometimes happened. In such circumstances the display would have taken a far less dismal form. This sort of incident lowered the spirits to an infinitely depressed level. Even though there might be less to do here than with the Battalion, no road-blocks to man, for example, there were also no amusements in the evening, beyond the grubby pubs of a small, down-at-heel town a mile or two away.

"There isn't a lot for the lads to do," said CSM Cadwallader.

He was watching, unsmilingly, a Red Indian war-dance a group of men were performing, led by Williams, I. G., whose eccentric strain probably accounted for his friendship with Lance-Corporal Gittins, the storeman. The dancers, with tent-peg mallets for tomahawks, were moving slowly round in a small circle, bowing their heads to the earth and up again, as they gradually increased the speed of their rotation. I thought what a pity that Bithel was not there to lead them in this dance.

"What about organising some football?"

"No other company there is to play, sir."

"Does that matter?"

"Personnel of the School, C.3., they are."

"But there are plenty of our own fellows. Can't they make up a game among themselves?"

"The boys wouldn't want that."

"Why not?"

"Another company's what they like to beat."

That was a good straightforward point of view, no pretence that games were anything but an outlet for power and aggression; no stuff about their being enjoyable as such. You played a game to demonstrate that you did it better than someone else. If it came to that, I thought, how few people do anything for its own sake, from making love to practising the arts.

"How do they amuse themselves when not doing Indian war-dances?"

"Some of the lads has found a girl."

The Sergeant-Major smiled quietly to himself, as if he might have been of that number.

"Corporal Gwylt?"

"Indeed, sir, Corporal Gwylt may have a girl or two."

Meanwhile, since my return from Aldershot, I was aware of a change that had taken place in Gwatkin, though precisely what had happened to him, I could not at first make out. He had been immensely gratified, so Kedward told me, to find himself more or less on his own as a junior commander, keenly jealous of this position in relation to the Castlemallock Commandant, always making difficulties with him when men were wanted for demonstrational purposes. On the other hand, Gwatkin had also developed a new vagueness, even bursts of apparent indolence. He would pass suddenly into a state close to amnesia, sitting at his table in the Company Office, holding in the palm of his hand, lettering uppermost, the rubber-stamp of the Company, as if it were an orb or other symbol of dominion, while he gazed out on to the cobbled yard, where outbuildings beyond had been transformed into barrack-rooms. For several minutes at a time he would stare into space, scanning the roofs as if he could descry beyond the yard and stables vision of battle, cavalry thundering down, long columns of infantry advancing through the smoke, horse artillery bringing up the guns. At least, that was what I supposed. I thought Gwatkin had at last "seen through" the army as he had formerly imagined it, was experiencing a casting out of devils within himself, the devils of his old military ideas. Gwatkin seemed himself to some extent aware of these visitations, because, as soon as they were passed, his "regimental" manner would become more obtrusive than ever. On such occasions he would indulge in tussles with the Commandant, or embark on sudden explosions of energy and extend hours of training. However, side by side with exertions that insisted upon an ever-increased standard of efficiency, he became no less subject to these lethargic moods. He talked more freely, too, abandoning all pretence of being a "man of few words," formerly one of his favourite roles. Again, these bursts of talkativeness alternated with states of the blackest, most silent gloom.

"Anything wrong with Rowland?" I asked Kedward.

"Not that I know of."

"He doesn't seem quite himself."

"All right, so far as I've heard."

"Just struck me as a bit browned off."

"Has he been on your tail?"

"Not specially."

"I thought he'd been better tempered lately. But, my God, it's true he's always forgetting things. We nearly ran out of Acquittance Rolls last Pay Parade owing to Rowland having shoved a lot of indents the CQMS gave him into a drawer. Perhaps you're right, Nick, and he's not well."

For some reason, the matter of the *Alarm* brought home to me these developments in Gwatkin. Command had issued one of their periodic warnings that all units and formations were to be on their guard against local terrorist action of the

Deafy Morgan sort, which, encouraged by German successes in the field, had recently become more common. A concerted attack by subversive elements was thought likely to take shape within the next week or two in the Castlemallock area. Accordingly, every unit was instructed to devise its own local *Alarm* signal, in addition to the normal *Alert*. The *Alert* was, of course, based on the principle that German invasion had taken place south of the Border, where British troops would consequently move forthwith. For training purposes, these *Alerts* were usually issued in code by telephone or radio—in the case of Gwatkin's company, routine procedure being to march on the main body of the Battalion. For merely local troubles, however—to which the warning from Command referred—different action would be required, therefore a different warning given. At Castlemallock, for example, the Commandant decided that any such outbreak should be made known by blowing the *Alarm* on the bugle. All ranks were paraded to hear the *Alarm* sounded, so that its notes should at once be recognised, if need arose. Afterwards, Gwatkin, Kedward, CSM Cadwallader and I assembled in the Company Office to check arrangements. The question obviously arose of those men insufficiently musical to register in the head the sound they had just heard.

"All those bugle calls have words to them," said Kedward. "What are the ones for the *Alarm?*"

"That's it," said Gwatkin, pleased at this opportunity to make practical use of military lore, "*Cookhouse*, for instance:

> Come to the cookhouse door, boys,
> Come to the cookhouse door,
> Officers' wives have puddings and pies,
> Soldiers' wives have skilly.

"How does the *Alarm* go, Sergeant-Major? That must have words too."

It was the only time I ever saw CSM Cadwallader blush.

"Rather vulgar words they are, sir," he said.

"Well, what are they?" said Gwatkin.

The Sergeant-Major seemed still for some reason unwilling to reveal the appropriate assonance.

"Think most of the Company know the call now, sir," he said.

"That's not the point," said Gwatkin. "We can't take any risks. There may be even one man only who won't recognise it. He'll need the rhyme. What are the words?"

"Really want them, sir?"

"I've just said so," said Gwatkin.

He was half irritated at the Sergeant-Major's prevarication, at the same time half losing interest. He had begun to look out of the window, his mind wandering in the manner I have described. CSM Cadwallader hesitated again. Then he pursed his lips and gave a vocalized version of the bugle blaring the *Alarm*:

> "Sergeant-Major's-got-a-horn!
> Sergeant-Major's-got-a-horn! . . ."

Kedward and I burst out laughing. I expected Gwatkin to do the same. He was normally capable of appreciating that sort of joke, especially as a laugh at CSM Cadwallader's expense was not a thing to be missed. However, Gwatkin seemed scarcely to have heard the words, certainly not taken in their import. At first I thought he had been put out by receiving so broadly comic an answer to his question, feeling perhaps his dignity was compromised. That would have been a possibility, though unlike Gwatkin, because he approved coarseness of phrase as being military, even though he might be touchy about his own importance. It was then I realized he had fallen into one of his trances in which all around was forgotten: the *Alarm*, the Sergeant-Major, Kedward, myself, the Battalion, the army, the war itself.

"Right, Sergeant-Major," he said, speaking abruptly, as if he had just woken from a dream. "See those words are promulgated throughout the Company. That's all. You can fall out."

By this time it was summer and very hot. The Germans

had invaded the Netherlands, Churchill become Prime Minister. I read in the papers that Sir Magnus Donners had been appointed to the ministerial post for which he had long been tipped. The Battalion was required to send men to reinforce one of the Regular Battalions in France. There was much grumbling at this, because we were supposed to be something more than a draft-finding unit. Gwatkin was particularly outraged by this order, and the loss of two or three good men from his company. Otherwise things went on much the same at Castlemallock, the great trees leafy in the park, all water dried up in the basins of the fountains. Then, one Saturday evening, Gwatkin suggested he and I should walk as far as the town and have a drink together. There was no Anti-Gas course in progress at that moment. Kedward was Duty Officer. As a rule, Gwatkin was rarely to be seen in the Mess after dinner. No one knew what he did with himself during those hours. It was possible that he retired to his room to study the *Field Service Pocket Book* or some other military manual. I never guessed he might make a practice of visiting the town. However, that was what his next remark seemed to suggest.

"I've found a new place—better than M'Coy's," he said rather challengingly. "The porter there is bloody marvellous. I've drunk it now several times. I'd like to have your opinion."

I had once visited M'Coy's with Kedward. It was, in fact, the only pub I had entered since being stationed at Castlemallock. I found no difficulty in believing M'Coy's could be improved upon as a drinking resort, but it was hard to guess why Gwatkin's transference of custom from M'Coy's to this new place should be an important issue, as Gwatkin's manner seemed to suggest. In any case, it was unlike him to suggest an evening's drinking. I agreed to make the trip. It would have been unfriendly, rather impolitic, to have refused. A walk into the town would be a change. Besides, I was heartily sick of *Esmond*. When dinner was at an end, Gwatkin and I set off together. We tramped along the drive in silence. We had almost reached the road, when he made an unexpected remark.

"It won't be easy to go back to the Bank after all this," he said.

"All what?"

"The army. The life we're leading."

"Don't you like the Bank?"

As Kedward had explained at the outset, most of the Battalion's officers worked in banks. This was one of the aspects of the unit which gave a peculiar sense of uniformity, of existing almost within a family. Even though one was personally outside this sept, its homogeneous character in itself offered a certain cordiality, rather than the reverse, to an intruder. Until now, no one had given the impression he specially disliked that employment, over and above the manner in which most people grumble about their own job, whatever it is. Indeed, all seemed to belong to a caste, clearly defined, powerful on its home-ground, almost a secret society, with perfect understanding between its members where outward things were concerned. The initiates might complain about specific drawbacks, but never in a way to imply hankering for another occupation. To hear absolute revolt expressed was new to me. Gwatkin seemed to relent a little when he spoke again.

"Oh, the bloody Bank's not that bad," he said laughing, "but it's a bit different being here. Something better to do than open jammed Home Safes and enter the contents in the Savings Bank Ledger."

"What's a Home Safe, and why does it jam?"

"Kids' money-boxes."

"Do the children jam them?"

"Parents, usually. Want a bit of ready. Try to break into the safe with a tin-opener. The bloody things arrive back at the office with the mechanism smashed to pieces. When the cashier gets in at last, he finds three pennies, a halfpenny and a tiddlywink."

"Still, brens get jammed too. It's traditional for machine-guns—you know, the Gatling's jammed and the Colonel's dead. Somebody wrote a poem about it. One might do the same about a Home Safe and the manager."

Gwatkin ignored such disenchantment.

"The bren's a soldier's job," he said.

"What about Pay Parades and Kit Inspection? They're soldiers' jobs. It doesn't make them any more enjoyable."

"Better than taking the Relief Till to Treorchy on a market day, doling out the money from a bag in old Mrs. Jones-the-Milk's front parlour. What sort of life is that for a man?"

"You find the army more glamorous, Rowland?"

"Yes," he said eagerly, "glamorous. That's the word. Don't you feel you want to do more in life than sit in front of a row of ledgers all day long? I know I do."

"Sitting at Castlemallock listening to the wireless announcing the German army is pushing towards the Channel ports isn't particularly inspiring either—especially after an hour with the CQMS trying to sort out the Company's sock situation, or searching for a pair of battledress trousers to fit Evans, J., who is such an abnormal shape."

"No, Nick, but we'll be in it soon. We can't stay at Castlemallock for ever."

"Why not?"

"Anyway, Castlemallock's not so bad."

He seemed desperately anxious to prevent me from speaking hardly of Castlemallock.

"I agree the park is pretty. That is about the best you can say for it."

"It's come to mean a lot to me," Gwatkin said.

His voice was full of excitement. I had been quite wrong in supposing him disillusioned with the army. On the contrary, he was keener than ever. I could not understand why his enthusiasm had suddenly risen to such new heights. I did not for a moment, as we walked along, guess what the answer was going to be. By that time we had reached the pub judged by Gwatkin to be superior to M'Coy's. The façade, it had to be admitted, was remarkably similar to M'Coy's, though in a back alley, rather than the main street of the town. Otherwise, the place was the usual large cottage, the ground floor of which had been converted to the purposes of a tavern. I followed Gwatkin through the low door. The interior was dark, the smell uninviting. No one was about when we entered, but voices came from a room beyond the bar. Gwatkin tapped the counter with a coin.

"Maureen . . ." he called.

He used that same peculiar cooing note he employed when answering the telephone.

"Hull-ooe . . . hull-ooe . . ." he would say, when he spoke into the instrument. Somehow that manner of answering seemed quite inappropriate to the rest of his character.

"I wonder whether what we call politeness isn't just weakness," he had once remarked.

This cooing certainly conveyed no impression of ruthless moral strength, neither on the telephone, nor at the counter of this pub. No one appeared. Gwatkin pronounced the name again.

"Maur-een . . . Maur-een . . ."

Still nothing happened. Then a girl came through the door leading to the back of the house. She was short and thick-set, with a pale face and lots of black hair. I thought her good-looking, with that suggestion of an animal, almost a touch of monstrosity, some men find very attractive. Barnby once remarked: "The Victorians saw only refinement in women, it's their coarseness makes them irresistible to me." Barnby would certainly have liked this girl.

"Why, it would be yourself again, Captain Gwatkin," she said.

She smiled and put her hands on her hips. Her teeth were very indifferent, her eyes in deep, dark sockets, striking.

"Yes, Maureen."

Gwatkin did not seem to know what to say next. He glanced in my direction, as if to seek encouragement. This speechlessness was unlike him. However, Maureen continued to talk herself.

"And with another military gentleman too," she said. "What'll ye be taking this evening now? Will it be porter, or is it a wee drop of whiskey this night, I'll be wondering, Captain?"

Gwatkin turned to me.

"Which, Nick?"

"Guinness."

"That goes for me too," he said. "Two pints of porter, Maureen. I only drink whiskey when I'm feeling down. Tonight we're out for a good time, aren't we, Nick?"

He spoke in an oddly self-conscious manner. I had never seen him like this before. We seated ourselves at a small table by the wall. Maureen began to draw the stout. Gwatkin watched her fixedly, while she allowed the froth to settle, scraping its foam from the surface of the liquid with a saucer, then returning the glass under the tap to be refilled to the brim. When she brought the drinks across to us, she took a chair, refusing to have anything herself.

"And what would be the name of this officer?" she asked.

"Second-Lieutenant Jenkins," said Gwatkin, "he's one of the officers of my company."

"Is he now. That would be grand and all."

"We're good friends," said Gwatkin soberly.

"Then why haven't ye brought him to see me before, Captain Gwatkin, I'll be asking ye?"

"Ah, Maureen, you see we work so hard," said Gwatkin. "We can't always be coming to see you, do you understand. That's just a treat for once in a while."

"Get along with ye," she said, smiling provocatively and showing discoloured teeth again, "yourself's down here often enough, Captain Gwatkin."

"Not as often as I'd like, Maureen."

Gwatkin had now recovered from the embarrassment which seemed to have overcome him on first entering the pub. He was no longer tongue-tied. Indeed, his manner suggested he was, in fact, more at ease with women than men, the earlier constraint merely a momentary attack of nerves.

"And what would it be you're all so busy with now?" she asked. "Is it drilling and all that? I expect so."

"Drilling is some of it, Maureen," said Gwatkin. "But we have to practise all kind of other training too. Modern war is a very complicated matter, you must understand."

This made her laugh again.

"I'd have ye know my great-uncle was in the Connaught Rangers," she said, "and a fine figure of a man he was, I can promise ye. Why, they say he was the best-looking young fellow of his day in all County Monaghan. And brave too. Why, they say he killed a dozen Germans with his bayonet when they tried to capture him. The Germans didn't like to meet the Irish in the last war."

"Well, it's a risk the Germans won't have to run in this one," said Gwatkin, speaking more gruffly than might have been expected in the circumstances. "Even here in the North there's no conscription, and you see plenty of young men out of uniform."

"Why, ye wouldn't be taking all the young fellows away from us, would ye?" she asked, rolling her eyes. "It's lonely we'd be if they all went to the war."

"Maybe Hitler will decide the South is where he wants to land his invasion force," said Gwatkin. "Then where will all your young men be, I'd like to know."

"Oh God," she said, throwing up her hands. "Don't say it of the old blackguard. Would he do such a thing? You think he truly may, Captain Gwatkin, do ye?"

"Shouldn't be surprised," said Gwatkin.

"Do you come from the other side of the Border yourself?" I asked her.

"Why, sure I do," she said smiling. "And how were you guessing that, Lieutenant Jenkins?"

"I just had the idea."

"Would it be my speech?" she said.

"Perhaps."

She lowered her voice.

"Maybe, too, you thought I was different from these Ulster people," she said, "them that is so hard and fond of money and all."

"That's it, I expect."

"So you've guessed Maureen's home country, Nick," said Gwatkin. "I tell her we must treat her as a security risk and not go speaking any secrets in front of her, as she's a neutral."

Maureen began to protest, but at that moment two young men in riding breeches and leggings came into the pub. She rose from the chair to serve them. Gwatkin fell into one of his silences. I thought he was probably reflecting how odd was the fact that Maureen seemed just as happy talking and laughing with a couple of local civilians, as with the dashing officer types he seemed to envisage ourselves. At least he stared at the young men, an unremarkable pair, as if there were something about them that interested him. Then it turned out Gwatkin's train of thought had returned to dissatisfaction with his own peacetime employment.

"Farmers, I suppose," he said. "My grandfather was a farmer. He didn't spend his time in a stuffy office."

"Where did he farm?"

"Up by the Shropshire border."

"And your father took to office life?"

"That was it. My dad's in insurance. His firm sent him to another part of the country."

"Do you know that Shropshire border yourself?"

"We've been up there for a holiday. I expect you've heard of the great Lord Aberavon?"

"I have, as a matter of fact."

"The farm was on his estate."

I had never thought of Lord Aberavon (first and last of his peerage) as a figure likely to go down to posterity as "great," though the designation might no doubt reasonably be applied by those living in the neighbourhood. His name was merely memorable to myself as deceased owner of Mr. Deacons's *Boyhood of Cyrus,* the picture in the Walpole-Wilsons' hall, which always made me think of Barbara Goring when I had been in love with her in pre-historic times. Lord Aberavon had been Barbara Goring's grandfather; Eleanor Walpole-Wilson's grandfather too. I wondered what had happened to Barbara, whether her husband, Johnny Pardoe (who also owned a house in the country of which Gwatkin spoke) had been recalled to the army. Eleanor, lifelong friend of my sister-in-law, Norah Tolland, was now, like Norah herself, driving cars for some women's service. Gwatkin by his words had certainly conjured up the past. He looked at me rather uncomfortably, as if he could read my mind, and knew I felt suddenly carried back into an earlier time sequence. He also had the air of wanting to elaborate what he had said, yet feared he might displease, or, at least, not amuse me. He cleared his throat and took a gulp of stout.

"You remember Lord Aberavon's family name?" he asked.

"Why, now I come to think of it, wasn't it 'Gwatkin'?"

"It was—same as mine. He was called Rowland too."

He said that very seriously.

"I'd quite forgotten. Was he a relation?"

Gwatkin laughed apologetically.

"No, of course he wasn't," he said.

"Well, he might have been."

"What makes you think so?"

"You never know with names."

"If so, it was miles distant," said Gwatkin.

"That's what I mean."

"I mean so distant, he wasn't a relation at all," Gwatkin said. "As a matter of fact my grandfather, the old farmer I was talking about, used to swear we were the same lot, if you went back far enough—right back, I mean."

"Why not, indeed?"

I remembered reading one of Lord Aberavon's obituaries, which had spoken of the incalculable antiquity of his line, notwithstanding his own modest start in a Liverpool shipping firm. The details had appealed to me.

"Wasn't it a very old family?"

"So they say."

"Going back to Vortigern—by one of his own daughters? I'm sure I read that."

Gwatkin looked uncertain again, as if he felt the discussion had suddenly got out of hand, that there was something inadmissible about my turning out to know so much about Gwatkin origins. Perhaps he was justified in thinking that.

"Who was Vortigern?" he asked uneasily.

"A fifth-century British prince. You remember—he invited Hengist and Horsa. All that. They came to help him. Then he couldn't get rid of them."

It was no good. Gwatkin looked utterly blank. Hengist and Horsa meant nothing to him; less, if anything, than Vortigern. He was unimpressed by the sinister splendour of the derivations indicated as potentially his own; indeed, totally uninterested in them. Thought of Lord Aberavon's business acumen kindled him more than any steep ascent in the genealogies of ancient Celtic Britain. His romanticism, though innate, was essentially limited—as often happens—by sheer lack of imagination. Vortigern, I saw, was better forgotten. I had deflected Gwatkin's flow of thought by ill-timed pedantry.

"I expect my grandfather made up most of the stuff," he said. "Just wanted to be thought related to a man of the same name who left three-quarters of a million."

He now appeared to regret ever having let fall this confidence regarding his own family background, refusing to be drawn into further discussion about his relations, their history or the part of the country they came from. I thought how odd, how typical of our island—unlike the Continent or America in that respect—that Gwatkin should put forward this claim, possibly in its essentials reasonable enough, be at once attracted and repelled by its implications, yet show no wish to carry the discussion further. Was it surprising that, in such respects, foreigners should find us hard to understand? Odd, too, I felt obstinately, that the incestuous Vortigern should link Gwatkin with Barbara Goring and Eleanor Walpole-Wilson. Perhaps it all stemmed from that ill-judged negotiation with Hengist and Horsa. Anyway, it linked me, too, with Gwatkin in a strange way. We had some more stout. Maureen was now too deeply involved in local gossip with the young farmers, if farmers they were, to pay further attention to us. Their party had been increased by the addition of an older man of similar type, with reddish hair and the demeanour of a professional humorist. There was a good deal of laughter. We had to fetch our drinks from the counter ourselves. This seemed to depress Gwatkin still further. We talked rather drearily of the affairs of the Company. More customers came in, all apparently on the closest terms with Maureen. Gwatkin and I drank a fair amount of stout. Finally, it was time to return.

"Shall we go back to barracks?"

This designation of Castlemallock on Gwatkin's part added nothing to its charms. He turned towards the bar as we were leaving.

"Good night, Maureen."

She was having too good a joke with the red-haired humorist to hear him.

"Good night, Maureen," Gwatkin said again, rather louder.

She looked up, then came round to the front of the bar.

"Good night to you, Captain Gwatkin, and to you, Lieutenant Jenkins," she said, "and don't be so long in coming to see me again, the pair of ye, or it's vexed with you both I'd be."

We waved farewell. Gwatkin did not open his mouth until we reached the outskirts of the town. Suddenly he took a deep breath. He seemed about to speak; then, as if he could not give sufficient weight to the words while we walked, he stopped and faced me.

"Isn't she marvellous?" he said.

"Who, Maureen?"

"Yes, of course."

"She seemed a nice girl."

"Is that all you thought, Nick?"

He spoke with real reproach.

"Why, yes. What about you? You've really taken a fancy to her, have you?"

"I think she's absolutely wonderful," he said.

We had had, as I have said, a fair amount to drink—the first time since joining the unit I had drunk more than two or three half-pints of beer—but no more than to loosen the tongue, not sufficient to cause amorous hallucination. Gwatkin was obviously expressing what he really felt, not speaking in an exaggerated manner to indicate light desire. The reason of those afternoon trances, that daydreaming while he nursed the Company's rubber-stamp, were now all at once apparent, affection for Castlemallock also explained. Gwatkin was in love. All love affairs are different cases, yet, at the same time, each is the same case. Moreland used to say love was like sea-sickness. For a time everything round you heaved about and you felt you were going to die—then you staggered down the gangway to dry land, and a minute or two later could hardly remember what you had suffered, why you had been feeling so ghastly. Gwatkin was at the earlier stage.

"Have you done anything about it?"

"About what?"

"About Maureen."

"How do you mean?"

"Well, taken her out, something like that."

"Oh, no."

"Why not?"

"What would be the good?"

"I don't know. I should have thought it might be enjoyable, if you feel like that about her."

"But I'd have to tell her I'm married."

"Tell her by all means. Put your cards on the table."

"But do you think she'd come?"

"I shouldn't wonder."

"You mean—try and seduce her?"

"I suppose that was roughly the line indicated—in due course."

He looked at me astonished. I felt a shade uncomfortable, rather like Mephistopheles unexpectedly receiving a hopelessly negative reaction from Faust. Such an incident in opera, I thought, might suggest a good basis for an *aria*.

"Some of the chaps you meet in the army never seem to have heard of women," Odo Stevens had said. "You never know in the Mess whether you're sitting next to a sex-maniac of nineteen or a middle-aged man who doesn't know the facts of life."

In Gwatkin's case, I was surprised by such scruples, even though I now recalled his attitude towards the case of Sergeant Pendry. In general, the younger officers of the Battalion were, like Kedward, engaged, or, like Breeze, recently married. They might, like Pumphrey, talk in a free and easy manner, but it was their girl or their wife who clearly preoccupied them. In any case, there had been no time for girls for anyone, married or single, before we reached Castlemallock. Gwatkin was certainly used to the idea of Pumphrey trying to have a romp with any barmaid who might be available. He had never seemed to disapprove of that. I knew nothing of his married life, except what Kedward had told me, that Gwatkin had known his wife all their lives, had previously wanted to marry Breeze's sister.

"But I'm married," Gwatkin said again.

He spoke rather desperately.

"I'm not insisting you should take Maureen out. I only asked if you had."

"And Maureen isn't that sort of girl."

"How do you know?"

He spoke angrily this time. Then he laughed, seeing, I suppose, that was a silly thing to say.

"You've only met Maureen for the first time, Nick. You don't realize at all what she's like. You think all that talk of hers means she's a bad girl. She isn't. I've often been alone with her in that bar. You'd be surprised. She's like a child."

"Some children know a thing or two."

Gwatkin did not even bother to consider that point of view.

"I don't know why I think her quite so wonderful," he admitted, "but I just do. It worries me that I think about her all the time. I've found myself forgetting things, matters of duty, I mean."

"Do you go down there every night?"

"Whenever I can. I haven't been able to get away lately owing to one thing and another. All this security check, for instance."

"Does she know this?"

"Know what?"

"Does Maureen know you're mad about her?"

"I don't think so," he said.

He spoke the words very humbly, quite unlike his usual tone. Then he assumed a rough, official voice again.

"I thought it would be better if I told you about it all, Nick," he said. "I hoped the thing wouldn't go on inside me all the time so much, if I let it out to someone. Unless it stops a bit, I'm frightened I'll make a fool of myself in some way to do with commanding the Company. A girl like Maureen makes everything go out of your head."

"Of course."

"You know what I mean."

"Yes."

Gwatkin still did not seem entirely satisfied.

"You really think I ought to take her out?"

"That's what a lot of people would do—probably a lot of people are doing already."

"Oh, no, I'm sure they're not, if you mean from the School of Chemical Warfare. I've never seen any of them there. It was quite a chance I went in myself. I was looking for a short cut. Maureen was standing by the door, and I asked her the way. Her parents own the pub. She's not just a barmaid."

"Anyway, there's no harm in trying, barmaid or not."

During the rest of the walk back to Castlemallock, Gwatkin did not refer again to the subject of Maureen. He talked of routine matters until we parted to our rooms.

"The Mess will be packed out again tomorrow night," he said. "Another Anti-Gas course starts next week. I suppose all that business will begin again of wanting to take my men away from me for their bloody demonstrations. Well, there it is."

"Good night, Rowland."

"Good night, Nick."

I made for the stables, where I shared a groom's room with Kedward, rather like the sleeping quarters of Albert and Bracey at Stonehurst. As Duty Officer that night, Kedward would not be there and I should have the bedroom to myself, always rather a treat. I was aware now that it had been a mistake to drink so much stout. Tomorrow was Sunday, so there would be comparatively little to do. I thought how awful Bithel must feel on parade the mornings after his occasional bouts of drinking. Reflecting on people often portends their own appearance. So it was in the case of Bithel. He was among the students to arrive at the School the following week. We should, indeed, all have been prepared for Bithel to be sent on an Anti-Gas course. It was a way of getting rid of him, pending final banishment from the Battalion, which, as Gwatkin said, was bound to come sooner or later. I was sitting at one of the trestle tables of the Mess, addressing an envelope, when Bithel peered through the door. He was fingering his ragged moustache and smiling nervously. When he saw me, he made towards the table at once.

"Nice to meet again," he said, speaking as usual as if he expected a rebuff. "Haven't seen you since the Battalion moved."

"How have you been?"

"Getting rockets, as usual," he said.

"Maelgwyn-Jones?"

"That fellow's got a positive down on me," Bithel said, "but I don't think it will be for long now."

"Why not?"

"I'm probably leaving the Battalion."

"Why's that?"

"There's talk of my going up to Division."

"On the staff?"

"Not exactly—a command."

"At Div HQ?"

"Only a subsidiary command, of course. I shall be sorry to leave the Regiment in some ways, if it comes off, but not altogether sorry to see the back of Maelgwyn-Jones."

"What is it? Or is that a secret?"

Bithel lowered his voice in his accustomed manner when speaking of his own affairs, as if there were always a hint of something dubious about them.

"The Mobile Laundry Unit," he said.

"You're going to command it?"

"If I'm picked. There are at least two other names in for

it from other units in the Division, I happen to know—one of them very eligible. As it happens, I have done publicity work for one of the laundries in my own neighbourhood, so I have quite a chance. In fact, that should stand very much in my favour. The CO seems very anxious for me to get the appointment. He's been on the phone to Division about it himself more than once. Very good of him."

"What rank does the job carry?"

"A subaltern's command. Still, it's promotion in a way. What you might call a step. The war news doesn't look very good, does it, since the Belgian Government surrendered."

"What's the latest? I missed the last news."

"Fighting on the coast. One of our Regular Battalions has been in action, I was told this morning. Got knocked about pretty badly. Do you remember a rather good-looking boy called Jones, D. Very fair."

"He was in my platoon—went out on the draft."

"He's been killed. Daniels, my batman, told me that. Daniels gets all the news."

"Jones, D., was killed, was he. Anyone else from our unit?"

"Progers, did you know him?"

"The driver with a squint?"

"That's the fellow. Used to bring the stuff up to the Mess sometimes. Dark curly hair and a lisp. He's gone too. Talking of messing, what's it like here?"

"We've had beef twice a day for just over a fortnight— thirty-seven times running, to be precise."

"What does it taste like?"

"Goat covered with brown custard powder."

We settled down to a talk about army food. When I next saw CSM Cadwallader, I asked if he had heard about Jones, D. Corporal Gwylt was standing nearby.

"Indeed, I had not, sir. So a bullet got him."

"Something did."

"Always an unlucky boy, Jones, D.," said CSM Cadwallader.

"Remember how sick he was when we came over the water, Sergeant-Major?" said Corporal Gwylt. "Terrible sick."

"That I do."

"Never did I see a boy so sick," said Corporal Gwylt, "nor a man neither."

This was the week leading up to the withdrawal through Dunkirk, so Jones, D. and Progers were not the only fatal casualties known to me personally at that period. Among these, Robert Tolland, serving in France with his Field Security Section, was also killed. The news came in a letter from Isobel. Nothing was revealed, then or later, of the circumstances of Robert's death. So far as it went, he died as mysteriously as he had lived, like many other young men to whom war put an end, an unsolved problem. Had Robert, as Chips Lovell alleged, lived a secret life with "night-club hostesses old enough to be his mother"? Would he have made a lot of money in his export house trading with the Far East? Might he have married Flavia Wisebite? As in musical chairs, the piano stops suddenly, someone is left without a seat, petrified for all time in their attitude of that particular moment. The balance-sheet is struck there and then, a matter of luck whether its calculations have much bearing, one way or the other, on the commerce conducted. Some die in an apparently suitable manner, others like Robert on the field of battle with a certain incongruity. Yet Fate had ordained this end for him. Or had Robert decided for himself? Had he set aside the chance of a commission to fulfil a destiny that required him to fall in France; or was Flavia's luck so irredeemably bad that her association with him was sufficient—as Dr. Trelawney might have said—to summon the Slayer of Osiris, her pattern of life, rather than Robert's, dominating the issue of life and death? Robert could even have died to escape her. The potential biographies of those who die young possess the mystic dignity of a headless statue, the poetry of enigmatic passages in an unfinished or mutilated manuscript, unburdened with contrived or banal ending. These were disturbing days, lived out in suffocating summer heat. While they went by, Gwatkin, for some reason, became more cheerful. The war increasingly revealed persons stimulated by disaster. I thought Gwatkin might be one of this fairly numerous order.

There turned out to be another cause for his good spirits. He revealed the reason one afternoon.

"I took your advice, Nick," he said.

We were alone together in the Company Office.

"About the storage of those live Mills bombs?"

Gwatkin shook his head, at the same time swallowing uncomfortably, as if the very thought of live grenades and where they were to be stored, brought an immediate sense of guilt.

"No, not about the Mills bombs," he said, "I'm still thinking over the best place to keep them—I don't want any interference from the Ordnance people. I mean about Maureen."

For a moment the name conveyed nothing. Then I remembered the evening in the pub: Maureen, the girl who had so greatly taken Gwatkin's fancy. Thinking things over the next day, I had attributed his remarks to the amount of stout we had drunk. Maureen had been dismissed from my mind.

"What about Maureen?"

"I asked her to come out with me."

"You did?"

"Yes."

"What did she say?"

"She agreed."

"I said she would."

"It was bloody marvellous."

"Splendid."

"Nick," he said, "I'm serious. Don't laugh. I really want to thank you, Nick, for making me take action—not hang about like a fool. That's my weakness. Like the day we were in support and I made such a balls of it."

"And Maureen's all right?"

"She's wonderful."

That was all Gwatkin said. He gave no account of the outing. I should have liked to hear a little about it, but clearly he regarded the latest development in their relationship as too sacred to describe in detail. I saw that Kedward, in some matters no great psychologist, had been right in saying that when Gwatkin took a fancy to a girl it was "like having the measles." This business of Maureen could be regarded only as a judgment on Gwatkin for supposing Sergeant Pendry's difficulties easy of solution. Now, he had himself been struck down by Aphrodite for his pride in refusing incense at her altars. The goddess was going to chastise him. In any case, there was nothing very surprising in this sort of thing happening, when, even after an exhausting day's training, the camp-bed was nightly a rack of desire, where no depravity of the imagination was unbegotten. No doubt much mutual irritation was caused by this constraint, particularly, for example, something like Gwatkin's detestation of Bithel.

"God," he said, when he set eyes on him at Castlemallock, "that bloody man has followed us here."

Bithel himself was quite unaware of the ferment of rage he aroused in Gwatkin. At least he showed no sign of recognising Gwatkin's hatred, even at times positively thrusting himself on Gwatkin's society. Some persons feel drawn towards those who dislike them, or are at least determined to overcome opposition of that sort. Bithel may have regarded Gwatkin's unfriendliness as a challenge. Whatever the reason, he always made a point of talking to Gwatkin whenever opportunity arose, showing himself equally undeterred by verbal rebuff or crushing moroseness. However, Gwatkin's attitude in repelling Bithel's conversational advances was not entirely based on a simple brutality. Their relationship was more complicated than that. The code of behaviour in the army which Gwatkin had set himself did not allow his own comportment with any brother officer to reach a pitch of unfriendliness he would certainly have shown to a civilian acquaintance disliked as much as he disliked Bithel. This code—Gwatkin's picture of it, that is—allowed, indeed positively kindled, a blaze of snubs directed towards Bithel, at the same time preventing, so to speak, any final dismissal of him as a person too contemptible to waste time upon. Bithel was a brother officer; for that reason always, in the last resort, handed a small dole by Gwatkin, usually in the form of an incitement to do better, to pull himself together. Besides, Gwatkin, with many others, could never finally be reconciled to abandoning the legend of Bithel's VC brother. Mythical prestige still hung faintly about Bithel on that account. Such legends, once taken shape, endlessly proliferate. Certainly I never heard Bithel himself make any public effort to extirpate the story. He may have feared that even the exacerbated toleration of himself Gwatkin was at times prepared to show would fade away, if the figure of the VC brother in the background were exorcised entirely.

"Coming to sit with the Regiment tonight, Captain Gwatkin," Bithel would say when he joined us; then add in his muttered, confidential tone: "Between you and me, there're not much of a crowd on this course. Pretty second-rate."

Bithel always found difficulty in addressing Gwatkin as "Rowland." In early days, Gwatkin had protested once or twice at this formality, but I think he secretly rather enjoyed the respect implied by its use. Bithel, like everyone else, possessed one or more initial, but no one ever knew, or at least seemed to have forgotten, the name or names for which they stood. He was always called "Bith" or "Bithy," in some ways a more intimate form of address, which Gwatkin, on his side, could never bring himself to employ. The relaxation Bithel styled "sitting with the Regiment" took place in an alcove, unofficially reserved by Gwatkin, Kedward and myself for our use as part of the permanent establishment of Castlemallock, as opposed to its shifting population of Anti-Gas students. The window seat where I used to read *Esmond* was in this alcove, and we would occasionally have a drink there. Since the night when he had first joined the Battalion, Bithel's drinking, though steady when drink was available, had not been excessive, except on such occasions as Christmas or the New Year, when no great exception could be taken. He would get rather fuddled, but no more. Bithel himself sometimes referred to his own moderation in this respect.

"Got to keep an eye on the old Mess bill," he would say.

"The odd gin-and-orange adds up. I have had the CO after me once already about my wine bill. Got to mind my p's and q's in that direction."

As things turned out at Castlemallock, encouragement to overstep the mark came, unexpectedly, from the army authorities themselves. At least that was the way Bithel himself afterwards explained matters.

"It was all the fault of that silly old instruction," he said. "I was tired out and got absolutely misled by it."

Part of the training on the particular Castlemallock course Bithel was attending consisted in passing without a mask through the gas-chamber. Sooner or later, every rank in the army had to comply with this routine, but students of an Anti-Gas course naturally experienced a somewhat more elaborate ritual in that respect than others who merely took their turn with a unit. A subsequent aspect of the test was first-aid treatment, which recommended, among other restoratives, for one poisonous gas sampled, "alcohol in moderate quantities." On the day of Bithel's misadventure, the gas-chamber was the last item on the day's programme for those on the course. When Bithel's class was dismissed after this test, some took the advice of the text-book and had a drink; others, because they did not like alcohol, or from motives of economy, confined themselves to hot sweet tea. Among those who took alcohol, no one but Bithel neglected the manual's admonition to be moderate in this remedial treatment.

"Old Bith's having a drink or two this evening, isn't he," Kedward remarked, even before dinner.

Bithel always talked thickly, and, like most people who habitually put an unusually large amount of drink away, there was in general no great difference between him drunk or sober. The stage of intoxication he had reached made itself known only on such rare occasions as his dance round the dummy. At Castlemallock that night, he merely pottered about the ante-room, talking first to one group of Anti-Gas students, then to another, when, bored with him, people moved away. He did not join us in the alcove until the end of the evening. Everyone used to retire early, so that Gwatkin, Kedward and myself were alone in the room by the time Bithel arrived there. We were discussing the German advance. Gwatkin's analysis of the tactical situation had continued for some time, and I was making preparations to move off to bed, when Bithel came towards us. He sat down heavily, without making his usual rather apologetic request to Gwatkin that he might be included in the party. For a time he listened to the conversation without speaking. Then he caught the word "Paris."

"Ever been to Paris, Captain Gwatkin?" he asked.

Gwatkin shot out a glance of profound disapproval.

"No," he said sharply.

The answer conveyed that Gwatkin considered the question a ridiculous one, as if Bithel had asked if he had ever visited Lhasa or Tierra del Fuego. He continued to lecture Kedward on the principles of mobile warfare.

"I've been to Paris," said Bithel.

He made a whistling sound with his lips to express a sense of great conviviality.

"Went there for a weekend once," he said.

Gwatkin looked furious, but said nothing. A Mess waiter appeared and began to collect glasses on a tray. He was, as it happened, the red-faced, hulking young soldier, who, weeping and complaining his back hurt, had made such a disturbance outside the Company Office. Now, he seemed more cheerful, answering Bithel's request for a final drink with the information that the bar was closed. He said this with the satisfaction always displayed by waiters and barmen at being in a position to make that particular announcement.

"Just one small Irish," said Bithel. "That's all I want."

"Bar's closed, sir."

"It can't be yet."

Bithel tried to look at his watch, but the figures evidently eluded him.

"I can't believe the bar's closed."

"Mess Sergeant's just said so."

"Do get me another, Emmot—it is Emmot, isn't it?"

"That's right, sir."

"Do, do get me a whiskey, Emmot."

"Can't sir. Bar's closed."

"But it can be opened again."

"Can't, sir."

"Open it just for one moment—just for one small whiskey."

"Sergeant says no, sir."

"Ask him again."

"Bar's closed, sir."

"I beseech you, Emmot."

Bithel rose to his feet. Afterwards, I was never certain what happened. I was sitting on the same side as Bithel and, as he turned away, his back was towards me. He lurched suddenly forward. This may have been a stumble, since some of the floorboards were loose at that place. The amount he had drunk did not necessarily have anything to do with Bithel's sudden loss of balance. Alternatively, his action could have been deliberate, intended as a physical appeal to Emmot's better feelings. Bithel's wheedling tone of voice a minute before certainly gave colour to that interpretation. If so, I am sure Bithel intended no more than to rest his hand on Emmot's shoulder in a facetious gesture, perhaps grip his arm. Such actions might have been thought undignified, bad for discipline, no worse. However, for one reason or another, Bithel lunged his body forward, and, either to save himself from falling, or to give emphasis to his request for a last drink, threw his arms round Emmot's neck. There, for a split second, he hung. There could be no doubt about the outward impression this posture conveyed. It looked exactly as if Bithel were kissing Emmot—in farewell, rather than in passion. Perhaps he was. Whether or not that were so, Emmot dropped the tray, breaking a couple of glasses, at the same time letting out a discordant sound. Gwatkin jumped to his feet. His face was white. He was trembling with rage.

"Mr. Bithel," he said, "consider yourself under arrest."

I had begun to laugh, but now saw things were serious. This was no joking matter. There was going to be a row. Gwatkin's eyes were fanatical.

"Mr. Kedward," he said, "go and fetch your cap and belt."

The alcove where we had been sitting was not far from the door leading to the great hall. There, on a row of hooks, caps and belts were left, before entering the confines of the Mess, so Kedward had not far to go. Afterwards, Kedward told me he did not immediately grasp the import of Gwatkin's order. He obeyed merely on the principle of not questioning an instruction from his Company Commander. Meanwhile, Emmot began picking up fragments of broken glass from the floor. He did not seem specially surprised by what had happened. Indeed, considering how far I knew he could go in the direction of hysterical loss of control, Emmot carried off the whole situation pretty well. Perhaps he understood Bithel better than the rest of us. Gwatkin, who now seemed to be in his element, told Emmot to be off quickly, to clear up the rest of the debris in the morning. Emmot did not need further encouragement to put an end to the day's work. He retired from the ante-room at once with his tray and most of the broken glass. Bithel still stood. As he had been put under arrest, this position was no doubt militarily correct. He swayed a little, smiling to himself rather foolishly. Kedward returned, wearing his cap and buckling on his Sam Browne.

"Escort Mr. Bithel to his room, Mr. Kedward," said Gwatkin. "He will not leave it without permission. When he does so, it will be under the escort of an officer. He will not wear a belt, nor carry a weapon."

Bithel gave a despairing look, as if cut to the quick to be forbidden a weapon, but he seemed to have taken in more or less what was happening, even to be extracting a certain masochistic zest from the ritual. Gwatkin jerked his head towards the door. Bithel turned and made slowly towards it, moving as if towards immediate execution. Kedward followed. I was relieved that Gwatkin had chosen Kedward for this duty, rather than myself, no doubt because he was senior in rank, approximating more nearly to Bithel's two pips. When they were gone, Gwatkin turned to me. He seemed suddenly exhausted by this output of disciplinary energy.

"There was nothing else I could do," he said.

"I wasn't sure what happened."

"You did not see?"

"Not exactly."

"Bithel *kissed* an Other Rank."

"Are you certain?"

"Haven't you got eyes?"

"I could only see Bithel's back. I thought he lost his balance."

"In any case, Bithel was grossly drunk."

"That's undeniable."

"To put him under arrest was my duty. It was the only course I could follow. The only course any officer could follow."

"What's the next step?"

Gwatkin frowned.

"Cut along to the Company Office, Nick," he said in a rather calmer tone of voice. "You know where the *Manual of Military Law* is kept. Bring it to me here. I don't want Idwal to come back and find me gone. He'll think I've retired to bed. I must have a further word with him."

When I returned with the *Manual of Military Law,* Gwatkin was just finishing his instructions to Kedward. At the end of these he curtly said good night to us both. Then he went off, the Manual under his arm, his face stern. Kedward looked at me and grinned. He was evidently surprised, not absolutely staggered, by what had taken place. It was all part of the day's work to him.

"What a thing to happen," he said.

"Going to lead to a lot of trouble."

"Old Bith was properly pissed."

"He was."

"I could hardly get him up the stairs."

"Did you have to take his arm?"

"Heaved him up somehow," said Kedward. "Felt like a copper."

"What happened when you arrived in his room?"

"Luckily the other chap there went sick and left the course yesterday. Bith's got the room to himself, so things weren't as awkward as they might have been. He just tumbled on to the bed, and I left him. Off to bed myself now. You're for the Company Office tonight, aren't you?"

"I am."

"Good night, Nick."

"Good night, Idwal."

The scene had been exhausting. I was glad to retire from it. Confused dreams of conflict pursued throughout the night. I was in the middle of explaining to the local builder at home—who wore a long Chinese robe and had turned into Pinkus, the Castlemallock Adjutant-Quartermaster—that I wanted the front of the house altered to a pillared façade of Isobel's own design, when a fire-engine manned by pygmies passed, ringing its bell furiously. The bell continued in my head. I awoke. It had become the telephone. This was exceptional in the small hours. There were no curtains to the room, only shutters for the blackout, which were down, so that, opening my eyes, I saw the sky was already getting light above the outbuildings of the yard. I grasped the instrument and gave the designation of the unit and my name. It was Maelgwyn-Jones, Adjutant of our Battalion.

"Fishcake," he said.

I was only half awake. It was almost as if the dream continued. As I have said, Maelgwyn-Jones's temper was not of the best. He began to get very angry at once, as it turned out, with good reason.

"Fishcake . . ." he repeated. "Fishcake—fishcake—fishcake . . ."

Obviously "Fishcake" was a codeword. The question was: what did it mean? I had no recollection ever of having heard it before.

"I'm sorry, I—"

"Fishcake!"

"I heard Fishcake. I don't know what it means."

"Fishcake, I tell you . . ."

"I know Leather and Toadstool . . ."

"Fishcake has taken the place of Leather—and Bathwater of Toadstool. What the hell are you dreaming about?"

"I don't think—"

"You've bloody well forgotten."

"First I've heard of Fishcake."

"Rot."

"Sure it is."

"Do you mean to say Rowland hasn't told you and Kedward? I gave him Bathwater a week ago—in person—when he came over to the Orderly Room to report."

"I don't know about Fishcake or Bathwater."

"Oh, Christ, is this one of Rowland's half-baked ideas about security? I suppose so. I told him the new code came into force in forty-eight hours from the day before yesterday. Didn't he mention that?"

"Not a word to me."

"Oh, Jesus. Was there ever such a bloody fool commanding a company. Go and get him, and look sharp about it."

I went off with all speed to Gwatkin's room, which was in the main part of the house. He was in deep sleep, lying on his side, almost at the position of attention. Only the half of his face above the moustache appeared over the grey-brown of the blanket. I agitated his shoulder. As usual, a lot of shaking was required to get him awake. Gwatkin always slept as if under an anaesthetic. He came to at last, rubbing his eyes.

"The Adjutant's on the line. He says it's Fishcake. I don't know what that means."

"Fishcake?"

"Yes."

Gwatkin sat upright in his camp-bed.

"Fishcake?" he repeated, as if he could hardly believe his ears.

"Fishcake."

"But we were not to get Fishcake until we had been signalled Buttonhook."

"I've never heard of Buttonhook either—or Bathwater. All I know are Leather and Toadstool."

Gwatkin stepped quickly out of bed. His pyjama trousers fell from him, revealing sexual parts and hairy brown thighs.

The legs were small and boney, well made, their nakedness suggesting something savage and untaught, yet congruous to his nature. He grabbed the garments to him and held them there, standing scratching his head with the other hand.

"I believe I've made a frightful balls," he said.

"What's to be done?"

"Didn't I mention the new codes to you and Idwal?"

"Not a word."

"God, I remember now. I thought I'd leave it to the last moment for security reasons—and then I went out with Maureen, and forgot I'd never told either of you."

"Well, I should go along to the telephone now, or Maelgwyn-Jones will have apoplexy."

Gwatkin ran off quickly down the passage, still holding up with one hand the untied pyjama trousers, his feet bare, his hair dishevelled. I followed him, also running. We reached the Company Office. Gwatkin took up the telephone.

"Gwatkin . . ."

There was the hum of the Adjutant's voice at the other end. He sounded very angry, as well he might.

"Jenkins didn't know . . ." Gwatkin said, "I thought it best not to tell junior officers until the last moment . . . I didn't expect to get a signal the first day it came into operation . . . I was going to inform them this morning . . ."

This answer must have had a very irritating effect on Maelgwyn-Jones, whose voice crepitated for several minutes. I could tell he had begun to stutter, a sure sign of extreme rage with him. Whatever the Adjutant was asserting must have taken Gwatkin once more by surprise.

"But Bathwater was to take the place of Walnut," he said, evidently appalled.

Once more the Adjutant spoke. While he listened, Gwatkin's face lost its colour, as always when he was agitated.

"To take the place of Toadstool? Then that means—"

There was another burst of angry words at the far end of the line. By the time Maelgwyn-Jones had ceased to speak, Gwatkin had recovered himself sufficiently to reassume his parade ground manner.

188   *Anthony Powell*

"Very good," he said, "the Company moves right away."

He listened for a second, but Maelgwyn-Jones had hung up. Gwatkin turned towards me.

"I had to tell him that."

"Tell him what?"

"That I had confused the codewords. The fact is, I forgot, as I said to you just now."

"Forgot to pass on the new codewords to Idwal and me?"

"Yes—but not only are the codewords new, the instructions that go with them are amended in certain respects too. But what I said was partly true. I had muddled them in my own mind. I've been thinking of other things. God, what a fool I've made of myself. Anyway, we mustn't stand here talking. The Company is to march on the Battalion right away. Wake Idwal and tell him that. Send the duty NCO to CSM Cadwallader, and tell him to report to me as soon as the men are roused—he needn't bother to be properly dressed. Get your Platoon on parade, Nick, and tell Idwal to do the same."

He hurried off, shaking up NCOs, delivering orders, amplifying instructions altered by changed arrangements. I did much the same, waking Kedward, who took this disturbance very well, then returning to the Company Office to dress as quickly as possible.

"This is an imperial balls-up," Kedward said, as we were on the way to inspect our platoons. "What the hell can Rowland have been thinking about?"

"He had some idea of keeping the codeword up his sleeve till the last moment."

"There'll be a God Almighty row about it all."

I found my own Platoon pretty well turned out considering the circumstances. With one exception, they were clean, shaved, correctly equipped. The exception was Sayce. I did not even have to inspect the Platoon to see what was wrong. It was obvious a mile off. Sayce was in his place, no dirtier than usual at a casual glance, even in other respects properly turned out, so it appeared, but without a helmet. In short, Sayce wore no headdress at all. His head was bare.

"Where's that man's helmet, Sergeant?"

Sergeant Basset had replaced Sergeant Pendry as Platoon Sergeant, since Corporal Gwylt, with his many qualities, did not seriously aspire to three stripes. Basset, basically a sound man, had a mind which moved slowly. His small pig eyes set in a broad, flabby face were often puzzled, his capacities included none of Sergeant Pendry's sense of fitness. Sergeant Pendry, even at the time of worst depression about his wife, would never have allowed a helmetless man to appear on parade, much less fall in. He would have found a helmet for him, told him to report sick, put him under arrest, or devised some other method of disposing of him out of sight. Sergeant Basset, bull-necked and worried, began to question Sayce. Time was getting short. Sayce, in a burst of explanatory whining, set forth a thousand reasons why he should be pitied rather than blamed.

"Says somebody took his helmet, sir."

"Tell him to fall out and find it in double-quick time, or he'll wish he'd never been born."

Sayce went off at a run. I hoped that was the last we should see of him that day. He could be dealt with on return. Anything was better than the prospect of a helmetless man haunting the ranks of my platoon. It would be the last straw as far as Gwatkin was concerned, no doubt Maelgwyn-Jones too. However, while I was completing the inspection, Sayce suddenly appeared again. This time he was wearing a helmet. It was too big for him, but that was an insignificant matter. This was no time to be particular, still less to ask questions. The platoon moved off to take its place with the rest of the Company. Gwatkin, who looked worried, but had now recovered his self-possession, made a rapid inspection and found nothing to complain of. We marched down the long drives of Castlemallock, out on to the road, through the town. As we passed the alley leading to Maureen's pub, I saw Gwatkin cast an eye in that direction, but it was too early in the morning for Maureen herself, or anyone else much, to be about.

"Something awful are the girls of this town," said Corporal Gwylt to the world at large, "never did I see such a way to go on."

When we reached Battalion Headquarters, there was a message to say the Adjutant wanted an immediate word with Captain Gwatkin. Gwatkin returned from this interview with a set face. It looked as if subordinates might be in for a bad time, such as that after the Company's failure to provide "support." However, Gwatkin showed no immediate desire to get his own back on somebody, though he must have had an unenjoyable ten minutes with Maelgwyn-Jones. We set out on the day's scheme, marching and counter-marching across the mountains, infiltrating the bare, treeless fields. From start to finish, things went badly. In fact, it was a disastrous day. Still, as Maelgwyn-Jones had said, it passed, like other days in the army, and we returned at length to Castlemallock, bad-tempered and tired. Kedward and I were on the way to our room, footsore, longing to get our boots off, when we met Pinkus, the Adjutant-Quartermaster, the malignant dwarf from the *Morte d'Arthur*. His pleased manner showed there was trouble in the air. He had a voice of horrible refinement, which must have taken years to perfect, and somewhat recalled that of Howard Craggs, the left-wing publisher.

"Where's your Company Commander?" asked Pinkus. "The Commander wants him pronto."

"In his room, I suppose. The Company's just been dismissed. He's probably changing."

"What's this about putting one of the officers of the course under arrest? The Commandant's bloody well brassed off about it, I can tell you—and, what's more, the Commandant's own helmet is missing, too, and he thinks one of your fellows has taken it."

"Why on earth?"

"Your Platoon falls in just outside his quarters."

"Much more likely to be one of the permanent staff on Fire Picquet. They pass just by the door."

"The Commandant doesn't think so."

"I bet one of the Fire Picquet pinched it."

"The Commandant says he doesn't trust your mob an inch."

"Why not?"

"That's what he says."

"If he wants to run down the Regiment, he'd better take it up with our Commanding Officer."

"Make enquiries, or there'll be trouble. Now, where's Gwatkin?"

He went off, mouthing refinedly to himself. I saw what had happened. In the stresses following realization that he had forgotten about the changed codewords, Gwatkin had also forgotten Bithel. During the exertions of the day in the field, I, too, had given no thought to the events of the previous night, at least none sufficient to consider how best the situation should be handled on our return. Now, back at Castlemallock, the Bithel problem loomed up ominously. Bad enough, in any case, to leave the matter unattended made it worse than ever. Even Kedward had no copybook solution.

"My God," he said, "I suppose old Bith ought to have been under escort all day. Under my escort, too, if it comes to that. It was Rowland's last order to me."

"Anyway, Bithel should have been brought up before the Commandant within twenty-four hours and charged, as a matter of routine. That's the regulation, isn't it?"

"Twenty-four hours isn't up yet."

"Still, it's a bit late in the day."

"Rowland's going to find this one tough to sort out."

"There's nothing we can do about it."

"Look, Nick," said Kedward, "I'll go off right away and see exactly what's happened before I take my boots off. Christ, my feet feel like balloons."

After a while, Kedward returned, saying Gwatkin was already with the Castlemallock Commandant, straightening out the Bithel affair. When I saw Gwatkin later, he looked desperately worried.

"That business of Bithel last night," he said harshly.

"Yes?"

"We'd better forget about it."

"OK."

"This Anti-Gas course is almost at an end."

"Yes."

"Bithel goes back to the Battalion."

"He may be going up to Division."

"Bithel?"

"Yes."

"What on earth for?"

"To command the Mobile Laundry."

"I hadn't heard that," said Gwatkin. "How do you know?"

"Bithel himself told me."

Gwatkin did not look best pleased, but he reserved judgment.

"The CO will be glad to be rid of him," he said, "no doubt about that. The point of what I'm saying now is that Bithel may have made a bloody swine of himself last night, but it's going to be too much of a business to see he gets his deserts."

"I can understand that."

"I suspect that Bithel himself got hold of the Mess waiter concerned. Between the two of them, they are prepared to swear that the whole thing was an accident. Bithel stayed in bed all day, saying he had 'flu."

"How did the Commandant know about the arrest?"

"It leaked out. He seemed to think I'd been officious. I suppose he was just waiting to get something back on me for trying to prevent him from standing between me and my own men and their training. He said Bithel may have had a few drinks, even too many, but, after all, he'd been through the gas-chamber, and, as it turned out, was also sickening for 'flu. The Commandant said, too, he didn't want a row of that undesirable sort at his School of Chemical Warfare. He'd already had trouble about that particular Mess waiter, and, if it came up for court-martial, there might be a real stink."

"Probably just as well to drop the whole affair."

Gwatkin sighed.

"Do you think that too, Nick?"

"I do."

"Then you really don't care about discipline either," said Gwatkin. "That's what it means. You're like the rest. Well,

well, few officers seem to these days—or even decent behaviour."

He spoke without bitterness, just regret. All the same, it
was perhaps a relief to him—as it certainly was to everyone
else—that the Bithel charge should be dropped. Nevertheless, matters had gone too far at the outset for the whole story
to be suppressed. Its discussion throughout the Castlemallock
garrison eventually spread to the Battalion; no doubt, in due
course, to the ears of the Commanding Officer. Bithel himself, as usual, took the whole business in his stride.

"I made a proper fool of myself that night," he said to me,
just before he left Castlemallock. "Ought to stick to beer
really. Whiskey is always a mistake on top of gin-and-orange.
Might have messed up my chances of getting that command.
Captain Gwatkin does go off the deep-end, though. Never
know what he's going to do next. The Commandant was very
decent. Saw my side. War news doesn't look too good, does
it? What do you think about Italy coming in? Just a lot of ice-
creamers, that's my opinion."

Then, one sweltering afternoon, returning with the Platoon
after practising attack under cover of a smoke-screen, I found
several things had happened which altered the pattern of life.
When I went into the Company Office, Gwatkin and Kedward were both there. They were standing facing each other.
Even as I came through the door and saluted, disturbance
was in the air. In fact tension could be described as acute.
Gwatkin was pale, Kedward rather red in the face. Neither
of them spoke. I made some casual remark about the afternoon's training. This was ignored by Gwatkin. There was a
pause. I wondered what had gone wrong. Then Gwatkin
spoke in his coldest, most military voice.

"There will be some changes announced in Part II Orders
next week, Nick," he said.

"Yes?"

"You'll like to know them before they appear officially."

I could not imagine why all this to-do should be made;
why, if there were to be changes, Gwatkin could not quite
simply state what the changes were, instead of behaving as

if about to notify me that the British Government had surrendered, and Kedward and I were to make immediate arrangements for our platoons to become prisoners-of-war. He
paused again. Behaviour like this was hard on the nerves.

"Idwal is your new Company Commander," Gwatkin said.

Everything was explained in a flash. There was nothing
to do but remain silent.

"There have been other promotions too," said Gwatkin.
He spoke as if this fact, that there were other promotions,
was at least some small consolation. I looked at Kedward.
Then I saw, what I had missed before, that he was in an
ecstasy of controlled delight. I had not at first noticed this to
be the reason for his tense bearing. The air of strain had
been imposed by an effort not to grin too much. Even Kedward
must have realized this was a painful moment for Gwatkin.
Now, the presence of a third party slightly easing the situation, he allowed a slight smile to appear on his face. It spread.
He could no longer limit its extent. The grin, by its broadness,
almost concealed his little moustache.

"Congratulations, Idwal."

"Thanks, Nick."

"And what about you, Rowland?"

I could hardly imagine Gwatkin was to be promoted major.
If that were to happen, he would be looking more cheerful.
There was a possibility he might be going to command
Headquarter Company, an appointment he was known to covet.
I doubted myself whether he were wholly qualified to deal
with Headquarter Company's many components, remembering, among other things, the incident with the bren-carrier.
All the same, I was not prepared for the answer I received,
even though I knew, as soon as I heard it, that the sentence
pronounced on him should have been guessed at the first
indication of upheaval.

"I'm going to the ITC," said Gwatkin.

"Pending—"

"To await a posting," Gwatkin said abruptly.

He could not conceal his own mortification. The corner

of his mouth worked a little. It was not surprising he was upset. There was no adequate comment at hand to offer in condolence. Gwatkin had been relieved of his Company. There was nothing more or less to it than that. He was being sent to the Regimental Depot—the Infantry Training Centre— whence he would emerge, probably posted to a Holding Battalion finding drafts for the First Line. His career as a military paragon was at an end, though not perhaps his visions as a monk of war, after the echoes and dreams of action died away. Gwatkin might get a company again, he might not. His Territorial captaincy at least was substantive, so that he could not, like holders of an emergency commission, be reduced in rank. However, a captaincy was not in every respect an advantage for someone who hoped to repair this catastrophe. An unreducible captain could find himself in some dead-end where three pips were by convention required, ship's adjutant, for example, or like Pinkus at Castlemallock. That would not be much of fate for a Stendhalian hero, a man bent on making a romantic career in arms, the sort of figure I had supposed Gwatkin only a few months before; in Stendhal, I thought this fate would be attributed to malign political intrigue, the work of Ultras or Freemasons.

"You can fall out, both of you, now," said Gwatkin, speaking with forced cheerfulness. "I'll straighten out the papers for you, Idwal. We'll go through them together tomorrow."

"What about the Imprest Account?" asked Kedward.

"I'll bring it up to date."

"And the other Company accounts?"

"Them, too."

"I only mention that, Rowland, because you're sometimes a bit behindhand with them. I don't want to have to waste a lot of time on paper work. There's too much to do about the Company without that."

"We'll check everything."

"Has that bren been returned we lent to the Anti-Gas School?"

"Not yet."

"I shall want it formally handed over again, before I sign for the Company's weapons."

"Of course."

"Then Corporal Rosser's promotion."

"What about it?"

"Did you decide to make him up?"

"Yes."

"Have you told him?"

"Not yet."

"Then don't tell him, Rowland."

"Why not?"

"I want to see more of Rosser before I decide he's to have a third stripe," said Kedward. "I shall think about it further."

Gwatkin's face took on a shade more colour. These were forcible reminders of Kedward's changed position. I was myself a little surprised at the manner in which Kedward accepted the Company as his undoubted right. In one sense, he could have behaved in a more tactful manner about the take-over, anyway leave such questions until they were going through the papers together; in another, as Company Commander designate, he was there to arrange matters in the Company's best interests—by Gwatkin's own definition—not to be polite or spare Gwatkin's feelings. Nevertheless, Gwatkin had not cared for being treated in this manner. He tapped with his knuckles on the blanket covering the trestle table, played with his beloved symbol, the rubber stamp. Gwatkin was deeply humiliated, even though keeping himself under control.

"I want to be alone now, boys," he said.

He began to rustle papers. Kedward and I retired. We went along the passage together, Kedward deep in thought.

"Rowland is taking this pretty hard," I said.

Kedward showed surprise.

"Losing the Company?"

"Yes."

"Do you think so?"

"I do."

"He must have seen it coming."

"I don't think he did for a moment."

"Rowland has been getting less and less efficient lately," Kedward said. "You must have noticed that. You said yourself something was wrong, when you came back from the Aldershot course."

"I somehow didn't expect him to be unstuck just like this."

"The Company needs a thorough overhaul," said Kedward. "There are one or two points I shall want altered in your own Platoon, Nick. It is far from satisfactory. I've noticed there's no snap about them when they march in from training. That's always a good test of men. They are the worst of the three platoons at musketry, too. You'll have to give special attention to the range. And another thing, Nick, about your own personal turn-out. Do get that anti-gas cape of yours properly folded. The way you have it done is not according to regulations."

"I'll see to all that, Idwal. Who are you getting as another subaltern?"

"Lyn Craddock. He'll go in senior to you, of course. I think Lyn should help pull the Company together."

"When do you put your pips up?"

"Monday. By the way, did I tell you Yanto Breeze is to become a captain too—in the Traffic Control Company. I just heard that this afternoon from one of the drivers who brought some stuff here. It isn't like getting a company in a battalion, but it's promotion all the same."

"Does Rowland know about Yanto?"

"I was just telling him when you came into the Company Office—saying it was funny two of his subalterns should become captain at the same moment."

"How did Rowland take it?"

"Didn't seem much interested. Rowland never liked Yanto. I don't know whether all that about his sister rankled. I say, Nick, do you know what?"

"What?"

"I'm going to write tonight and arrange about the wedding on my next leave."

"When's that going to be?"

"Getting the Company may mean a postponement, but even then it won't be far off. By the way, I've got a new snap of my fiancée. Like to see it?"

"Of course."

We gazed at the photograph.

"She's altered her hair," Kedward said.

"So I see."

"I'm not sure I like it the new way," he said.

Nevertheless, he gave the photograph its routine kiss before putting it away. His promotion, his fiancée, the wedding in prospect, were matters of fact to him, not, as to Gwatkin, dreams come true. When Gwatkin was given the Company, that must have seemed the first important step in a glorious career; when he first took out Maureen, entry into an equally glorious romance. Kedward, it was true, accepted accession of rank with enthusiasm, but without the smallest romanticism, military or otherwise. As Moreland would have said, it is just the way you look at things. We crossed the hall. Emmot, the Mess waiter, appeared from a doorway. The whole Bithel affair had greatly cheered him up. He looked positively a new man. It was hard to believe he had been sobbing like a child only a few weeks before.

"You're wanted on the phone, sir," he said, grinning, as if he and I had shared most of the fun of the Bithel incident, "your unit."

I went to the telephone in the Duty Officer's room.

"Jenkins here."

It was the Adjutant.

"Hold on a moment," he said.

I held on. At the other end of the line Maelgwyn-Jones began to talk to someone in the Orderly Room. I waited. He returned at last.

"Who is that?"

"Jenkins."

"What do you want?"

"You rang up for me."

"What was it? Oh, yes. Here's the chit. Second-Lieutenant Jenkins. You will report to Divisional Headquarters, DAAG's office, by 1700 hours. tomorrow, taking all your kit with you."

"Do you know what I'm to do there?"

"No idea."

"For how long?"

"No idea of that either."

"What's the DAAG's name?"

"Also unknown. He's a new appointment. Old Square-arse got bowler-hatted."

"How shall I get to Division HQ?"

"There's a truck going up tomorrow with some details for hospital treatment. I'll tell it to pick you up at Castlemallock on the way. I expect you've heard about certain changes in your Company."

"Yes."

"Strictly speaking, this instruction should have been issued by me through your Company Commander, but, to avoid confusion, I thought I'd tell you direct. There was another reason, too, why I wanted to speak personally. If the new DAAG is an approachable chap, find out about that Intelligence course I'm supposed to be going on. Also about those two officer reinforcements we've been promised. All right?"

"All right."

"Report what I've just told you about yourself to the two officers concerned—Rowland and Idwal—right away. Tell them they'll get it in writing tomorrow. All right?"

"Yes."

Maelgwyn-Jones hung up. Castlemallock was to be left behind. I heard the news without regret; although in the army—as in love—anxiety is an ever-present factor where change is concerned. I returned to Kedward and told him what was happening to me.

"You're leaving right away?"

"Tomorrow."

"What are you going to do at Division?"

"No idea. Could be only temporary, I suppose. I may reappear."

"You won't if you once go."

"You think not?"

"As I've said before, Nick, you're a bit old for a subaltern in an operational unit. I want to make the Company more mobile. I was a little worried anyway about having you on my hands, to tell the truth."

"Well, you won't have to worry any longer, Idwal."

These words of mine expressed, on my own part, no more, no less, than what they were, a mere statement of fact. They did not convey the smallest reverberation of acerbity at being treated so frankly as a more than doubtful asset. Kedward dealt in realities. There is much to be said for persons who traffic in this corn, provided it is always borne in mind that so-called realities present, as a rule, only a small part of the picture. On this occasion, however, I was myself in complete agreement with Kedward's view about my departure, feeling even stimulated by a certain excitement at the thought of being on the move.

"You'd better tell Rowland right away."

"I'm going to."

I returned to the Company Office. Gwatkin was surrounded with papers. He looked as if he were handing over an Army in the field, rather than a Company on detachment for security duties. He glared when I came through the door at this disobeying of an order that he should be left undisturbed. I repeated Maelgwyn-Jones's words. Gwatkin pushed back his chair.

"So you're leaving the Battalion too, Nick?"

"The Adjutant didn't say for how long."

"You won't come back, if you go to Division."

"That's what Idwal said."

"What can it be? They'd hardly give you a staff appointment. It's probably something like Bithel. I hear he's going to the Mobile Laundry. The CO must have rigged that."

I saw that even Bithel's new command was painful to Gwatkin, destined himself for the ITC. My own unexplained move was scarcely less disturbing to him. He frowned.

"This must be part of a general shake-up," he said. "CSM Cadwallader is leaving the Battalion too."

"Why is the Sergeant-Major going?"

"Age. I don't understand why Maelgwyn-Jones did not pass the order about yourself to me in the first instance."

"He said he spoke to me personally because he wanted to explain about some questions I was to put to the new DAAG."

"He should have done that through me."

"He said you would get it in writing tomorrow."

"If the Adjutant ignores the correct channels, I don't know what he expects other officers to do," said Gwatkin.

He laughed, as if he found some relief in the thought that the whole framework of the Company, as we had known it together, was now to be broken up; not, so to speak, given over unimpaired to the innovations of Kedward. There was no doubt, I saw now, that Gwatkin would have preferred almost anyone, rather than Kedward, to succeed him.

"Idwal will get either Phillpots or Parry in your place, I expect," he said.

He began to fiddle with his papers again. I turned to go. Gwatkin looked up suddenly.

"Doing anything special tonight?" he said.

"No."

"Come for a stroll in the park."

"After Mess?"

"Yes."

"All right."

I went off to pack, and make such other preparations as were required for departure the following day. Gwatkin came in to dinner late. I was already sitting in the anteroom when he joined me.

"Shall we go?"

"Right."

We left the house by the steps leading to what remained of the lawn, its turf criss-crossed now with footpaths worn by the feet of soldiers taking short cuts. Shrubberies divided the garden from the park. When we were among the trees, Gwatkin took the way leading to Lady Caro's Dingle. After the heat of the afternoon, these woods were wonderfully cool and peaceful. The moon was full, the sky almost as light as day. Now that I was about to leave Castlemallock, I began to regret having spent so little time in this park. All I knew was the immediate neighbourhood of the house. To have frequented its woods and glades would perhaps have only increased the melancholy inherent in the place.

"Do you know, Nick," said Gwatkin, "although the Company used to mean everything to me, it's leaving the Battalion that's the real blow. Of course there will be up-to-date training at the ITC, opportunity to get to know the latest weapons and tactics thoroughly, not just rush through them and instruct, as we have to here."

I did not know what to say to that, but Gwatkin was just getting it off his chest. He did not require answers.

"Idwal is pretty pleased with himself now," he said. "Let him see what it's like to be skipper. Perhaps it isn't as easy as he thinks."

"Idwal certainly enjoys the idea of being a company commander."

"Then there's Maureen," Gwatkin said. "This means leaving her. That was what I wanted to talk to you about."

I had supposed that to be the reason for our coming to the park.

"You'll at least have time to say goodbye to her."

That did not sound much consolation. It seemed to me he was well rid of Maureen, if she really was disturbing him to the extent that it appeared; but being judicious about other people's love affairs is easy, often merely a sign one has not understood their force or complexity.

"I'm going to try and get down there tomorrow," he said, "take her out for the evening."

"Have you been seeing much of her?"

"Quite a bit."

"It's bad luck."

"I know I've made a bloody fool of myself," Gwatkin said, "but I don't know that I'd do different if I started again. Anyway, it isn't quite over."

"What isn't?"

"Maureen."

"In what way?"

"Nick—"

"Yes?"

"She's pretty well said—you know—"

"She has?"

"I believe if I can manage to see her tomorrow—but I don't want to talk about it. She can't make up her mind, you see. I understand that."

I thought of Dicky Umfraville's comment: "Not tonight, darling, I don't love you enough—not tonight, darling, I love you too much . . ." It sounded as if Gwatkin had had his share of such reservations. As we walked, his mind continually jumped from one aspect of his vexations to another.

"If I'm at the ITC and there's an invasion," he said, "I'll at least be nearer the scene of action than here. I don't think the Germans will try this country, do you? There'd be no difficulty in landing here, but it would mean mounting another operation after their arrival."

"Hardly worth it, I'd have thought."

"Idwal didn't take long to get hold of the idea he was to command the Company."

"He certainly did not."

"Do you remember my saying what we call good manners are just a form of weakness?"

"Very well."

"I suppose if that's true, Idwal was right to speak as he did."

"There's a lot to be said for going straight to the point."

"But that's what I've always tried to do since I've been in the army," Gwatkin said. "It doesn't seem to have worked in my case. Here I am being sent back to the ITC as a dud. It's not because I haven't been keen, or slacked in any way— except I know I forgot about those bloody code words—and other people make balls-ups too."

He spoke without self-pity, just lack of understanding; deep desire to know the answer why, so far as he was concerned, things had gone so wrong. It would be no good attempting to explain. I was not even sure I knew the explanation myself. All Gwatkin said was true. He had worked hard. In many respects he was a good officer, so far as he went. He was even conscious of such moral aspects of military life as the fact that the army is a world of the will, accordingly, if the will is weak, the army is weak. I could see, however, that one of the fallacies that made him so vulnerable was the supposition that manners, good or bad, had anything to do with the will as such.

"I loved commanding the Company," Gwatkin said. "Don't you enjoy your Platoon, Nick?"

"I might have once. I don't know. It's too late now. That's certain. Thirty men are merely a responsibility without the least compensatory feeling of power. They only need everlasting looking after."

"Do you really feel that?" he said, astonished. "When the war broke out, I was thrilled at the thought I might lead men into action. I suppose I may yet. This could be only a temporary set-back."

He laughed unhappily. By this time we were approaching the dingle, a glade enclosed by a kind of shrubbery. A large stone seat was on one side of it, ornamental urns set on plinths at either end. All at once there was a sound of singing.

> "Arm in arm together,
> Just like we used to be,
> Stepping out along with you
> Meant all the world to me . . ."

It was a man's voice, a familiar one. The song, recalling old fashioned music-hall tunes of fifty years before, was, in fact, contemporary with that moment, popular among the men, perhaps, on account of such nostalgic tones and rhythm. The singing stopped abruptly. A woman began giggling and squeaking. Gwatkin and I paused.

"One of our fellows?" he said.

"It sounds to me like Corporal Gwylt."

"I believe you're right."

"Let's have a look."

We skirted the dingle by way of a narrow path among the bushes, stepping quietly through the undergrowth that surrounded the glade. On the stone seat a soldier and a girl were sprawled in a long embrace. The soldier's arm bore two white stripes. The back of the huge head was unmistakably that of Corporal Gwylt. We watched for a moment. Suddenly Gwatkin gave a start He drew in his breath.

"Christ," he said very quietly.

He began to pick his way with great care through the shrubs and laurels. I followed him. I was not at first aware why he was moving so soon, nor that something had upset him. I thought his exclamation due to the scratch of a thorn, or remembrance of some additional item to be supervised before handing over the Company. When we were beyond the immediate outskirts of the dingle, he began walking quickly. He did not speak until we were on the path leading back to the house.

"You saw who the girl was?"

"No."

"Maureen."

"God, was she?"

There was absolutely no comment to make. This was even more unanswerable than the news that Gwatkin had been superseded in his command. If you are in love with a woman— and Gwatkin was undoubtedly in love—you can recognise her a mile off. The fact that I myself had failed to identify Maureen in the evening light did not make Gwatkin's certainty in the least suspect. The statement could be accepted as correct.

"Corporal Gwylt," he said. "Could you believe it?"

"It was Gwylt all right."

"What do you think of it?"

"There's nothing to say."

"Rolling about with him."

"They were certainly in a clinch."

"Well, say something."

"Gwylt ought to pray more to Mithras."

"What do you mean?"

"You know—the Kipling poem—'keeping us pure till the dawn.'"

"My God," said Gwatkin, "you're bloody right."

He began to laugh. That was one of the moments when I felt I had not been wrong in thinking there was some style about him. We reached the house, parting without further discussion on either side, though Gwatkin had again laughed loudly from time to time. I made my way up the rickety stairs of the stable. The light was out in the bedroom, the blackout down from the window, through which moonlight shone on to the floor. This would usually have meant Kedward was asleep. However, as I came through the door, he sat up in bed.

"You're late, Nick."

"I went for a walk in the park with Rowland."

"Is he browned off?"

"Just a shade."

"I couldn't get to sleep," Kedward said. "Never happened to me before. I suppose I'm so bloody pleased to get command of the Company. I keep on having new ideas about running it. I was thinking, I'll probably get Phillpots or Parry in your place, now that you're going up to Div."

"Phillpots is a nice chap to work with."

"Parry is the better officer," said Kedward.

He turned over, in due course going to sleep, I suppose, in spite of these agitations induced by the prospect of power. For a time I thought about Gwatkin, Gwylt and Maureen, then went to sleep myself. The following day there were farewells to be said. I undertook these in the afternoon.

"I hear you're leaving the Battalion too, Sergeant-Major."

"That I am, sir."

"I expect you're sorry to go."

"I am that, sir, and then I'm not. Nice to see home again, that will be, but there needs promotion for these younger lads that must be getting on."

"Who is going to take your place?"

"It will be Sergeant Humphries, I do believe."

"I hope Humphries does the job as well as you have."

"Ah, well, sir, Humphries is a good NCO, and he should be all right, I do think."

"Thank you for all your help."

"Oh, it was a pleasure, sir . . ."

Before CSM Cadwallader could say more—not a man to take lightly opportunity to speak at length on the occasion of such a leave-taking, he was certainly going to say more, much more—Corporal Gwylt came running up. He saluted perfunctorily. Evidently I was not the object of his approach. He was tousled and out of breath.

"Excuse me, sir, may I speak to the Sergeant-Major?"

"Go ahead."

Gwylt could hardly contain his indignation.

"Somebody's broke in and stole the Company's butter, Sergeant-Major, and the lock's all bust and the wire ripped out of the front of the meat-safe where it was put, and the Messing Corporal do think it be that bugger Sayce again that has taken the butter to flog it, so will you come and see right away, the Messing Corporal says, that we have your witness, Sergeant-Major, if there's a Summary of Evidence like there was those blankets . . ."

CSM Cadwallader shortened his speech in preparation to a mere goodbye and grip of the hand. There was no alternative in the circumstances. He looked disappointed, but characteristically put duty before even the most enjoyably sententious of valedictions. He and Corporal Gwylt hurried off together. By this time the truck that was to take me to Divisional Headquarters had driven up. An NCO was parading the men who were to travel up in it for medical treatment. Gwatkin appeared. He had been busy all the morning, but had promised he would turn up to see me off. We talked for a minute or two about Company arrangements, revisions proposed by Kedward. Gwatkin had resumed his formality of manner.

"Perhaps you'll arrive at the ITC yourself, Nick," he said,

"on the way to something better, of course, but it's used as a place of transit. I trust I'll be gone by then, but it would be good to meet."

"We may both turn up on the same staff," I said, without great seriousness.

"No," he said gravely, "I'll never get on the staff. I don't mind that. All I want is to carry out regimental duties properly."

He tapped his gaiter with the swagger stick he carried. Then his tone changed.

"I had some rather bad news from home this morning," he said.

"You're not in luck."

"My father-in-law passed away. I think I told you he had been ill for some time."

"You did. I'm sorry. Did you get on very well with him?"

"Pretty well," said Gwatkin, "but this will mean Blodwen's mother will have to move in with us. I like her all right, but I'd rather that didn't have to happen. Look, Nick, you won't speak to anyone about last night."

"Of course not."

"It was bloody awful," he said.

"Of course."

"But a lesson to me."

"One never takes lessons to heart. It's just a thing people talk about—learning by experience and all that."

"Oh, but I do take lessons to heart," he said. "What do you think then?"

"That one just gets these knocks from time to time."

"You believe that?"

"Yes."

"You really believe that everyone has that sort of thing happen to them?"

"In different ways."

Gwatkin considered the matter for a moment.

"I don't know," he said, "I can't help thinking it was just because I was such a bloody fool, what with Maureen and making a balls of the Company too. I thought at least I was being some good as a soldier, but I was bloody wrong."

I thought of Pennistone and his quotations from Vigny.

"A French writer who'd been a regular officer said the whole point of soldiering was its bloody boring side. The glamour, such as it was, was just a bit of exceptional luck if it came your way."

"Did he?" said Gwatkin.

He spoke without a vestige of interest. I was impressed for the ten thousandth time by the fact that literature illuminates life only for those to whom books are a necessity. Books are unconvertible assets, to be passed on only to those who possess them already. Before I could decide whether it was worth making a final effort to ram home Vigny's point, or whether further energy thus expended was as wasteful of Gwatkin's time as my own, Kedward crossed the yard.

"Rowland," he said, "come to the cookhouse at once, will you. It's serious."

"What's happened?" said Gwatkin, not pleased by this interruption.

"The Company butter's been flogged. So far as I can see, storage arrangements have been quite irregular. I'd like you to be present while I check facts with the CQMS and the Messing Corporal. Another thing, the galantine that's just arrived is bad. It's disposal must be authorized by an officer. I've got to straighten out this butter business before I do anything else. Nick, will you go along and sign for the galantine. Just a formality. It's round at the back by the ablutions."

"Nick's just off to Division HQ," said Gwatkin.

"Oh, are you, Nick?" said Kedward. "Well best of luck, but you will sign for the galantine first, won't you?"

"Of course."

"Goodbye, then."

"Goodbye, Idwal, and good luck."

Kedward hastily shook my hand, then rushed off to the scene of the butter robbery, saying: "Don't be long, Rowland."

Gwatkin shook my hand too. He smiled in an odd sort of way, as if he dimly perceived it was no good battling against Fate, which, seen in right perspective, almost always provides a certain beauty of design, sometimes even an occasional good laugh.

"I leave you to your galantine, Nick," he said. "Best of luck."

I gave him a salute for the last time, feeling he deserved it. Gwatkin marched away, looking a trifle absurd with his little moustache, but somehow rising above that. I went off in the other direction, where the burial certificate of the galantine awaited signature. A blazing sun was beating down. For this, my final duty at Castlemallock, Corporal Gwylt, who was representing the Messing Corporal, elsewhere engaged in the butter investigation, had arranged the galantine, an immense slab of it, in its wrappings on a kind of bier, looking like a corpse in a mortuary. Beside the galantine, he had placed a pen and the appropriate Army Form.

"Oh, that galantine do smell something awful, sir," he said. "Sign the paper without smelling it, I should, sir."

"I'd better make sure."

I inclined my head with caution, then quickly withdrew it. Corporal Gwylt was absolutely right. The smell was appalling, indescribable. Shades of the *Potemkin*, I thought, wondering if I were going to vomit. After several deep breaths, I set my name to the document, confirming animal corruption.

"I'm leaving now, Corporal Gwylt. Going up to Division. I'll say goodbye."

"You're leaving the Company, sir?"

"That I am."

The Battalion's form of speech was catching.

"Then I'm sorry, sir. Good luck to you. I expect it will be nice up at Division."

"Hope so. Don't get into too much mischief with the girls."

"Oh, those girls, sir, they never give you any peace, they don't."

"You must give up girls and get a third stripe. Then you'll be like the Sergeant-Major and not think of girls any longer."

"That I will, sir. It will be better, though I'll not be the man the Sergeant-Major is, I haven't the height. But don't you believe the Sergeant-Major don't like girls. That's just his joke. I know they put something in the tea to make us not want them, but it don't do boys like me no good, it seem, nor the Sergeant-Major either."

We shook hands on it. Any attempt to undermine the age-old army legend of sedatives in the tea would be as idle as to lecture Gwatkin on Vigny. I returned to the truck, and climbed up beside the driver. We rumbled through the park with its sad decayed trees, its Byronic associations. In the town, Maureen was talking to a couple of corner-boys in the main street. She waved and blew a kiss as we drove past, more as a matter of routine, I thought, than on account of any flattering recognition of myself, because she seemed to be looking in the direction of the men at the back of the truck, who, on passing, had raised some sort of hoot at her. Now they began to sing:

> "She'll be wearing purple socks,
> And she's always in the pox,
> And she's Mickey McGilligan's daughter,
>   Mary-Anne . . ."

There were no villages in the country traversed, rarely even farms or hovels. One mile looked like another, except when once we passed a pair of stone pillars, much battered by the elements, their capitals surmounted by heraldic animals holding shields. Here were formerly gates to some mansion, the gryphons, the shields, the heraldry, nineteenth century in design. Now, instead of dignifying the entrance to a park, the pillars stood starkly in open country, alone among wide fields: no gates; no wall; no drive; no park; no house. Beyond them, towards the far horizon, stretched hedgeless ploughland, rank grass, across the expanses of which, like the divisions of a chess-board, squat walls of piled stone were beginning to rise. The pillars marked the entrance to Nowhere. Nothing remained of what had once been the demesne, except these chipped, over-elaborate coats of arms, emblems probably of some lord of the Law, like the first Castlemallock, or business magnate, such as those who succeeded him. Here, too, there had been no heirs, or heirs who preferred to live elsewhere. I did not blame them. North or South, this country was not greatly sympathetic to me. All the same, the day was sunny, there was a vast sense of relief in not being required to settle the Company butter problem, nor take the Platoon in gas drill. Respite was momentary, but welcome. At the back of the vehicle the hospital party sang gently:

> "Open now the crystal fountain,
> Whence the healing stream doth flow:
> Let the fire and cloudy pillar
> Lead me all my journey through:
>   Strong Deliverer,
>   Strong Deliverer
> Be thou still my strength and shield . . ."

Gwatkin, Kedward and the rest already seemed far away. I was entering another phase of my war. By this time we had driven for an hour or two. The country had begun to change its character. Mean dwellings appeared more often, then the outer suburbs of a large town. The truck drove up a long straight road of grim houses. There was a crossroads where half a dozen ways met, a sinister place such as that where Oedipus, refusing to give passage, slew his father, a locality designed for civil strife and street fighting. Pressing on, we reached a less desolate residential quarter. Here, Divisional Headquarters occupied two or three adjacent houses. At one of these, a Military Policeman stood on duty.

"I want the DAAG's office."

I was taken to see a sergeant-clerk. No one seemed to have heard I was to arrive. The truck had to move on. My kit was unloaded. The DAAG's office was consulted from the switchboard, a message returned that I was to "come up." A soldier-clerk showed the way. We passed along passages, the doors of which were painted with the name, rank and appointment of the occupants, on one of them:

Major-General H. de C. Liddament, DSO, MC.
Divisional Commander

The clerk left me at a door on which the name of the former DAAG—"Old Square-arse," as Maelgwyn-Jones designated him—was still inscribed. From within came the drone of a voice apparently reciting some endless chant, which rose and fell, but never ceased. I knocked. No one answered. After a time, I knocked again. Again there was no answer. Then I walked in, and saluted. An officer, wearing major's crowns on his shoulder, was sitting with his back to the door dictating, while a clerk with pencil and pad was taking down letters in shorthand. The DAAG's back was fat and humped, a roll of flesh at the neck.

"Wait a moment," he said, waving his hand in the air, but not turning.

He continued his dictation while I stood there.

". . . It is accordingly felt . . . that the case of the officer in question—give his name and personal number—would be more appropriately dealt with—no—more appropriately regulated—under the terms of the Army Council Instruction quoted above—give reference—of which para II, sections (d) and (f), and para XI, sections (b) and (h), as amended by War Office Letter AG 27/9852/73 of 3 January, 1940, which, it would appear, contemplate exceptional cases of this kind . . . It is at the same time emphasised that this formation is in no way responsible for the breakdown in administration—no, no, better not say that—for certain irregularities of routine that appear to have taken place during the course of conducting the investigation of the case, *vide* page 23, para 17 of the findings of the Court of Inquiry, and para VII of the above quoted ACI, section (e)—irregularities which it is hoped will be adjusted in due course by the authorities concerned . . ."

The voice, like so many other dictating or admonitory voices of even that early period of the war, had assumed the timbre and inflexions of the Churchill broadcast, slurred consonants, rhythmical stresses and prolations. These accents, in certain

circumstances, were to be found imitated as low as battalion
level. Latterly, for example, Gwatkin's addresses to the
Company could be detected, by an attentive ear, to have veered
away a little from the style of the chapel elder, towards the
Prime Minister's individualities of delivery. In this, Gwatkin's
harangues lost not a little of their otherwise traditional charm.
If we won the war, there could be no doubt that these rich,
distinctive tones would be echoed for a generation at least. I
was still thinking of this curious imposition of a mode of
speech on those for whom its manner was totally incongruous,
when the clerk folded his pad and rose.

"Will you sign these, sir?" he asked.

"'For Major General,'" said the DAAG, "I'll sign them 'for
Major-General.'"

He turned in his chair.

"How are you?" he said.

It was Widmerpool. He brought his large spectacles to
bear on me like searchlights, and held out his hand. I took
it. I felt enormously glad to see him. One's associations with
people are regulated as much by what they stand for, as by
what they are, individual characteristics becoming from time
to time submerged in more general implications. At that moment, although I had never possessed anything approaching
a warm relationship with Widmerpool, his presence brought
back with a rush all kinds of things, more or less desirable,
from which I had been cut off for an eternity. I wondered
how I could ever have considered him in the disobliging light
that seemed so innate since we had been at school together.

"Sit down," he said.

I looked about. The shorthand clerk had been sitting on
a tin box. I chose the edge of a table.

"Anyway, between these four walls," said Widmerpool,
"don't feel rank makes a gulf between us."

"How did you know it was me when I came into the room?"

Widmerpool indicated a small circular shaving-mirror,
which stood on his table, almost hidden by piles of documents.
He may have thought this question already presumed too far
on our difference in rank, because he stopped smiling at once,

and began to tap his knee. His battle-dress, like his civilian clothes, seemed a little too small for him. At the same time, he was undeniably a somewhat formidable figure in his present role.

"I'll put you in the picture right away," he said. "In the first place, I do not mean to stay on this staff long. That is between ourselves, of course. The Division is spoken of as potentially operational. So far as I am concerned, it is a backwater. Besides, I have to do most of the work here. Ack-and-Quack, a Regular, is a good fellow, but terribly slow. He is not too bad on supply, but possesses little or no grasp of personnel."

"What about the General?"

Widmerpool took off his spectacles. He leant towards me. His face was severe under his blinking. He spoke in a low voice.

"I despair of the General," he said.

"I thought everyone admired him."

"Quite a wrong judgment."

"As bad as that?"

"Worse."

"He has a reputation for efficiency."

"Mistakenly."

"They like him in the units."

"People love buffoonery," said Widmerpool, "soldiers like everyone else. Incidentally, I don't think General Liddament cares for me either. However, that is by the way. I make sure he can find nothing to complain of in my work. As a result, he contents himself with adopting a mock-heroic style of talk whenever I approach him. Very undignified in a relatively senior officer. I repeat, I do not propose to stay with this formation long."

"What job do you want?"

"That's my affair," said Widmerpool, "but in the meantime, so long as I remain, the work will be properly done. Now it happens lately there has been a spate of courts-martial, none of special interest, but all requiring, for one reason or another, a great deal of work from the DAAG. With his other duties, it has been more than one man can cope with. It was too much for my predecessor. That was to be expected. Now I thrive on work, but I saw at once that even I must have assistance. Accordingly, I have obtained War Office authority for the temporary employment of a junior officer to aid me in such matters as taking Summary of Evidence. Various names were put forward within the Division, yours among them. I noticed this. I had no reason to suppose you would be the most efficient, but, since none of the others had any more legal training than yourself, I allowed the ties of old acquaintance to prevail. I chose you—subject to your giving satisfaction, of course."

Widmerpool laughed.

"Thanks very much."

"I take it you did not find yourself specially cut out to be a regimental officer."

"Not specially."

"Otherwise, I doubt if your name would have been submitted to me. Let's hope you will be better adapted to staff duties."

"We can but hope."

"I remember when we last met, you came to see me with a view to getting help in actually entering the army. How did you get in?"

"In the end I was called up. As I told you at the time, my name was already on the Emergency Reserve. I merely consulted you as to the best means of speeding up that process."

I saw no reason to give Widmerpool further details about that particular subject. It had been no thanks to him that the calling-up process had been accelerated. By now he had succeeded in dispelling, with extraordinary promptness, my earlier apprehension that army contacts were necessarily preferable with people one knew in civilian life. I began to wonder whether I was not already regretting Gwatkin and Kedward.

"Like so many units and formations at this moment," said Widmerpool, "the Division is under-establishment. You will be expected to help while you are here in other capacities than purely 'A' duties. When in the field—on exercises, I mean—you will be something of a dogsbody, to use a favourite army phrase with which you are no doubt familiar. You understand?"

"Perfectly."

"Good. You will be in F Mess. F is low, but not the final dregs of the Divisional Headquarters staff, if staff they can be called. The Mobile Bath Officer, and his like, are in G Mess. By the way, a body from your unit, one Bithel, is coming up to command the Mobile Laundry."

"So I heard."

"Brother of a VC, I understand, and was himself a notable sportsman when younger. Pity they could not find him better employment, for he should be a good type. But we must get on with the job, not spend our time coffee-housing here. Your kit is downstairs?"

"Yes."

"I will give orders for it to be taken round to your billet— you had better go with it to see the place. Come straight back here. I will run through your duties, then take you back to the Mess to meet some of the staff."

Widmerpool picked up the telephone. He spoke for some minutes about my affairs. Then he said to the operator: "Get me Major Farebrother at Command."

He hung up the receiver and waited.

"My opposite number at Command is one, Sunny Farebrother, a City acquaintance of mine—rather a slippery customer to deal with. He was my Territorial unit's Brigade-Major at the beginning of the war."

"I met him years ago."

The telephone bell rang.

"Well, get cracking," said Widmerpool, without commenting on this last observation. "The sooner you go, the sooner you'll be back. There's a good deal to run through."

He had already begun to speak on the telephone when I left the room. I saw that I was now in Widmerpool's power. This, for some reason, gave me a disagreeable, sinking feeling within. On the news that night, motorized elements of the German army were reported as occupying the outskirts of Paris.